A Taste of Gold

MIRACLES ON HARLEY STREET, BOOK 5

SARA ADRIEN

ARE YOU SIGNED UP FOR DRAGONBLADE'S BLOG?

You'll get the latest news and information on exclusive giveaways, exclusive excerpts, coming releases, sales, free books, cover reveals and more.

Check out our complete list of authors, too!

No spam, no junk. That's a promise!

Sign Up Here

www.dragonbladepublishing.com

Dearest Reader;

Thank you for your support of a small press. At Dragonblade Publishing, we strive to bring you the highest quality Historical Romance from some of the best authors in the business. Without your support, there is no 'us', so we sincerely hope you adore these stories and find some new favorite authors along the way.

Happy Reading!

CEO, Dragonblade Publishing

DEDICATION

For my parents and my grandfather.

PREFACE

All the characters in this book are fictitious. Yet the difficulties they face are rooted in real history. For more on these challenges, please see my Author's Note.

And now, welcome to Harley Street!

Felix and the other doctors you'll meet in this story are part of my beloved *Miracles on Harley Street* series. Their tales are works of fiction, inspired by both historical realities and my imagination, crafted to transport you to another time.

The conflicts and events you'll encounter are drawn from historical inspiration. However, I've taken creative liberties—including inventing fictional royals and political struggles that actually occurred later in history but received their spark around the time this story is set. The medical techniques and tools featured have been carefully researched to reflect the innovations of their era, within a three- to five-year historical window.

If you'd like to know more about the history woven into this tale and where I've added artistic flair, you'll find details in the Author's Note at the end.

So, let the adventure begin—step into a world where history and romance intertwine, and enjoy the journey.

And if you are new to the Doctors on Harley Street and this is your first story, keep the following short overview handy, so you already know who is coming back from other books. Think of the doctors on Harley Street as a group of friends, almost like in television shows such as Grey's Anatomy or Friends, in which the stories bring everyone back, even though the focus may only be on one person and his or her love interest.

Philippa "Pippa" Mae Pemberton, in Book 1, is the cousin of the heroine in Book 2, Lady Beatrice Wetherby, also known as "Bea." In book 1, *A Sight to Behold*, Pippa fell in love with Dr. Nicholas Folsham, "Nick," who is one of the doctors at 87 Harley Street. Bea lived with Pippa at Cloverdale House, a large estate surrounded by parks with an adjoining orangery, which belonged to Pippa's family and was being converted into a rehabilitation center throughout the series.

Dr. Nicholas "Nick" Folsham is an oculist at 87 Harley Street and the best eye surgeon in London. He studied in Vienna with Alfie Collins and some of the others, including Felix. Nick's story is book 1, *A Sight to Behold*. He's Wendy Folsham's older brother and, with his wife Pippa, moved to a townhouse close to the practice at 87 Harley Street. Wendy also lives there with Nick and Pippa.

Alfie Collins is the apothecary at 87 Harley Street. His and Bea's romantic story is book 2, *The Scent of Intuition*. He studied in Vienna and completed an apprenticeship in ayurvedic medicine in Delhi, India, before he returned to London and opened the practice with his friends. In his story, he administered a truth serum to Baron von List, which gives rise to some of the tension fueling the plot in the story you are about to read.

Dr. Andre Fernando, the orthopedist at 87 Harley Street, originally from Florence, Italy, is quite the heartbreaker. Although his past overlaps with that of his friends Alfie and Felix, his future has very different surprises in store because he falls in love with Princess Thea, the sister of Prince Stan. Andre's story is in book 3, *A Touch of Charm*.

Wendy Folsham is Nick's younger sister and the nurse who lives and works at 87 Harley Street. Alfie, Andre, and Felix treat Wendy as their little sister, too, watching over her and keeping her safe. In reality, it's Wendy's wisdom and good heart that help the young men. Her story is in book 4, *The Sound of Seduction*.

Dr. Felix Leafley (formerly named Faivish Blattner, before he came to England) is the dentist at 87 Harley Street, and a master of his craft. He suffers from a broken heart because he hasn't been able to be reunited with the love of his life. You're about to read his story in book 5, *A Taste of Gold*.

Baron Wolfgang von List is a Prussian villain in this series and some of my other series, too. To put it mildly, his morals are questionable, his methods brutal, and his intentions violent. For more books with this villain and his story, please visit www.Sara Adrien.com—this is also where you can find out when he will be gloriously defeated by the heroes and heroines in my other books.

Several other medical professionals regularly visit 87 Harley Street and the nearby clinic. Find those stories as part of my contributions to the *Lyon's Den* series. For more information and a complete list of Sara Adrien's novels, please visit www.Sara Adrien.com.

Prologue

Harley Street, London, 1817

MIRACLES AT HARLEY Street came in many forms: spectacles from Nick, the oculist, for the far-sighted to read again, ointments from Alfie, the apothecary, to soothe irritated skin, splints from Andre, the orthopedist, for those whose legs needed to be supported, bandages from Nurse Wendy who cured with her kindness as much as her hands, and gold fillings from the dentist on the second floor.

And so it was again when Felix Leafley allowed himself a rare, clean satisfaction upon finishing the treatment of the girl in his chair: a gold foil filling set exactly right, a young patient spared a future of needless toothaches because his training and patience had met and bested the problem.

He lifted the oral mirror and watched the surface catch light and reflect brightness where there'd been darkness before. Another quiet rescue. He was the one dentist in London who packed gold so fine it behaved like tooth, the one whose Royal Warrant brought the ton to his door. He was the only one who reduced a painful cavity to a mere speck of gold gleaming on a tooth.

But being the only one meant being alone.

And he couldn't change that because the name on his door was not the name his love knew. As long as Baron von List built secret registries—names, addresses, trades—and used licenses and patrols to harry Jewish businesses and silence anyone pressing for equality, Felix kept to an English alias no clerk would flag. He would not risk his patients who needed him. Nor would he ever risk the practice or the people who kept it standing: Nurse Wendy, Alfie, Nick, Andre—family at 87 Harley Street.

I must keep silent.

Because names leave trails, trails lead to doors. Baron von List opens those doors—and people vanish.

But he had not given up. He would not. He would never stop trying to find *her.*

"Is it all done, then?" The young countess's voice, careful and bright, cut into his thoughts when his young patient, Emily, hopped off the chair.

Felix turned to mother and daughter. The girl had her bright curls tied with a ribbon so he could work; her fingers gripped the pelisse folded in her lap as if it could steady her better than any hand. He kept his tone even, the one that lowered shoulders and unfurled breaths.

"Open once more for your mother, Miss Emily."

She did, brave in the way children are when bravery is shown to them. Felix held the mirror so her mother could see his work. The small mirror caught a neat golden gleam; no ridge, no gap.

"Bite," he said, and she obeyed. As she clenched her teeth to show her mother her smile, there was no sign of his work. The countess tilted, searching.

"It's tiny now," she said with palpable relief, and he knew it was meant as a compliment. His work must be invisible; so must his name.

Emily tipped up her chin, shamelessly proud. The new gold winked only when she opened wide. Her mother let out the breath she'd seemed to have been holding during the treatment.

"Oh, Dr. Leafley, you've worked a miracle for Emily." The distance of rank slipped; only a relieved mother remained. "Others would have waited until it grew worse or—well." Her lips pinched against the thought she would not name.

"We did not wait." He stripped off his gloves and set them square on the brass tray. "You brought her early. We needed only the smallest fillings."

"In a few years she'll make her debut," the countess said, eyes warm with gratitude and calculation both. "Her smile must be impeccable. Thanks to you, it will be." Her gaze drifted to his hands. "Where did you learn such precise work? It shines—so small, so smooth."

"In Vienna, your grace." He let a contained smile touch his mouth. "Many years ago."

In another life entirely.

"You're much too young to speak so." Her voice softened. "Thank you, Dr. Leafley."

Emily made a proper curtsey, grave as a duchess. "Thank you, sir."

"Bravely done," he told her, and meant it. "If it troubles her in the future, send word. I will call."

"We shall." The countess adjusted her daughter's shawl with hands that trembled now, the need for stillness had passed. Fine muslin whispered; the door murmured shut behind them.

Felix stood a moment with his palm flat to the brass tray, feeling the last warmth the metal had stolen from his hands. These tiny gold fillings would hold if they were minded.

Nurse Wendy slipped into his treatment room with hot water; steam loosened the sharp scent of clove oil. Her apron sat crisp at her waist; her gaze combined affection and practicality in equal measure.

"She did very well," Wendy said.

"Indeed." He lifted the tray so she could pour.

"A boy waits in the hall," Wendy added. "Kitchen maid's son from number seven. He tried to be a man about it, but—" a small tilt of her hand "—he's frayed."

His schedule ran tight as clean stitches: a gentleman at the hour; a nervous lady at the half; two more beyond. He could keep to it and no one would fault him. He pictured a boy with a cap crushed between his palms, pride held together with stubborn thread.

"Bring him in, please," Felix said.

The boy entered with his jaw set for battle. Tall but thin. Felix rolled his sleeves—not for show, only to feel the work in his forearms—and warmed his instrument in his palm so the metal wouldn't startle.

"Name?"

"Tom, sir."

"Tom." Felix tipped the lamp a fraction, coaxing clean light across the chair.

"How old?"

"Twelve." Tom tightened his grip on the cap. "My mother said you could help me."

"Let me see." The front tooth told its story at once: a fall, a split edge. Not a case for gold but porcelain. "Market cart?"

A flush rose in patches. "I might've slipped. To show I could."

"Of course, you could." Felix brushed clove oil to the gum and spoke while he worked. "We'll make it neat. Then you may boast properly."

Tom's lip trembled once. "I can't pay, sir."

"Does your mother make the delightful plum tarts?" Felix asked.

"Yes, sir."

"Then consider this our thanks for the smell of her plum tart drifting up our stairs." He raised his voice a shade. "Wendy, is there anyone else waiting for me?"

"Not yet," came her dry answer from the passage.

"Then I'll tend to our young acrobat right away."

Tom's chest rose as if a button might pop. He managed a strangled "Thank you, sir," and ducked his head. When the door closed behind Wendy, Felix let himself take one long breath that reached the tight place under his ribs. *This is the work. This is what matters.*

A short while later, the boy left lighter and with another

appointment in a day. The nervous Lord Chesterfield followed; he left steadier than he arrived. Outside, the lamplighter's pole flashed in the window and moved on. Inside, Felix's hands did exactly what they'd been trained to do: swift when swiftness spared pain, patient when patience protected what could be saved.

Between one patient and the next, Vienna rose in his mind again.

It had taught him how to seal gold so it held like enamel—no show, only strength. It had taught him to see a flinch before it arrived, to pause a heartbeat longer than pride advised, to trust what lived in his fingertips. His mentor had covered his hand once and waited until the urge to rush quieted.

He had believed he'd never leave that room with its cold air and varnished benches and stern windows. He had believed he would give anything to stay because she was near. In the end, he had given more than he had counted.

And London asked its price still. The notice on his desk—dull paper, thin ink—requested the particulars of every tradesman with a Royal Warrant for the sake of "order." Names. Birthplaces. Affiliations. Lists chase of Jews.

Alfie had set his palm over another notice this morning and said, very mildly, "Let it sit."

Now, Felix stared at the threat as if it had been no different than the one all those years ago in Vienna.

He trimmed the lamp's wick until the flame burned clean. The burnisher lay curved and faithful on the linen. He set it down too carefully, as if it might break. Warmth stirred under his breastbone at the memory that always arrived with Vienna; then a practiced chill swept it aside.

He had lost her.

Maisie.

All those years ago.

Harley Street—his name on the door, his days full, his nights honest—had come at a cost that did not leave visible marks. So he kept working. He kept his borrowed name tidy and his care exact. He hid his hope where it could not be used against them. Felix did not speak her name into the room. He let it rest, where it had learned to be muted. Then he turned back to his chair, to the next small rescue, and—because hope never learned its lesson—allowed one promise to settle with the weight of a vow.

One day, I'll find you, Maisie.

My love.

Chapter One

Vienna, Spring 1812

> *University of Vienna—Faculty of Dental Medicine*
> *By Order of the Rector*

It is hereby announced that, in the final examinations of the graduating class of 1812, the following gentlemen have obtained the highest distinction:

1. *Faivish Blattner*
2. *Herr Karl-Heinz von Altenburg*
3. *Herr Georg Wittelsbach*
4. *Herr Matthias Bismarck*

The first-named, by virtue of his achievement, is appointed apprentice to Professor Ephraim Morgenschein.

Faivish read the list twice, though once was enough. Every other name wore its polite little Herr, neat as epaulets. His name stood bare—just Faivish Blattner, sitting above three aristocrats like an ink blot no one wanted on the parchment.

The corridor behind him swelled with boots and voices, laughter echoing sharp as the stone beneath his feet.

A shove caught his shoulder, jolting him forward.

"You think you belong there?" Karl-Heinz von Altenburg's voice was smooth as cream, smug as ever. "That place is mine. The only reason your name sits at the top is because Morgenschein is a Jew like you. Morning shine—what sort of name is that? The sun shines, not mornings."

The cluster behind him laughed, brittle as glass.

Faivish's fists curled. Every instinct urged him to answer. But he lifted his chin instead, walked on. Give them nothing. Let them choke on silence.

At the far end of the corridor, Alfie Collins leaned against the wall, arms folded.

"Well?" Alfie asked.

Faivish allowed himself a small smile. "Yes. First. I'll be Professor Morgenschein's apprentice."

"I knew it." Alfie clapped his shoulder. "Knew you'd be the best."

Faivish nodded, though the omission on the parchment burned hotter than the praise. Being first always came with a price—and enemies.

Alfie had been his roommate since their first term, studying alchemy and chemistry while dreaming of his own apothecary. Faivish's dream was different, but this paper tucked in his pocket carried him closer—not only to becoming a dentist worthy of the professor he admired, but to working under the same roof as the professor's daughter. Maisie Morgenschein.

The girl he'd been watching like a star he couldn't reach.

"So you'll be in the practice?" Alfie asked as they stepped into the cold air. Their breath visible in the corridor.

"Yes," Faivish said. One syllable, but it held everything.

Alfie grinned, too knowingly. "She'll be there, then. Not just across a hall—you'll actually have to speak to her."

"I know." Maisie.

He'd glimpsed her at the university, escorting her father, just enough to lose his breath each time. But the memory that haunted him wasn't her face—it was her voice. That day at the practice when he'd borrowed Morgenschein's kiln, he'd heard her humming Tumbalalaika from the back rooms.

The Yiddish melody had slipped under his skin, impossible to forget, just like her.

Topping his class had been his ambition for four years. But working beside her? That felt like standing on top of the world.

⇒⟫⟫⟪⟪⇐

THE HANDHELD MIRROR on the brass tray caught the light and flared like a small sun. Maisie rubbed at it until her own face swam in the steel—ghostly, stretched. She smoothed her apron after, forcing her restless hands to be still. Her mother had stood here once, polishing these same tools before Father's most important patients. That was seven years ago. Illness had carried her off, leaving Maisie with a three-year-old sister and the certainty that she could never again be only a girl. Not after that.

The muffled rumble of wheels outside drifted in through the shutters. The air carried the clean, sharp bite of clove oil from the practice below.

Then came footsteps. Heavier than Father's. Slower, deliberate. And a voice—a ripple of English vowels through the doorway.

The Marquess of Stonebridge.

One of Father's most loyal patients. An exiled English nobleman whose reserve melted only when he spoke of his boy back in England. Maisie was used to his polite nods when she appeared with towels or filled the basin. But today his voice carried a different weight.

"...my wife has taken a turn for the worse," he said. "When she's gone, our little John will be all I have left. And if something happens to me, my sister is nearly an invalid. She cannot raise a boy and protect the marquisate till John's of age."

Father's reply was gentle, but the edge in it was firm. "Bring him here. Vienna has every advantage—art, culture, medicine at the forefront of Europe."

"Medicine, yes, but it is as riddled with politics as the stage," the Marquess returned with a wry twist of the mouth. "Still… without you, Morgenschein, I might not have a single tooth left."

Maisie stepped forward, balancing a folded towel and a pitcher. The Marquess's eyes flicked to her—measuring, considering. Then he lowered himself into the chair.

"If society allowed it," he said suddenly, "I'd trust a capable woman like your daughter to watch over John."

The words hit strangely. Impossible, of course. Her place was here, not in some English estate. Yet the thought lodged, faint as a blur.

He settled back. "So, with this new technique, you can restore a smile?"

Father's pride warmed his tone. "Yes. The latest method. Not yet released for general use." But Maisie saw it then—the faint tremor in his hand as he gestured toward the tray.

Before she could think about it, a knock sounded.

"That will be my new apprentice," Father said, and pride softened his whole face. "First in his class every year since he enrolled—Faivish Blattner."

Maisie turned. And nearly lost her grip on the pitcher.

The student was not what she had pictured. His dark hair looked wind-tossed, a sun-touched strand falling over his brow. His eyes—brown, clear, alive with intelligence. His coat could not disguise the breadth of his shoulders or the easy strength in his stride. She had imagined nimble, scholarly hands. Instead, they were broad, veins visible beneath smooth, tanned skin.

He bowed to the Marquess, then looked at Father with a smile. Warm. Unassuming. Admiring in a way that sent a strange flutter through her chest.

Rolling up his sleeves, he made his way to the basin. Water splashed, mingling with the bite of clove oil. His movements were deliberate, almost meditative, as though the work began before he even touched the tools.

He let his gaze drift over the tray. Did he nod to her?

The mirror caught the light again in his hand. He tested the mallet and weighed it. Even the air around him seemed charged with purpose.

Father began to explain, gesturing, and again—the tremor.

Maisie's breath caught. She had noticed it before, that tiny quiver. But never like this. The ache of it pressed into her chest. For a heartbeat, she forgot anyone else was in the room—until Faivish's gaze met hers.

He spoke gently. "If I may, Professor." He lifted the plaster model for the Marquess to see. "Porcelain fused over gold caps, cemented in place. We can halt decay without extraction. Your teeth, restored—and lasting a lifetime."

"You made these for me?"

"Yes," Faivish said.

"Under my supervision," Father added quickly. Pride sharpened his voice. "With the newest techniques at the university."

Maisie found herself watching Faivish's hands again. Deft. Steady. Gentle.

The hour slid past in the soft hum of steel and water, the rise and fall of low voices. Even the Marquess's stiff frame eased under Faivish's careful touch. Grateful—that was the word. He looked almost grateful.

Maisie worked quietly, clearing the tray, replacing towels. And when she stepped back into the hall for fresh supplies, she caught herself humming—*Tumbalalaika*. A tune her mother had once filled this house with.

When she returned, Faivish's eyes lifted. A faint smile touched them. "I know that song," he murmured, just for her. "But never quite like that."

Heat rose to her cheeks. She set down the towels, busying her hands. Their rhythm fell in step again—she anticipated his reach, he nodded in wordless thanks—the scrape of metal, the clink of porcelain, the quiet cadence of doctor and nurse.

She told herself it was only efficiency. But when his fingers brushed hers, steadying the plaster model as she set it down after the last crown was fixed, she felt it. That spark and danger. And beneath the scent of clove oil and the rustling of cloth, the risk echoed like a shadow: sometimes, the impossible was exactly what the heart began to want.

Chapter Two

Two months later, Vienna...

THE LAST PATIENT of the day had scarcely stepped out into the street when Faivish rinsed his hands in the porcelain basin. Soapy foam slid over his knuckles, and he listened to the house shift into a quieter evening rhythm.

From the kitchen drifted the scrape of cutlery, the clink of bowls, a burst of laughter that could only belong to Deena. Nine years old and thus eleven years younger than Maisie, was incapable of being still.

Drawn to the friendly sound, he stepped into the doorway.

The Morgenschein kitchen glowed like a hearth—lamplight gilding the plaster walls, a bowl of strawberries crowned with whipped cream at the center of the oak table, adorned with a simple woven center cloth. The window was propped open to the street; outside, a carriage rumbled over cobblestones, a hawker's call trailing faintly behind.

Maisie sat close to her father's right hand, sleeves pushed back, her braid loosened by the day's labor. One delightfully stubborn blonde wisp had slipped free and curved against her cheek, catching the lamplight. The sight of it made his fingers ache—an almost physical pull—to reach across and smooth it into place. To touch her. Hold her.

Instead, he lingered where he was. Watching.

Her gaze lifted to his. And even though his eyes held hers, his heart stopped. "Would you like to stay for dinner?" she asked.

He'd noticed the simple spread on the counter, likely reserved for after the meal—bread torn thick, a wedge of cheese, apples sliced clean, and of course, the berries bright as jewels against the porcelain. Before he could answer, Deena bounced in her seat, curls springing. *"Ananas mit Schlagobers!"* she declared, though there wasn't a pineapple in sight. Ananas meant pineapple, except in Viennese German where it meant strawberries. Whipped cream was named after the heavy cream rising to the top of the milk, which, well, was whipped to its fluffy perfection like the one on the table.

Faivish chuckled. "That looks delicious."

"As we call it in Vienna," she shot back, chin high with the pride of belonging.

Professor Morgenschein's knife paused mid-slice on a piece of apple. His tone was mild, but the words had an edge. "You were born Jewish. That is the only truth that follows us. Nationality—no matter what we give to them—never sticks."

Maisie's spoon hovered over her bowl, her lashes dropping like shutters.

The air shifted. Faivish knew that silence. The same taut quiet that always crept in when prejudice pressed too close to their door. He thought of Rector Hofstätter, of the man's endless disputes with the professor, and felt heat rise at the back of his neck.

"He demands I use the porcelain work under his roof," Professor Morgenschein muttered as if he'd known that Faivish knew why he'd corrected Deena as the older man resumed his slice with more force than needed. "The building belongs to the university, he says. As if thirty years of my work do not count."

Every corner of this place bore Morgenschein's mark—his wife's, too, before illness stole her away. They had built not just a practice, but a refuge. And still, men like Hofstätter would call it borrowed.

The professor gestured toward the empty chair. Faivish sat,

the wood warm from recent use. Deena smeared cream across her chin, giggling, while Maisie leaned over now and then to steady her little sister's hand or nudge the bowl closer. Quiet efficiency. But also, devotion. She was the axis around which this household turned.

Faivish felt it then—an ache low and steady. She belonged here, in this house, in this role. And yet, somehow, he wanted her for himself.

"You know, Professor," he said, aiming his voice low enough for Maisie to hear, "I'm to meet Alfie Collins tonight at the Spanish Riding School."

The words hung in the air. Maisie's spoon slowed.

The professor nodded. "Ah, yes, the apothecary. Ambitious for a British student. He'll have his shop one day, I'm sure."

Maisie traced slow circles in the cream with her spoon. "What business do you and Alfie have there?" The question was soft, almost reluctant, but it carried a spark of curiosity that thrilled him.

"Alfie's been asked to bring ointments for the horses. Have you ever seen the Lipizzaners?"

Her eyes flicked toward him, quick as a heartbeat, then shifted to her father. The professor sliced another apple, precisely as a surgeon.

"No," she said. "Since Mother passed… Father works so much."

He heard what she left unsaid: outings had not been theirs to enjoy.

"Would you both like to come?" His voice was light, though his pulse wasn't. "Deena, too. Alfie will be there. I'll see you home before dark. Entirely proper."

Professor Morgenschein looked up, surprised, but waved a hand. "Yes, yes. Go on, children. Maisie, keep an eye on your sister."

Deena's whole face lit. "Please, Maisie?"

A moment's hesitation stretched thin as wire. Faivish held his breath.

At last, Maisie nodded. "All right."

The word landed like a stone in still water, rippling through him. He'd longed to take Maisie out for so long, and this was as close as he could manage to the honor.

They finished the meal, but he barely tasted it. Outside, the city was turning to honey with the afternoon sun. Two months of imagining her beyond the bright walls of the practice—and tonight, it would be real.

Sometimes, it seemed, beginnings started with strawberries and cream.

THE LATE-AFTERNOON SUN lingered on Maisie's shoulders as she and Deena reached the wrought-iron gates. A small plaque beside the arch read *Spanische Hofreitschule*—the Spanish Riding School. She had heard of it since childhood: the oldest institution in Europe devoted to the art of classical horsemanship, where riders trained for years to master the white Lipizzaner stallions.

Warm metal gleamed under her fingertips as she pressed the gate open, and above, the imperial crest caught the light—the double-headed eagle staring down as if it had been taking the measure of its visitors for centuries. Maisie tilted her chin up, uneasy beneath its gaze. All that history—emperors, audiences, performances polished to perfection—pressed against her like a weight, neatly contained within one legendary building. Beyond the gates, marble columns and glittering chandeliers waited to preside over a spectacle older than she could truly grasp.

Faivish had brought them here in barely ten minutes, walking with that measured stride of his. His coat was buttoned to the throat, his shoulders straight enough to make other men look careless. Beside him, Maisie was suddenly conscious of her own steps, how her hem whispered over the stones.

Another figure stood waiting near the archway. Dark blond

hair, broad chest, and a wooden crate balanced easily on one hip. It looked like the sort of box a greengrocer might have used for cabbages, but instead it brimmed with squat jars sealed with cork. Even from here, the contents caught the light—green-gold, glimmering—and the sharp-sweet tang reached Maisie's nose, herbs and something biting underneath. She wondered at the smell, but her gaze slid back to Faivish almost at once, as if drawn by gravity.

"This is Alfie Collins, my roommate," Faivish said.

Alfie set the crate down and bent over her hand with a bow that belonged more to a ballroom than a stable yard. "A pleasure, Miss Morgenschein," he said, vowels polished, clipped with English precision. He repeated the bow for Deena, and her giggle burst out, hands flying to her mouth.

"I've been pounding herbs all day for this liniment," Alfie went on, throwing Faivish a conspirator's grin. "If I reek of *Pferdesalbe*, forgive me."

Maisie caught the name—an ointment for horses, camphor, and menthol meant to ease muscles. Now that she knew, the scent rose sharper, threaded with rosemary, pungent but not unpleasant.

Deena's eyes went wide as saucers. "So you're a true apothecary? Can you make perfume? Rose pomade? Poison?"

"Yes," Alfie said cheerfully, "though I'd never put all three in the same jar."

That was enough to entice her younger sister. Deena skipped to his side, peppering him with more questions until Alfie tipped back his head and laughed outright.

Maisie fell into step a pace behind, beside Faivish. She let her eyes climb the pale façade of the Riding School. Stucco curved into flourishes, each line drawing the gaze higher and higher. "Baroque," she murmured without thinking. "See how the façade pulls your eyes upward? That was the point—to raise the soul as much as the sight."

Faivish looked down at her, and the curve of his mouth softened into something that wasn't quite a smile. "I'm beginning to believe you could make anything sound like poetry."

Her breath caught. The words struck too close, and yet she didn't look away. When he offered his arm, she hesitated only a heartbeat. To take his arm felt like admitting something she had spent too long denying. Yet her hand moved of its own accord, sliding into the crook of his elbow.

The wool of his sleeve was warm beneath her palm, and the strength of his arm was steady, unyielding. Heat crept into her chest, spiraling outward until she had to steady her breath. It was nothing more than a gentleman's courtesy and yet so much more.

Her fingers pressed lightly, as if testing the reality of him, and she was startled by the answering jolt low in her belly. The world seemed to narrow to his strong arm, offered just to her. The closeness was more daring than his kind smile—because it was public, because it was real, because it was *him*.

They stepped together beneath the arch into shadow. The air shifted at once—cool and heavy with leather and hay, carrying the warm musk of horses. Somewhere beyond, unseen hooves struck stone in a slow, deliberate rhythm, each strike echoing against the high, whitewashed vaults above. Even the sound seemed ceremonial, as though it belonged not to animals at all, but to emperors and centuries.

Maisie tightened her grip by the smallest fraction, unwilling to let go.

"This way," Alfie called, striding ahead with Deena skipping at his side. Framed engravings lined the passage: stallions frozen mid-leap, hooves tucked, riders stern.

And then—the passage ended, and the hall revealed itself.

Maisie stopped where she stood.

Light cascaded from tall arched windows, spilling across sand raked into perfect lines. Chandeliers dripped overhead like frozen rain. Crimson draperies fell in rich folds against the bright walls, and the marble columns stood in solemn rows, giving the whole place the sensation of a cathedral. Even the air smelled sanctified—clean sand, polished leather, a faint sweetness of hay.

Deena gasped and tugged on Alfie's sleeve. "It's beautiful," she whispered. Her voice carried in the vast hush, and then she was off again, leaning over the railing as if she could drink the scene straight into her bones.

Four riders already circled the arena, each astride a gleaming white Lipizzaner. The men's boots gleamed, coats sharp at the waist, bicorne hats shadowing eyes that never strayed from their horses. The stallions' tails had been braided with ribbon; their forelegs lifted and fell with a precision that made Maisie's heart stumble.

The air seemed to pulse with the rhythm—thud of hooves, jingle of harness, soft snort of a stallion.

She let out a quiet gasp. "It's… like something out of a fairy tale."

Turning to share the wonder, she found Faivish watching her, not the horses.

The chandeliers caught in his eyes, scattering flecks of gold through the dark brown. The warmth there unsettled her, loosening something deep inside. He didn't look away. Neither did she.

Somewhere, Deena resumed questioning Alfie about peppermint oil. Somewhere, the horses struck their rhythm into the sand. But between her hand resting on his arm and the weight of his gaze, Maisie felt the air alter around them. She should have withdrawn. She didn't.

And he gave her no reason to.

MAISIE NOTICED RIGHT away that the back stables were cooler than the grand hall. The air smelled of hay, saddle oil, and warm animal breath. Afternoon light streamed through narrow windows, stripping the stalls in gold. Somewhere behind her, Deena gave a small sneeze, and Maisie thought—not for the first time and with a heavy heart—that soon Faivish would insist on taking them home.

A tall rider in a spotless brown tailcoat appeared from the shadows, boots clicking on the stone as if every sound were meant to remind them who owned the space. His chin tipped at an angle of entitlement like that of a man accustomed to others stepping aside.

"Collins," he said, eyes darting to the crate in Alfie's arms.

Alfie set it down without hurry. "My lord," he answered, calm and unbothered. "The salve for the Lipizzaner's joints, as you ordered."

The man's gaze shifted, landing on Faivish. The flicker of politeness vanished. His lips curled faintly. "Best mind yourself. This stallion belongs to Baron von List, Rector Hofstätter's nephew. He wouldn't take kindly to..." He let the sentence dangle, but the look that accompanied it was enough.

Maisie's stomach pinched tight at the mention of Hofstätter. The one with the sneer she'd never forgotten, who measured worth by lineage and nothing more, no matter how hard father worked and how many times he'd proved he was indispensable to the faculty.

Yet, Alfie seemed to ignore the insult. He crouched, uncorked one of the jars, and let the sharp, resinous scent of herbs spill into the air. The horse shifted, ears flicking, a tremor racing through its foreleg.

"Step back," Faivish murmured, quiet but firm, and Maisie found herself pulling Deena behind her, skirts whispering through straw.

The stallion tossed his head, muscles bunching.

Alfie looked up quickly. "Careful, Faivish—"

"Better if you call off the Jew," the rider cut in, tone sharp.

Maisie's face went hot. She saw Faivish's jaw tighten, the faint tic of restraint, but before he could reply, Alfie rose smoothly, voice bright as if to mask steel.

"Not my position, my lord. He's a doctor—and my best friend. Almost a doctor, if you must be exact, but always the better man."

"Almost?" The rider's tone cut like a whip. "And yet he touches the horse?"

Alfie's brows climbed. "Are you a doctor tending your horse? Or the stableboys? If titles are the only requirement, perhaps the Emperor should do it himself."

The silence stretched, taut as a bowstring.

Again, the horse shifted, growing visibly restless. Faivish didn't step back. Instead, he moved closer, steady, his hand rising to rest against the stallion's forehead and with each slow stroke down the white blaze of its face, the tremors eased. "Easy, boy," he whispered, voice low, coaxing. "That's it. Easy now."

The stallion's breath steadied. The tension melted out of his frame as though thawing from ice.

Maisie couldn't look away from Faivish because he exuded such calm and certainty. In that moment, she felt as if she'd glimpsed the truest part of him, something no slur could diminish. He healed.

⟫⟪

AFTER THEY LEFT the Riding School, the city swallowed them again. Vienna's streets were narrower here, caught between tall façades that still held the warmth of the day. The wooden crate was back in Alfie's arms, though this time only the empty jars he'd exchange for the full ones clinked together as he shifted the weight when they neared Maisie's home.

"Well then," he said, tipping his hat with a grin that included all three of them. "Goodnight, you two. And you, young lady." He gave Deena a little bow as though she were a duchess, and she burst into giggles, curtsying before darting ahead toward their door.

You two? The words caught Maisie squarely in the stomach. Did Alfie know something she hadn't yet admitted, even to herself? Best friends always knew but she couldn't even name it yet.

Before she could collect her thoughts, the crate and Alfie's easy demeanor faded down the lane. The door clicked shut behind Deena, leaving Maisie and Faivish standing alone in the cooler early evening air.

He looked at her, then offered his arm again. "Let me see you home." There were five, perhaps six steps, left to the door.

Still, she didn't hesitate. Her hand slid into place as if they could stretch the moment, and together they walked beneath the lamps just flickering to life. Their glow stretched long over the cobblestones. The air smelled faintly of roasting chestnuts and river damp from the Danube drifting through the alleys.

She loved this city—its carved palaces, glittering shop windows, gardens spilling roses. And yet none of it was ever truly hers. For Jews, Vienna was a stage on which they were permitted to play but never to own.

At the corner, crickets began their steady song. She turned to Faivish, words slipping out before she could stop them. "I was afraid, back in the stables. That the horse might have kicked you."

He smiled slowly, the sort of smile that made her knees feel unreliable. "If he had, I'd have kicked back."

She laughed—bubbled, unguarded—and the sound seemed to draw his eyes to her mouth. "You wouldn't," she teased, breath catching. Heat rushed low in her belly.

He pressed a hand to his chest in mock offense. "Wouldn't I?"

"You're a healer," she said softly, still smiling. "You calmed him like no one else could. You were..." She faltered, then finished with a truth that made her cheeks heat. "Wonderful."

"Me? *Wonderful?*" he asked, quiet now, teasing threaded with something deeper.

She couldn't look away. "You know you are."

He stepped closer, and the lamplight caught the hard line of his jaw, the bronze warmth of his skin. She gripped her skirts to stop her hand from rising to his cheek.

"You've no idea," he said, voice low, "how long I've wanted to see you outside the practice."

Her heart kicked. "Since you started the apprenticeship in May?" she whispered.

His mouth curved, not quite a smile. "No. Since that day in the amphitheater—when you carried your father's notes. Almost four years ago."

Her breath stalled. "Four years?"

"Yes." The single syllable felt like a vow. "I worked harder every year because of it. Because I liked you then, and I never stopped."

Her throat tightened. "Faivish…"

He reached for her hand. Tentative, giving her the chance to pull away. She didn't. His fingers closed around hers, his thumb tracing slow circles across her knuckles.

"I've been more grateful than I could say, for every time you've asked me to stay for dinner," he said softly. "Not only because of the food but because I could linger near you."

She smiled, lips trembling. "I… always hoped you'd say yes."

The quiet between them thickened, heavy with things unsaid.

"And if your father caught us in… less than a proper moment?" he asked, half teasing, half daring.

Her breath hitched. "I think… I'd be afraid."

"So would I," he admitted, leaning closer. "But only because I want the chance to ask him—to ask you—properly."

Her heart pounded wildly and recklessly, but now she had to know, or she thought she'd faint right then. "You want to court me?"

"For months, I didn't dare ask," he said. "But tonight… may I?"

She didn't answer with words. She lifted her chin and he was already so close. His lips brushed hers, tentative at first, offering her every chance to pull back. But she'd never! And then, he deepened the kiss, gentle and certain, and her knees went weak.

His hand cupped her jaw with the care of a man who could heal but never harm. She pressed into him, fingers fisting in his coat, every bit of her coming alive.

When he finally drew back, he lifted her hand and kissed her knuckles, slow and reverent.

"Goodnight, Maisie," he whispered.

But she caught his coat, tugged him back down to her, and this time her kiss was urgent, hungry, her voice breaking against his lips. "Teach me how to kiss you properly. I've waited long enough."

Chapter Three

THE NEXT MORNING, she was everywhere. First in the hall, slipping past him with a tray balanced on her hands, then lingering by the treatment room door. She had no reason to hover, and yet her shoulder brushed his sleeve each time she passed. Lavender clung to her like a secret, threaded with the sharper tang of clove oil. The scent lodged in his throat until he could hardly swallow and Faivish longed for nothing more than to press his lips to hers for another kiss.

Teach me how to kiss you properly.

Her words. Simple and innocent. He'd not been able to sleep all night after he had, in fact, taught her. And yet, he had so much more to show her.

I just can't wait.

But he needed her father's permission to court her, it was the respect his professor, mentor, and her only living parent deserved. She was precious and deserved his utmost respect and honor.

By mid-morning, Faivish was bent over his instruments when she appeared again, tray in hand—and a thin line of red glistening across her finger.

"Maisie," he said, sharper than he meant, crossing to her before she could set the tray down. "You've cut yourself."

"It's nothing—"

"Let me see." The command left his mouth before he could temper it. He caught her hand gently but firmly, turning it into the light. The nick was shallow, but the bead of blood shone bright against her skin. He pressed a clean cloth to it, steady as though she were a patient in the chair, not the woman he thought of every single second of his life.

She watched him, lashes lowered, her breathing slowing until it matched the measured rhythm of his own. The room seemed to shrink to the fragile weight of her hand in his and the soft flutter of her pulse beneath his thumb.

Without thinking, he lifted her hand just enough to bare the curve of her fingertips. He brushed his lips there—careful, not against the cut, but close enough that the warmth of his mouth drew the sting away. The thought came swift and undeniable: if he could, he would take every hurt from her. Always and forever.

Her lashes flickered, a small start of surprise. But she didn't pull back. He felt the moment she yielded, her fingers softening until they curled lightly around his, keeping him there. His thumb traced her skin, slow and deliberate, finding the quickened beat beneath. That pulse thrummed through him like a tether, intoxicating.

He held her gaze, memorizing the lamplight on her cheek, the faint parting of her lips, the way each breath seemed to catch before it left her. Lavender. Clove. Her. He would never breathe them again without remembering this exact moment.

And she let him press his mouth to her hand. She let him hold her there, suspended on the thin edge between propriety and something far more dangerous.

The scrape of shoes broke the spell.

He glanced up. Professor Morgenschein stood in the doorway, silent. His gaze fell to where Faivish still cradled Maisie's hand. It lingered, unreadable, before it rose again to meet his eyes. No anger—only recognition, and something else that weighed heavier than words.

Faivish released her slowly, but the imprint of her hand

burned in his palm. Morgenschein inclined his head once, as if he'd seen enough, and turned away.

Faivish's resolve hardened. He would ask permission. Now.

It wasn't infatuation, nor the kind of careless tryst that Vienna's gossips might imagine. Faivish wanted a life with Maisie. And after last night—after the way she'd kissed him back, the way her hand had lingered in his—he knew she would welcome his offer if her father gave his blessing. Today, he told himself, he would ask.

But the moment never came.

When he lingered in the hallway, waiting for a pause between patients, the professor brushed past him with a ledger in hand. Faivish opened his mouth, only to find himself dismissed with a curt, "Check the appointment book—Mrs. Adler insists her crown be moved up a day."

Later, when Faivish carried in the sterilized instruments, he tried again. "Professor—"

But Morgenschein didn't look up from the tray. "Pass me the forceps, will you? No, the larger pair. Thank you." His tone was even, polite, yet it built a wall Faivish couldn't scale.

By midday, Faivish caught his mentor at the basin, sleeves rolled as he washed his hands. The light from the window fell across the man's face, etching hollows beneath his eyes. Faivish said quietly, "There's something important I'd like to ask—"

Morgenschein reached for the towel, rubbing briskly, his gaze fixed on the brass mirror on the counter. "You've a steady hand with gold foil, Faivish. Better than mine." A compliment, but also a diversion. The words landed with more finality than praise.

Again and again, the professor turned aside. A ledger to be signed, a patient to be soothed, a tray to be polished. Each time Faivish swallowed back the words burning his tongue. Each time, Morgenschein's mouth pressed into that same thin, pained line— as though he carried a truth too heavy to share, one that made every request to speak dissolve on Faivish's lips.

By the time the last patient left, Faivish's throat was dry from silence, his resolve frayed by the loss of so many missed chances.

"You've done well with the Marquess," Morgenschein said at last, polishing a brass tray as though it needed one more gleam. "Better than I expected."

Faivish's chest leapt—was this his moment? "Thank you, Professor. It means so much to—"

Morgenschein cut across him, voice low. "It's more than praise. It's an opportunity. The Marquess has written to a colleague in Calcutta. There's an apprenticeship there. A rare one. They'll take you."

The words struck like a dropped mallet.

"Calcutta?" Faivish repeated, almost disbelieving. "In India?"

"Yes." Morgenschein's gaze slipped past him. "A city growing faster than you can imagine. Medicine is hungry for skilled hands. It's a chance of a lifetime, Faivish. The sort of post that would open doors that will always remain locked to you here."

He meant Vienna. He meant Hofstätter.

Not an opportunity—an escape.

Faivish set down the mirror he'd been drying. His knuckles whitened on the brass. "Professor, I have no wish to go to India. My place is here. With you."

"And with Maisie?" Morgenschein asked quietly, the question dropping like a stone.

Faivish did not flinch. "If you would allow it—yes. I came to you for dentistry. But I found more than that. I would be honored to stay, to work with you, for as long as you'll have me."

For an instant, light broke across the older man's eyes. Then it dimmed, leaving only weariness etched in its place.

"You've learned all I can teach you," he said slowly. "But I cannot shield you forever. Hofstätter has tolerated you because you are under my name. The moment I am gone…" His voice thinned. "I wish I were strong enough. I wish it were enough."

"You are," Faivish said, the words rough with feeling. "You are everything—to me, to your patients—"

"Not in a world where malice holds influence," Morgenschein interrupted, his tone carrying a finality that made Faivish's stomach clench. "I am old. The Rector is relentless. He wants my methods under his name, and you will be in his sights the moment he can make it so."

Faivish's chest tightened. He had not expected this—not Calcutta dangled like salvation, not Hofstätter's shadow stretching over everything. Yes, he knew the Indian dentists' molten-gold crowns were famed, and yes, part of him ached to see it. But not at this cost. Not at the cost of being with Maisie.

"My place is here," he said again, softer, because the truth burned steadily. "India may be an opportunity. But this is the life I want. Here. With you. With her."

The professor's sigh carried both pain and pride. He set the brass tray aside, his hands trembling faintly. "Leave it, Faivish. Go and rest."

But Faivish hesitated. "The ledger says the Marquess is coming. Shall I prepare—?"

"No," Morgenschein interrupted gently. "Not for treatment. You did well with that."

"Then why—?"

"I need to speak with him," the professor said, his voice suddenly older than Faivish had ever heard it.

A knot twisted tight in Faivish's chest. Something was being kept from him. Something that made the thought of asking for Maisie's hand feel as though it were slipping, just out of reach.

⊱❯❯❯✦❮❮❮⊰

MAISIE SPENT THE afternoon half-distracted from her work but entirely aware of him in every room. He glanced at her more than once—she was certain of it—but the look never lasted long enough to leave proof. In the cramped treatment room, their fingers brushed as she passed him a mirror. The contact sparked through her so sharply she nearly dropped it. And yet he said nothing.

When she asked, lightly, if he might stay for dinner, her father answered for him.

"No. The Marquess is coming," he said, brisk enough to cut short any protest.

The dismissal stung.

So when Faivish stepped out into the dusk, coat folded over one arm, she followed. Coal smoke lingered in the air, sharp against the fading scent of leaves. Her heartbeat fell into step with her hurried feet. At the side alley, where lamplight failed to reach, shadows pooled deep and silent.

She caught his sleeve. "Faivish!"

He turned—surprise flashing in his eyes—just as she rose onto her toes and kissed him. Not tentative, not proper. A kiss pressed from days of restraint and every look they had not dared name.

The coat slid from his arm. His free hand found her waist, steadying, drawing her nearer. He kissed her back with a smile she could feel more than see, as if he had been waiting for her to be the one to cross that line.

Her hands knotted in his shoulders, unwilling to let go. His thumb brushed her side, unhurried, memorizing her shape.

She pulled back for breath, lips tingling.

"When will you speak to him?" she whispered.

"As soon as he lets me," he said low enough for his breath to graze her skin. "Tomorrow. Together with you, perhaps. If he allows."

The certainty in his tone left her dizzy. She kissed him once more, quick and fierce, before stepping away.

And the promise clung to her even more than his kiss as she slipped inside. But she stopped short in the darkened hall. Voices floated from the kitchen—low, urgent. She knew the Marquess's timbre, but the other was Father's.

"...Hofstätter... the faculty..."

She froze. Words tangled, muffled, but fragments broke free: "*...trouble for all of us... Jewish...*" Then another phrase, sharp enough to raise the hairs on her arms: "*...Eleanor Spencer is dead now... but nobody needs to know...*"

The voices dropped again, too low to catch, before rising just long enough for the Marquess to ask, "And what about Deena?"

Maisie's hand tightened on the knob. She stood motionless, her pulse pounding, the echo of her kiss already eclipsed by a dread far larger—whatever lay waiting behind that kitchen door?

Chapter Four

Later that summer...

MAISIE WAS LATE.

Again.

Silk hissed at her sleeves, louder than it should have been and clashing with the muted rise and fall of voices drifting up from her father's practice below. She lingered at the looking glass, one hand pressing against her chest as if she might steady the thrum inside her. It wasn't the silly flutter she'd known earlier this year but deeper now, heavier and the kind that left no air between one pulse and the next.

Faivish's kiss still burned at her mouth: the one from last night, after Father and Deena had gone to sleep. His promise had lingered there too—I'll marry you as soon as your father allows. And they'd based everything on this hope.

But father dismissed them every time they'd broached the issue. Had something shifted in that low exchange with the Marquess—the conversation she wasn't supposed to hear? Did Faivish even know what secrets her father kept folded away like dangerous letters?

The clock struck, brisk and cold. She closed the clasp of the pearls at her ears with fingers that wouldn't stay steady. The mirror gave back a tidy girl, cheeks faintly flushed, hair smoothed into place. But that reflection told none of the story thrumming under her ribs.

Another chime. Now she was later than late.

Her palms prickled with damp as she reached for her shawl. If only her mind would line itself in order like Father's neat rows of labeled ledgers. Instead, it circled back, again and again, to those words overheard in the kitchen—*Hofstätter. Jewish trouble. Eleanor Spencer is dead. What about Deena?* The words that felt like stones she'd hidden in her bodice. Something about that conversation, she suspected, was why Father didn't give Faivish official permission to ask for her hand. And yet, he treated Faivish like a son, as if he were family already.

She ran downstairs, slippers whispering on polished boards. The air shifted, sharp with antiseptic. And there it was—the sight she both longed for and dreaded.

The waiting room brimmed with young women. Ribbons at their sleeves, silk reticules clenched in pale hands, eyes bright and watchful.

He's here.

Whispers fluttered like wings, handkerchiefs twisted, and fans tapped against gloved palms. All of them are waiting for the same person.

Maisie didn't need to ask who.

Doctor *in spe* Faivish Blattner. Almost a doctor, already Father's pride. Her love.

As always, the women followed him. They didn't know the taste of him in the dark, or the way his breath had broken across her skin when he swore tomorrow would be theirs. They hadn't felt his hand steady her waist or the promise in his gaze. Yet every hour that tomorrow slipped further away, Maisie feared Father had other plans—plans that might send him out of her reach.

Through the half-open door, she caught his profile: tall, shoulders squared from habit, his voice a quiet balm to some nervous patient. His hair caught the sun slanting through the window, casting a glow she resented the others seeing.

But then his eyes found hers. And in that look, there was nothing of a doctor, nothing of Father's apprentice. It was the look of a man holding a secret. Their secret.

Every Tuesday and Thursday, the practice swelled like this—queues spilling into the street, chatter buzzing through the waiting room. And still, amid all that noise, Faivish always found a way. A glance that lingered too long. Fingers brushing hers when no one noticed. Sparks she carried away like contraband.

Maisie twisted the fringe of her shawl tight around her fingers, watching as he coaxed a frightened boy with some quiet jest, calmed a man twice his size with nothing more than a hand at the shoulder. She knew those hands in another way—the silent reassurance pressed into her skin when no one was watching.

Then suddenly his head turned. His gaze caught hers full on, direct as a struck match. His mouth quirked—just a sliver, enough to set warmth racing down her spine—before he vanished back through the door.

Too late for them, she thought with a glance at the women waiting. *He is mine.* And she was the only one who knew his laugh when it spilled out unguarded, bright and boyish, as if the world were kinder than it seemed.

The truth pressed at her ribs. Women could not be doctors. Discovery meant marriage at once—something she wanted with an ache that left her breathless, but not if it cost him the future he'd worked for. So she stayed at Father's side, a nurse with her tray, her secrets tucked between teacups and polished mirrors.

Tea. That was her excuse to go back to him.

A few minutes later, she steadied the tray with both hands, jasmine scent curling upward. The waiting women's shawls brushed against her as she passed, eyes flicking with envy at her effortless entrance. They didn't know he had already chosen her. That every time she set tea in his hand, she was not only serving, but claiming her place beside him.

The treatment room was bright with the smell of eucalyptus and lavender. Father glanced up, silver hair glinting under the lamplight, while a patient dabbed delicately at her lips.

Maisie set the tray aside. But her gaze went to Faivish, as it always did.

He dried his hands with calm care, the faint tug at his mouth betraying a warmth meant only for her.

The patient lingered, reluctant to leave. "And Dr. Blattner."

Her father's eyes flicked—Faivish, then her, then back again. The heft of it made her breath falter.

He knows. Or suspects.

I have to tell him—

Not now.

The patient lingered in the doorway, a woman of thirty or so, her smile just a little too eager. "And Dr. Blattner."

Faivish inclined his head, that faint curl at his mouth betraying no more than polite acknowledgment. "Only *in spe*," he said—soon to be. The title rolled easily from him now. His diploma was only ink and parchment away.

The woman's gloved fingers reached for his. "Vienna is fortunate to have you. Such skilled hands." Her gaze clung to him longer than courtesy allowed.

He touched her hand only briefly, bowing away like contact meant little. "You are kind, madam." He used the same measured tone he usually did with everyone but her.

Maisie knew the difference. Knew it in the way his eyes, after that small exchange, lifted across the room until they caught hers.

Heat shot up her throat. That glance was not for the woman in the chair. It was for her alone. And in it lay everything unspoken—the brush of his lips in the alley, the promise of tomorrow, the secret that tied them together so tightly she could hardly breathe.

Her pulse stumbled. She willed her hands steady as she adjusted the tray on the side table. Steady, steady. She could not let the tremor show. Not here, not in front of Father.

"My dear."

The sound of her father's voice sliced the moment. She startled, turning toward him. He held out his empty teacup, his eyes gentler than his tone.

"Would you?"

The porcelain was harmless enough, but Maisie's breath snagged when she saw the way Father's gaze shifted. First to Faivish. Then back to her. A flicker of something unreadable passed across his face. Not anger, not yet. But knowing. Or suspecting.

She felt the blood rush to her cheeks. *He knows. He must know.*

Her fingers closed around the cup, her knuckles white against the handle. Words pressed at the back of her throat—I must tell him. I have to tell him about us so he hears it from me.

But not now. Time never seemed right.

Not with the patient still in the room. Not with Faivish standing close enough that she could feel the ponderousness of his silence.

So she lowered her head, took the cup, and busied herself with the simplicity of pouring tea—while the truth she longed to speak lodged like a stone inside.

Returning to her task, she poured the steaming brew into the waiting porcelain. The air between the three of them felt almost too tight, as if every word, every glance, carried a second meaning. The tension didn't ease, though she felt Faivish's presence behind her—close enough that the warmth of him brushed her back—as he moved to take the emptied tray.

Father smiled fondly at him, a rare light in his proud eyes. "The most talented student I've had in thirty years, and using porcelain for dental crowns instead of just teacups," he declared, a touch of reverence slipping into his tone.

SOON, MAISIE THOUGHT, Faivish would be even busier at the practice when he could restore a tooth with white porcelain instead of gold. Patients were fond of the idea that their oral repairs would be undetectable. It would be a medical marvel— her Faivish performing miracles in plain sight, as if it were nothing at all. If only the university allowed Jewish students the same access to advanced techniques as their peers, instead of keeping such methods reserved for nobility—a truth everyone pretended not to notice, yet no one dared name aloud.

Maisie glanced at her father, reading the genuine pride etched into his expression. Then, almost against her will, she looked at Faivish again. His face betrayed no reaction to the compliment other than the polite inclination of his head. But in that brief flick of his gaze toward her, she felt it—the quiet vow, the unspoken "I'm doing this for us."

Her heartbeat quickened.

The door clicked shut behind the departing patient, sealing them in an almost palpable silence. Maisie smoothed the creases of her apron as if the gesture could settle the rising unease within her. "The waiting room is crowded," she said, looking at her father as she poured his tea. "I don't know if they're here for their teeth—"

"They're definitely here for him," Father jested, though his smile didn't quite reach his eyes. "And they're right to be." He chuckled, warm and fleeting—but the sound faltered, as if laughter cost him something. He reached for the cup she offered, and his hand, frail and speckled with age, trembled visibly.

Maisie's breath hitched as the teacup clattered against its saucer, a thin stream of tea sloshing over the rim.

"Father," she murmured, her voice low but steady, setting the pot down. She reached to steady his hand, but he waved her off with a tight smile.

"I'm alright, my dear. Nothing to fuss over."

But the lie settled heavily in her chest. The tremors had worsened. Now, even the smallest movements seemed to require an effort he could barely summon.

If Father could no longer practice… what would become of them all? Deena still needed watching over, and their lives ran on such a delicate thread. And Faivish—if he were to step into Father's place, not merely as his pupil but as… she hardly dared think it, yet it was always on her mind—her future husband?

Yes, she wanted that more than she could say. But never at

this cost.

And underneath it all was the question she didn't dare voice: did Father's late-night talk with the Marquess have anything to do with this? Or the whispers about poor Eleanor Spencer, whoever she was? She couldn't shake the thought that something—someone—was steering all their futures, and not in her favor.

Behind her, Faivish stepped closer, the sound of his boots soft against the floorboards. His gaze shifted from her father's trembling hands to her face, and something unspoken passed between them. The usual ease in his features hardened into seriousness.

She wasn't alone in this fear. He felt it too.

And certainty washed over her: that she was not alone in her worry. Everything about Faivish's careful glance at Father bore the dense responsibility already pressing on his own future.

"Thank you for taking over, Faivish," her father said, breaking the awkward silence as he lowered his hand to rest it firmly on the small table.

"It was nothing," Faivish replied, his voice measured, his eyes still fixed on the older man. Maisie caught the flicker of something in his expression. Not pity. Respect, perhaps. Or concern. Deeply so.

"It was everything." Her father shook his head, shoulders slumping slightly. "These tremors…" His voice trailed off, and he raised the teacup again, though this time it barely made it to his lips before his hand faltered, spilling more of the cooling tea into the saucer. Muttering something under his breath, he set the cup down with as steady a movement as he could manage. "I can't practice anymore, my boy. And you cannot hold them off for me much longer."

"Who?" Maisie asked, the words tumbling out before she could stop them. Her gaze darted to Faivish, who had turned now and stood near the window, his frame tall and still as stone. "What does he mean?"

Father sighed, folding his hands in his lap. It seemed to cost him something to look her in the eye. "I—I couldn't manage the mallet earlier. My hands … they wouldn't do it. Faivish stepped in. He did the gold foil fillings. He's as good as I was before the tremors."

The knot in Maisie's stomach pulled tighter. Her deepest hope sat within reach—Faivish at her side, her father still at the heart of the practice, Deena safe under their roof. It should have been happiness. It nearly was.

But sometimes, wishes came true at the wrong cost.

She'd imagined her father placing Faivish's hand in hers with pride under the *chuppah*, a wedding canopy decorated with flowers for them. Instead, Father's tremors had worsened. And lately, his gaze lingered on her not with joy, but with a quiet sorrow she couldn't name—creases etching deeper at his brow, his mouth tugged downward as if some unspoken regret lived there.

She wanted to help and would have given everything to see Father smile again. But the truth sat heavy in her chest: he was fading. Slowly, perhaps. But unmistakably. And Faivish's place beside her felt less like a celebration and more like preparation. If only she knew how and what to prepare for… her heart dropped.

Not because Faivish wasn't worthy. But because it meant her father could no longer carry the weight himself. What if this was as close to her dream as she'd ever stand—a future shaped by fear and tenderness, always one pane of glass away from shattering?

"I'm afraid I can't work alone now," Father said. "I will soon retire to mere paperwork and lectures for the faculty. You'll be essential in carrying the highest standard for our patients into the future."

Maisie blinked, her lips parting, the surge of emotions caught somewhere between disbelief and worry. She turned her attention to Faivish, whose gaze briefly lifted to meet hers before darting away again. His profile, outlined by the soft glow through the window, betrayed absolutely no self-congratulation.

"I'm not permitted the highest standard," Faivish said quietly, finally breaking the silence. "Otherwise, the university would allow me access to the new techniques." His words were clipped but steady, though Maisie heard the undercurrent of frustration.

She knew what he meant. Civil rights or not, prejudice still lurked in the corridors of the faculty, polite enough to smile at him in lecture halls but cold enough to bar the doors to certain privileges. The techniques Father had brought back from the university—ones that could transform a patient's smile—had been offered to other students without hesitation. Gentile students. Preferably titled ones.

Faivish had been Father's most gifted pupil, but still, Rector Hofstätter had found reason to delay his training in them at university, and only Father had taught him privately. Maisie knew that now.

Vienna might grant Jews the right to live and work openly, but it did not grant them the same welcome.

Faivish downed the tea she had poured for him, setting the cup down with a precision that belied the anger behind it. His self-control was immaculate; only in his eyes could she glimpse the turmoil beneath.

She caught the faint downturn of Faivish's lips as he moved to the treatment chair, his hands deftly adjusting the headrest and smoothing the clean white linen across its surface. His shoulders squared—not with pride, but as if bracing for a weight that would never lift.

"I don't understand." She heard the words, she knew the facts, but the why still stung. Faivish adjusted the headrest, smoothing the linen with precise care. "On paper," he said at last, "I have every right to the same instruction as any other student. Yet somehow, invitations to special lectures are misplaced. Demonstrations begin just before I arrive. Newer methods always seem to be taught to others."

His voice was steady, but Maisie heard the controlled strain beneath it, the bitterness of years spent swallowing the same truth. It wasn't law that kept him on the margins—it was the quiet narrowing of eyes, the polite omissions, the doors left half-shut.

She wanted to reach out, to pull him into a world where the air wasn't so sharp, where he didn't have to carry the burden of being acknowledged, yet never fully embraced.

"Don't worry about it, Maisie. It's hardly worth noting," Father said. His voice was light, brushing past an awkward moment. Yet, the tightness around his mouth always came at the cost of leaving things unspoken. "Just university politics," he added, and the words fell slower now, weighted with the truth Maisie had come to fear.

"Politics, indeed," Faivish muttered, and though his voice stayed even, Maisie heard the bitter edge beneath it—one she'd learned to recognize over the past few months. It was the sound of him holding back more than he said for fear of trespassing into dangerous territory. He'd told her that this was a promise he'd given his mother the night his parents had been taken from their shop and killed. He'd keep his head low. And yet, she could tell how he bristled against it.

Father exhaled heavily, his hand settling beside the half-spilled tea. His gaze fixed on Faivish for a long, unreadable moment, as though weighing something important. "Perhaps it is time you knew—" he began, but then stopped abruptly, his mouth tightening.

Faivish straightened a fraction in his chair, the movement subtle but alert. "Professor—there's something I've been meaning to—"

Father's hand lifted in quiet interruption, his eyes softening in a way that sent a shiver down Maisie's spine. Whatever passed between them was invisible to her, but she felt it like a sudden draft through the room.

From her place across the table, Maisie's fingers tightened into the folds of her apron. The silence between the two men seemed to stretch, filling the space with unspoken things that pressed against her chest. "T—tell me what is wrong!" she blurted, the words tumbling out before she could stop herself.

Faivish turned toward her, his expression smooth as glass. She searched for a crack, a flicker of truth—but all she met was that calm mask he wore whenever he wanted to spare her worry. He glanced once at Father, a look that felt like a plea for leave to speak. But Father's gaze was steady. Closed.

"Perhaps another time," Faivish said at last with a sigh that resonated with the one Maisie suppressed. His voice had gentled, but the words still landed like a door shutting. He set the brass tray on the table and aligned the instruments, each click of metal against metal too careful, as though order might erase the moment. "The next patient is waiting."

The murmur of women carried in from the waiting room— light, eager voices that belonged to a world untouched by the heaviness pressing in here. Father said nothing. Maisie stood rooted, her arms slack at her sides, the weight of unsaid things settling heavier than any tray. She narrowed her eyes, watching Faivish step into the corridor, the door closing softly between them.

The swell of voices outside rose momentarily, then dimmed again, as if the practice itself held its breath.

Father sighed, the sound worn, and reached for his tea. His hand trembled before the cup touched his lips, and he set it down untouched. "Another time," he murmured—not to her, not even to Faivish, but as though repeating a thought he'd carried too long.

From the other side of the door came Faivish's steady tone, muffled but sure: "You're the best now, Professor. You'll take my place someday."

"I promise I'll do everything you've taught me."

Father exhaled, as if those words gave him a moment's peace. But for Maisie, there was no comfort in them.

Her mind churned like an unquiet sea. Was this silence—this refusal to name what they both knew—linked to the Marquess's visit? The hushed conversation she had overheard through the kitchen door the night before? She remembered the fragments she wished she could forget: *Hofstätter... Jewish troubles... Eleanor Spencer is dead... nobody needs to know.* And, softest of all: *What about Deena?*

The names tangled inside her, barbed and sharp. What could Father possibly have meant?

Nothing about the future felt steady now—not Father's work, not the practice, not the promise Faivish had whispered into her hair. And as the waiting room's voices lifted again, as eyes turned toward her with idle curiosity, Maisie held herself very still, aching for the day she would be something more than a fleeting glance in Faivish Blattner's crowded world.

$$\sim\!\!\diamond\!\!\sim$$

Chapter Five

FAIVISH COUNTED THE hours until he could see her again. Every lecture dragged like penance, the drone of professors a wall between him and the quiet world he wanted most—Maisie's world. Chalk dust clung to the air in the anatomy halls, dry and insistent, as though even the silence wanted to keep him from her. Outside, the corridors hummed with a sharper unrest: pipe smoke curling under the arches, boots striking stone, the restless buzz of students too eager for slogans and marching songs. One clash of heels against flagstones and the clock seemed to lurch another torturous second away from her.

He adjusted the satchel strap, biting into his shoulder, the familiar weight grounding him as he cut toward the courtyard gate.

Alfie caught him there, voice low. "Walk with me."

He didn't slow until they were under the colonnade's shade, away from the knots of students in uniform who lingered as if itching for a quarrel.

Faivish frowned. "What's happened?"

Alfie kept his eyes on the far arch. "Word is the *Burschenschaft* is planning another march. They're talking about driving Jewish students out of the cafés. Not with pamphlets—worse."

Faivish stopped short. He'd heard the muttering, but hearing it from Alfie—who could drift unnoticed into those same circles—tightened something in his chest. "They've threatened it before."

"This is different." Alfie's jaw set. "They've got numbers. And a list. You're on it."

Faivish didn't ask what kind of list. The answer was in Alfie's tone. "I can handle myself."

"Against one man, maybe. Not a mob." Alfie's glance was sharp. "And you can't help Maisie—or Deena—if you're bleeding in a gutter."

The truth of it struck harder than he cared to admit. He walked on, his boots unsteady against the cobbles. "Professor Morgenschein wants me to take an apprenticeship in Calcutta," he said finally. His voice dropped. "Says it's the chance of a lifetime." Was this why he'd offered it as an escape? Could it be that the professor was more concerned with keeping Faivish safe than hasting giving his blessing to him and Maisie?

Alfie's head snapped toward him. "India?"

Faivish nodded once. "He thinks it will keep me safe. That it'll open doors Vienna will never unlock for me."

"And Maisie?"

The name lodged in his throat. He swallowed. "I'd ask for her hand tomorrow if I thought—" His words faltered. He fixed his eyes on the stones beneath his boots. "Do you not think we're safe here anymore?"

Alfie looked over his shoulder and let the silence stretch before answering. "Take her somewhere else if you can." His voice was low, deliberate. "You'll need more than Vienna gives you. You'll need every skill you can gather. The professor's idea is rather brilliant, you know? India could give you everything you need for a better future with Maisie."

Faivish lifted his eyes, wary. "And you?"

Alfie's grin carried both challenge and loyalty. "I'm not letting you vanish to the far side of the world without me. India's possibly a chance for me, too. Ayurveda, natural remedies—medicine they don't even whisper about here. The professor told me about it."

Faivish slowed, caught off guard. "You'd leave everything?"

"For a future worth building? Yes. Wouldn't you?" Alfie's look was steady, the weight of it pressing in. "You can't take Maisie anywhere if you don't live to try. And if you take her, you take Deena too. You know that."

Faivish's mouth tugged into the faintest smile. "You've thought this through."

"Of course, I have." Alfie's tone lightened, though his eyes stayed serious. "It's not only your chance. It's mine. The professor knows it too. If it keeps you breathing long enough to marry his daughter, all the better."

Faivish turned away, staring at the long stretch of courtyard where the light fell in pale stripes across the stones. Maisie's face filled his mind—the quick way her smile broke through restraint, the tilt of her chin when she refused to be cowed, the warmth of her hand when it lingered just a little too long in his. The wanting pressed heavily in his chest, matched only by the danger that shadowed it.

Danger, he had never once underestimated. Not since the night the men dragged his parents from their shop and left him standing in the street with blood on the cobblestones. The aristocrats who had jeered never faced consequences. Jews always did—every whisper of resistance was met with punishment harsher than the crime, while the powerful walked away untouched. That truth had been branded into him, as permanent as any scar.

It was an unwritten law to let them get away with it. Even the newspapers were silent on the matter. No traces, no harm. Faivish groaned at the cruelty of the world.

But not all hurt was inflicted through crime.

He had noticed the professor's tremor worsening, the tools being set down with careful deliberation that betrayed strain. Alfie had noticed too. Neither of them had yet told Maisie how swiftly her father was succumbing to his disease.

Faivish exhaled, the severity of the choice closing around him. "I'll think about it."

Alfie clapped his shoulder, brisk but not unkind. "Think quick. Vienna isn't holding its breath, and they've been watching us both."

They stepped back into the brighter lane together. The clamor of the city rushed to meet them, yet the shadow of decision walked with Faivish long after the crowd had swallowed them.

Chapter Six

N OT MUCH LATER *that summer…*

The door slammed hard enough to rattle the glass jars. Maisie's pen jerked, spilling ink across her father's ledger.

Faivish came in half-carrying Alfie. The smell hit before the sight—lamp oil, sweat, and blood.

"Chair," Faivish ordered, easing him down.

The lamplight showed Alfie's swollen face, a lip split wide. Maisie's breath snagged.

"*Burschenschaft* students," Alfie muttered. He spat pink into a handkerchief, then darker red. "Von Altenburg. Wittelsbach. Bismarck. Vienna's finest names." His grimace twisted toward a grin. "They wanted some sport."

Faivish lifted the lamp, his hands steady in motion but rigid with control. "Not sport. Envy. My grades."

Maisie's brow knit, shaken. "But Father's exams—"

"Numbers, not names," Faivish said, laying his instruments in a ruthless line. "Merit, not pedigree. They can't stomach it. So they took him instead of me."

Alfie groaned, bloodied but defiant. "And Hofstätter's son was with them."

The lamp's brass burned against Maisie's palm.

"They could have killed you," Alfie groaned. "Would have."

"They tried." Faivish's glance at her was brief, raw when he looked at Maisie. "If Alfie hadn't stepped in…" He looked back at his tray. "We'll use porcelain."

Her breath caught. "That's forbidden—"

"So is their violence. And yet it goes unpunished." His voice carried a weight that silenced her. "Porcelain on gold is stronger. He deserves it."

She moved closer, her shoulder brushing his. "If they find out—"

"They will. But tonight, he's my patient. And you'll help me, won't you?"

Her throat tightened, but she tilted the lamp to where he needed it.

The hiss of flame filled the silence, broken by Alfie's ragged breathing and the faint clink of tools. He lowered the cloth, showing the jagged break. "What are we waiting for? Until one of us doesn't get back up?"

Maisie flinched.

"It's why your father arranged Calcutta," Alfie said. "It's a safer escape and a chance…"

The words hit harder than the slam of the door had.

Faivish didn't deny it. His hands stayed on the instruments, though the muscle in his jaw worked.

Maisie's stomach dropped. *Father knew.* Knew this city would devour them. Knew that keeping Faivish in Vienna meant losing him.

"When this is done," Alfie pressed, "we're leaving. He'll take the apprenticeship. I'll study Ayurveda. We'll come back stronger."

Her voice cracked. "So it's decided for me?"

Faivish finally looked at her. Not the careful composure he showed patients—something stripped bare. "Your father's condition worsens. You've seen it. The tremors. What comes after?"

The unspoken words chilled her: Deena.

Her pulse thundered. "So I stay. You go." The words didn't

even feel like her own.

"I'm saying," Faivish said quietly, "that if I vow myself to you, I vow myself to her, too. That means being strong enough to keep you both safe. Not just a wedding, Maisie. A marriage. A lifetime."

Maisie's throat ached with the truth she'd stumbled into—that her father had always known their love would demand sacrifice. And that cost would fall, as it always had, on her.

Alfie groaned, pressing the towel harder to his cheek.

Faivish caught Maisie's eye. She knew that look—it meant there were things he couldn't say in front of Alfie. He set down the instrument, wiped his hands, and drew her gently into the shadowed hallway.

"When I go," he said, "it won't be to run. It'll be good to come back, the man who can give you a life beyond fear."

Her breath failed her. "Calcutta?" she whispered. The word tasted like unfathomable distance.

He nodded once. "I'll learn everything there, everything they'll never allow me here. And when I return, no one—no arrogant rider, no aristocrat—will be able to deny us."

Her hand trembled in his. "But it's so long!"

His grip firmed, anchoring her. "No matter how long or how far, I'll still find you. Even if you're on the other side of the world, I'll walk until I hold you in my arms and make it last forever."

The air seemed to thicken between the narrow walls. She could hear her own heartbeat above the lamp's hiss. Instead of words, she moaned. It was protest as much as acceptance.

"I don't only want a wedding," he went on, softer now, but edged with something fierce. "I want years with you. Waking beside you, hearing you laugh, growing old with your hand in mine. I want Deena safe, and your father proud to see his daughter loved as she deserves."

Her vision blurred. She swallowed hard. "Then stay," she whispered. "Stay, and we can start now."

His thumb brushed her knuckles—a tender refusal. "If I stay, I can't protect you. If I go, I come back strong enough to guard you both. That's why your father sent for the apprenticeship—he knows this city will eat me alive if I don't leave it."

The words cut through her, hollow and sharp.

"You're asking me to wait."

His voice roughened. "I'm asking you to believe in us. Enough for me to fight for it. Enough to walk away now, so I can return to you for the rest of my life."

She couldn't trust her voice. She only nodded, sharp and sure, because anything else might break her.

He touched her cheek, lifted her face, and kissed her. Not long—just enough to brand her as his, enough to burn the air out of her lungs. When he drew back, she felt changed, claimed. "I love you," she whispered before fear could stop her. "I think I loved you from the moment you first stepped through this door."

His mouth curved, a smile worn thin with wonder. "And I loved you when you opened your father's notes for me in the amphitheatre. You knew the right page. You knew without asking."

Her laugh escaped as a sob. "You remember that?"

"How could I forget?" His thumb traced the corner of her damp lashes. "You handed out notes to all the students, but I was the only one who gave you his heart in return. Keep it for me."

Maisie pressed his hand to her cheek. "I'll keep it safe."

He lingered one more breath, then stepped back into the lamplight, toward Alfie's battered form.

"Hold the light steady," he said, and his voice seemed already composed. "This has to be perfect."

SILENCE PRESSED IN, thick and close. The lamp hissed faintly, its glow spilling over Faivish's hands as he steadied the first tool.

The moment the metal touched Alfie's tooth, he flinched

hard, a sound torn out of him—and Faivish's jaw locked.

It should have been me.

That thought had burned through him since the alley: the glint of steel, the step he'd shifted without thinking, Alfie moving in—taking the blow meant for him. The knife's iron pommel had cracked across Alfie's face. Not bone-breaking, but enough to shear the tooth nearly to the root, too.

Faivish had lived his whole life by one rule: keep your head down, keep your body whole. Jews didn't fight aristocrats; they endured. And when the smoke cleared, it was always the Jews who paid.

He had never forgotten. Not the night his parents were dragged from their shop, nor the stink of lamp oil and scorched cloth clinging to the rafters. The crowd had called it a riot. But riots ended. Hatred didn't. His father was a harmless merchant, his mother gentler than butterflies—and still they were beaten down while the mob walked away untouched. Aristocrats broke Jews with no repercussions; Jews were punished for breaking or even just thinking about fighting back. That was the unspoken law.

His mother's voice haunted him still: *Keep low. Survive. Don't throw yourself to justice—the bad men always prevail.* By morning, he had nothing left but his books and a grief that threatened to strangle him.

Professor Morgenschein had found him then, sharp-eyed, commanding, and said: *Do well, not despite your mourning, but because of it.* Achievement was the only revenge allowed him. And then, his beautiful daughter had handed him a syllabus he'd clung to for dear life.

So Faivish had lived by silence, by sidestepping. Survive. Survive. And tonight, Alfie bled for it.

Maisie shifted the lamp, her hand trembling, but her chin high. She hated what Calcutta meant; he could feel it. Yet she nodded. She would not leave him to it alone.

"Hold still," Faivish murmured, voice steady as stone. "Any

other clinic would've pulled the tooth before you sat down."

Alfie's lips twisted around the gauze. "That's what they wanted. To mark me. To take the smile first. It's the smile people remember—take that away, and every door's already closed."

Faivish swallowed hard. He knew. For a Jew, scars became proof. Evidence of inferiority. And aristocrats knew it.

"Porcelain on gold," he said, turning the blade in the lamplight. "Stronger than anything they can break. You'll keep your immaculate smile."

Maisie's hand stilled on the towel. "Why isn't it used at the university?"

His voice cut sharper than the steel in his hand. "Because porcelain is reserved for men with crests. Their teeth, like their titles, must appear unbroken. We craft perfection for them, but we may never wear it ourselves. Alfie has no title, no crest. He doesn't count."

Her breath hitched. "And if they find out?"

"They'll call it theft." His tone was calm, almost too calm. "And then they'll make certain I never practice again in Europe. That's why your father is sending me away—before they do worse."

Alfie groaned low, pain thick in his throat. "They tried tonight."

The truth settled over the room like lead.

Faivish bent forward again, steel probe catching the light. He could hear Maisie's breathing behind him, the weight of her trust heavy as the lamp she held steady. If he failed, Alfie would lose more than a tooth. Maisie lost the man she loved. Deena lost the brother he had promised to become.

He caught Maisie's reflection in the polished brass tray. Her eyes, wide, fixed on him—not the instruments, not the wound, but him.

And Faivish thought: *Please, let me be enough.*

Chapter Seven

THE NEXT NIGHT, Faivish cemented the porcelain crown. When Alfie leaned toward the looking glass, it was almost as though nothing had happened at all. The tooth gleamed—whole, unmarred—as if pain, panic, and the attack meant for Faivish had been erased.

Almost.

The purpling shadow along Alfie's cheekbone still told the truth.

He touched it with two fingers, thoughtful, then dabbed the corner of his mouth with the towel Maisie offered. His swagger began to seep back—slow as sap rising after winter, steady but not yet certain. "You two," Alfie said, gaze flicking between them, "are remarkable. Truly. Thank you—for saving my smile."

From the tool table, Faivish felt the words land deeper than he'd expected. "No, thank you, Alfie. You stood in the way when it should have been me."

Alfie shrugged one shoulder into his coat sleeve as if it cost him nothing. "I stand by good people. You're my friends. That's all that matters. And if science has taught us anything, it's that every vein carries the same blood, there's no way to distinguish people by color or religion, only by their hearts."

The truth of it weighed between them. Science knew it, but Vienna's laws did not. Faivish pressed his lips flat, catching

Maisie's mirrored gesture at the edge of his sight—an unspoken pact sparking like a wire touched by flame.

"I have to go to India," he said at last. "If I'm to be known, let it be for the work of my hands, not for the syllables of my name."

Alfie's mouth twitched. "I'll stand by you." He winced when his cheek strained under the attempted smile, then forced a grin softened with sincerity. His glance shifted to Maisie. "You were right to trust him with your heart. I trust him with my life."

Color rose to her cheeks, though she held his look without blinking.

Alfie nodded toward the curtained window, where a draft stirred the velvet folds. "And now, I'll slip out the back. Fewer eyes."

Faivish followed him into the vestibule. His steps were quiet but heavy, carrying more than his friend's coat. The lamplight caught Alfie's bruise, gilding the damage into something almost noble. Faivish clasped his hand and wrinkled the coat but he was instantly sorry when he gave it to Alfie.

Finally, at the threshold, Alfie paused, his eyes catching the light. "You're both good—good enough to believe you can mend the world, one tooth at a time. I hope you'll always be happy together, no matter what."

The night took him, bruise and all.

Faivish lingered. The streetlamp's glow cut a line across his brow, picking out the sheen of sweat and strain. "That could have gone terribly wrong."

From behind him, Maisie's voice was quiet, steady. "But it didn't. Because you were brilliant."

His mouth tilted in a small, private smile. "You held the lamp steady."

"You held justice in your hands."

Something passed between them, unspoken, fragile as spun glass. When her fingertips brushed his sleeve, her voice was almost a plea: "Don't go yet."

He couldn't have left, even if he'd wanted to.

He stepped closer, drawn by a pull as certain as a tide to the moon. A wild curl brushed her cheek; the lamplight burnished her hair into bronze. He lifted his hand, feeling the air shift, as if her soft and supple skin had been waiting all this time.

"I haven't told you in words," he said quietly, "what you've become to me. You've stood with me when it would have been easier to turn away. You've given me more than I thought I could hold. If your father would only allow it... I'd spend my life proving myself worthy of you. Every part of me already belongs to you."

Her lashes dipped; her lips softened, not with surprise but with a quiet, aching acceptance. He turned her hand palm-up, pressed his mouth to it gently, as though afraid the dream might vanish. Her fingers trembled, then closed around his, sure as a vow.

The kiss that followed was quieter than breath, warmer than flame. The last days—the secrecy, the fear—dissolved in that hush. She leaned into him, her body fitting his as though it had always known the way. His hand slid to her nape, holding her as if the world might tear them apart if he loosened his grip.

He drew back just enough for their foreheads to rest together, breath mingling.

"You hold my heart," he whispered.

"And you mine," she sighed against him, her fingers fisting gently in his coat. In that small hold, he felt something greater than longing: a bone-deep rightness.

"Thank you," he said roughly. "For trusting me with your father's instruments. For standing with me."

"You've been his hands longer than he admits," she murmured.

He looked toward the treatment room. "Let me clear everything—no trace left."

She shook her head. "You've done enough. Rest. And if we are healers, then let us heal. Care should never be hidden behind rules that wound more than they mend."

Her words sank deep. But before he could answer, the patter of bare feet overhead made them both still.

"Maisie?"

Deena stood on the landing, hair rumpled, nightgown slipped at one shoulder.

Maisie went to her, smoothing the child's hair, whispering words Faivish couldn't hear. The girl lingered, then disappeared into her room, the door clicking shut, leaving behind a silence too delicate to break.

Faivish let out the breath he'd been holding. "That was close," he murmured, the words more relief than sound.

Maisie stepped toward him, her smile quick, wry, and edged with weariness. "Everything is."

He reached for the doorknob—

—but never touched it.

The latch snapped with a sharp, metallic click. The door swung wide.

Two men filled the frame of the winter night. Professor Morgenschein—her father—stood first, his face pale yet thunderous, two storms wrestled behind his eyes as if he'd met a lynching man. Beside him loomed Rector Hofstätter.

Her father's gaze swept toward the treatment room, where the air still carried the bitter tang of heated porcelain and dental cement, faint smoke of the kiln clinging like guilt. His mouth thinned to a line that cut deeper than words.

"You've been busy."

The syllables dropped like stones, and the cold from the open door seemed to flood the room until even their breathing felt dangerous.

Rector Hofstätter stepped past, chin angled high, his gait deliberate, proprietary. Clearing his throat, he let the silence stretch before saying, "So, so, so. The nightly use of university resources."

In that suspended moment, with Maisie's kiss still lingering on his lips, Faivish understood with perfect clarity: *We're caught.*

THE KNOCK NEVER came.

The latch snapped instead—sharp, metallic, final. The door swung wide, letting in the night.

Maisie's breath hitched. Her father stood there, frost still clinging to his coat, his face drained and thunderous at once—as if two storms wrestled for dominion beneath his skin. Beside him, Rector Hofstätter's folder glinted like a seal of judgment—a weapon already drawn.

The cold rushed in with them. She could still smell porcelain and cement in the air, hot and faintly acrid, the unmistakable scent of what they had done. Her father's gaze swept the room, landed on the instruments, and his mouth pinched tight.

The air shifted. Maisie caught the faint, bitter tang of porcelain still cooling in the back room. Her father's gaze went straight there. His mouth thinned. "You've been busy."

Rector Hofstätter strode in without waiting for an answer. "So. The nightly use of university resources. Porcelain. Cement. A crown, then." His lip curled. "For whom?"

Faivish didn't flinch. "For a man attacked in the street. Beaten by the *Burschenschaft*. By your son among them."

The words landed like a stone in still water. Hofstätter's pause was brief—deliberate. "My son," he said smoothly, "is a devoted scholar. He carries honor into our halls."

"He carries a knife pommel," Faivish shot back. "I saw it."

"Oh please. Boys scuffle." Hofstätter's voice carried the lazy dismissal of a man too accustomed to being obeyed. His lip curled in disdain. "Better they learn their duty early—Vienna must be kept clear of vermin."

The word landed hard, as if the air itself recoiled. Maisie's father flinched, his voice cracking. "Vermin?"

Faivish stepped forward, every line of him taut with anger. "Your son was among them. You condone their violence?"

The Rector's smile was slow, deliberate, teeth catching the lamplight. "I applaud it. They understand what must be done to preserve Vienna." His gaze slid to the cooling porcelain crown on the tray. "And now it is my duty to preserve the university as well."

The lamp trembled in her father's grip, glass chiming faintly. Maisie had not seen him like this since the night her mother died—fragile, unmoored, as if the flame he carried might gutter out and take him with it.

"Tomorrow." Hofstätter's tone dropped lower, gaining weight. "Nine o'clock. You will present yourselves before the Faculty Council of Medicine. Every senior professor will sit in judgment." He savored the silence before striking. "And there we strip away the illusion you've built. We return the place you've stolen to better men. Not Jews."

"Faivish Blattner earned his place as the best in his class." Her father lifted his chin, voice thin but steady. "Examinations are anonymous. Numbers, not names. My pupil's work speaks for itself."

"Spare me your sermons on fairness," Hofstätter cut in, folder snapping open with a sound like a blade leaving its sheath. "Life is not fair. Life is a position. My son studies until dawn, yet you let him be discredited by this boy? Enough."

The lamp shook again, the flame dancing wildly. Her father's eyes flicked to hers—pleading, helpless—and Maisie felt the world tilt. For the first time, she saw him not as the master craftsman of gold and porcelain, but as a man hollowed by fear.

She swallowed words that clawed her throat. All she could do was lock eyes with Faivish. The warmth of his kiss still lingered, but what she saw in him now was clear: Hofstätter meant to break him.

Faivish's voice cut the silence. "He wasn't discredited. He escaped while Alfie was beaten. They came at night because I surpassed them on merit."

Hofstätter turned the folder in his hand, as if testing its

weight. "Still this slander. My son doesn't dirty himself in alleys. He prepares to inherit his station."

Maisie's fists curled into her skirts. Her voice broke free before she could stop it. "I held the lamp. I saw the wound. Without the crown, infection would have spread. He'd have lost more than a tooth."

The Rector looked at her, not truly at her—through her, as though she were nothing more than a shadow that dared to speak. "And this," he said to her father, "is the rot you permit. A nurse with opinions. You've forgotten your place, Morgenschein."

The ivory knob of her father's cane creaked under his grip. His reply was quiet but unyielding. "Do not speak to my daughter."

Hofstätter's smile dropped away. What replaced it was colder. "You tremble, old man. Then hear me plainly. Your anarchy ends tonight. Keys to the kiln. Now."

Her father's hand moved slowly, reluctant. The key scraped against metal, then fell into Hofstätter's palm.

"You will not light it again. You will not let this boy claim what he has not earned. And tomorrow morning, you face the wrath of the entire academic committee."

"Under oath?" Faivish asked, his voice iron.

"Under mercy," Hofstätter said, almost lightly. "If any remains."

Maisie thought of Deena asleep upstairs, of the house worn soft by her mother's steps. She thought of Faivish's hand on her jaw only an hour ago—and how this man could twist that tenderness into danger.

At the threshold, Hofstätter paused, eyes drilling into her father. "Position, Professor. Learn it—or I will teach it."

The door slammed shut, rattling the shelves.

Her father sank into a chair, a tremor running up his arm. When he looked at Maisie, it was with the same broken calculation she remembered from years ago: how to shield a child when there was no shield left.

Chapter Eight

FATHER HAD BEEN at the university in the morning but he hadn't told Maisie what the committee had decided. Nor what they'd done. He didn't need to, she could see how bad it was in his expression.

Later in the afternoon, after the last patient left with a stiff bow, the practice sagged into quiet. The air still carried its mix of sharp clove oil and the faint bitterness of antiseptic, but without voices to cut through, the silence felt suspiciously as if walls were listening.

Maisie latched the door and turned back to the treatment chair. Her cloth moved in practiced, even strokes across the leather, but every swish of damp linen seemed to echo. No Faivish to murmur instructions. No steady rhythm of his hands setting instruments to order. The room felt emptier for it— emptier than she could bear.

He hadn't come. Not once.

And her father had not spoken his name.

She rinsed the cloth and worked faster, as though brisk movements alone might scrub away the dread rising in her chest. She wanted Faivish near, more than she'd ever dared put into words. Not as her father's pupil but as her husband and partner in life. She wanted to assist him and care for him. Her pulse jumped at the thought of mornings that might follow nights full of his kisses—perhaps more. Heat rushed under her collar, and she pressed her palm to her brow, trying to smother the thought before it carried her away.

At the desk, her father sat too still. His eyes moved to the clock again, and again, and again. Normally he timed everything precisely—patients never waiting more than a heartbeat past the hour. But this was different. This was waiting. And his hands trembled worse than she had seen in weeks.

She noticed the rest too: the unnerving clarity of the desk. No stack of patient records, no half-finished sketch of a tooth, no pencil left to roll. Just the pen, perfectly aligned with the inkwell, as though the desk had been prepared for some solemn ritual.

"Father?" Her voice was careful, almost hushed. She dried her hands on her apron. "Are you expecting someone?"

His swallow was sharp, the line of his throat jerking. "Yes."

The answer had barely settled when a knock rapped through the silence.

Maisie's palm dampened on the knob. She opened the door and there he was—Faivish. Solemn, composed, his dark coat brushed clean of snow. His eyes caught hers, and she knew at once this wasn't a visit for pleasantries or tea.

"Come in, Faivish," Father said.

He stepped inside, ungloved, hat in hand. His boots left faint wet marks across the mat. Her father remained behind the desk, hands clasped tight as if they alone kept him steady.

"The university has decided." His voice was taut, like wire about to snap. "You will graduate. But you may not walk in the ceremony. And you are to leave Vienna."

The words hit her chest like a mallet striking stone.

If Faivish did not take his place on the dais, the *Bruderschaft* boys—Hofstätter's son among them—would rise instead. They would seize the honors he had earned. They would win.

"Vile opportunists," she muttered, the words slipping past before she could stop them.

Both men looked at her. And in their eyes—for one fleeting

moment—she saw not correction, not reprimand, but softness.

"Yes," her father said quietly. "But that is the world we live in. And it is the world I would spare you—and Deena—because I cannot change what I will soon leave behind. The future belongs to you."

The words landed in her chest like stones, heavy and final. She tried to breathe but could not seem to let the air out.

Faivish's jaw tightened. His nod was slight, but resolute. "I understand."

Her father's gaze flicked briefly to her, then back to Faivish. "I believe you care for my daughter."

Faivish did not hesitate. "I do."

"Then here is my condition." The professor's voice softened, though the tonnage of it filled the room. "Go to India. Take the apprenticeship. Work. Learn. A year from now, if your feelings remain—and hers do as well—you may return and claim her hand. If your love is true, a year will prove it."

Maisie swallowed hard, the cry rising in her throat. A year? A year was an ocean. She lifted her chin, tried to let her eyes thank him, tried to show gratitude, but inside she was screaming.

Faivish's gaze met hers and held it. And in that look, she knew he heard her scream as if she had spoken aloud.

"I will go," he said. His voice carried the solemnity of an oath. "And I will come back."

Her father inclined his head, as if the matter had been sealed. "Then I expect to be here when you return."

Maisie kept her face still, but her fists tightened against her skirts until her nails bit half-moons into her palms.

When Faivish bowed his head in thanks, it was not only to her father. It was to her.

FROM THE DORMITORY window, Vienna's night crept in on scraps of sound: carriage wheels grinding over cobblestones, the faint jangle of a harness bell, a burst of laughter from the beer hall, rough and sudden. Somewhere below, a cat yowled, then was shooed into silence.

Inside, the noises were smaller, lonelier—the groan of the water pipes, the steady tick of the wall clock that had marked out every day of his studies. Faivish knelt beside his open trunk, folding shirts with deliberate care, smoothing each crease as though neatness might steady what felt dangerously close to unraveling.

Across the room, Alfie sprawled in the only chair, his bruised cheekbone catching the lamplight like a dark bloom.

"So it's real then," Alfie said at last. "We're leaving on the morning carriage to the port? Before graduation." His tone wasn't surprised, only worn down, the ring of someone who'd braced for the blow. "Bloody unfair. I thought we had more time."

Faivish's hands didn't pause, but his jaw tightened.

I thought so too.

"It's the world," he said, the words flat on his tongue. He could almost feel Maisie's hand on his sleeve again, hear her whisper asking him not to go. But memory pressed back harder—his mother's last warning: *Keep your head low. Don't waste yourself for justice. The bad men always prevail.*

He'd believed she was wrong, once. Tonight, with Hofstätter's verdict still ringing in his ears, with Morgenschein's trembling voice laying out conditions for Maisie's hand, he feared she'd always been right.

Alfie leaned forward, elbows braced on his knees, his bruised face lit sharp by the lamp. "If they're forcing you out, we make it count. I've got the fare. Dawn, we take the coach to Trieste. Ship across the Mediterranean, past Sicily, through the Red Sea. Camels over Egypt. Then the Arabian Sea toward Calcutta."

Faivish let out a short huff—half laugh, half disbelief. "You've planned every mile."

"Of course I have." Alfie's mouth tilted, but his gaze stayed earnest. "It's the road to my apothecary. And to you coming back with more than a diploma. You'll come back for her."

Her.

Maisie.

Her name thrummed through him like a low chord. He saw her as she'd been the night before—hair tumbling from its pins, eyes lit with stubborn faith in him. He wanted her laughter in his home, her hand steadying his instruments, her breath warm in the quiet between one heartbeat and the next. He wanted her, everywhere, always.

Alfie's voice cut in. "Why don't you ask her to come with us?"

"Come with us?" Faivish blinked hard. "You know her father's ill. And there's Deena." The thought twisted sharp inside him. *Does Maisie even know how close he is to failing? How much is waiting to fall on her shoulders?*

"Poor little thing," Alfie said, his voice rough. "She needs someone."

And Maisie... I thought that someone would be me.

Alfie sat back, a half-smile shadowing his bruises. "Then that's the plan, just like the professor said. We go. We learn. We come back stronger. And next time..." His tone hardened. "Next time, we don't just survive. We win."

Faivish shut the trunk. The latch clicked with a finality that made his chest tighten. His palm rested there longer than it should have, as if holding the lid shut might keep him from losing the vision inside his head—Maisie, standing in a doorway, smiling at him as though he already belonged.

But instead of reaching for her, he dragged out the second trunk from beneath his bed and snapped it open.

I'm preparing for a journey I never wanted. And leaving behind the only one I do.

Chapter Nine

A few hours later at the University of Vienna, still 1812.

A FAINT CHILL hung in the corridor as Maisie crept through the student dormitory, her father's old cloak trailing at her ankles, smelling faintly of tobacco and time. The floorboards carried the stale perfume of young men's lives—cheap liquor, cold coffee, the sour tang of ink left too long in its pot. She'd slipped out while her father was still speaking over supper, his voice full of other people's stories: Jews in England, Rachel-this and Rachel-that, starting over after flights from Switzerland. Each word had pressed on her ribs until she felt caged in her own skin. She couldn't bear the room with its polite disapproval, the silences that said more than the words. So she had come here.

Beyond the shuttered windows, Vienna sprawled in lamplight and frost. The spire of *Stephansdom* carved its black silhouette into the winter sky. Oil lamps shivered on the cobbles; alleys breathed woodsmoke, dung, and roasted chestnuts hawked by shivering vendors. A carriage slammed its door somewhere, wheels clattering away. A night watchman's cry echoed off the stone— *Alles sicher! Safe!*—but the sound felt hollow, as if even the walls knew it was a lie.

She tightened the cloak at her throat. Every street she had known since childhood now seemed altered, the very stones shifting beneath her as though Vienna itself had turned against them. And still she walked, heart hammering, not sure if she was seeking Faivish or simply refusing to let him vanish without her.

The dormitory was stark, foreign: bare plaster streaked with water stains, plain doors lined up like soldiers at attention. Brass handles dulled by years of use. At the end of the hall, one candle guttered in its sconce, its light running along the wainscoting in jagged shadows.

25B.

Her pulse leapt. She remembered the number etched on the key he always carried. Her hand hovered above the latch, trembling, empty of words but full of need. She couldn't face a dawn where he had gone and she hadn't tried. She knocked.

Alfie opened. His bruised cheek looked oddly tender in the lamplight. She slipped past quickly; the room's warmth hit her at once. Soap. Leather. And underneath, the faint trace that was unmistakably him.

Faivish was crouched over a trunk. He looked up. Froze. Then rose, slowly, until he stood to his full height. For a breath their eyes caught—flared—and then his gaze shuttered.

"Maisie," he said, glancing toward Alfie.

"I don't need to be here," Alfie murmured. Apology in his voice, heavy enough to sting. "I'm sorry, Maisie. All of this—it's mine to bear."

"I let it happen," she whispered.

"No—I caused it." He tugged his coat from the nail on the wall. He and Faivish exchanged a look that carried more than words—shared blame, shared loss—and then Alfie slipped out. The latch shut behind him, sharp as a sentence.

Maisie slid the bolt.

Faivish stood at his desk, folding a shirt with mechanical care, as if neat creases could shield him from what lay between them.

"No girls allowed in the dormitory," he said at last. A joke so thin it nearly tore.

"You've broken worse rules," she said, keeping her voice steady though her heart skittered. "One more won't count."

"I'm not expelled. Just... exiled a little." His lips pressed into something between bitterness and defiance. *A little. Not funny.*

Her gaze swept the shelves—stripped bare. The emptiness made her throat ache. "You're truly packing for India?"

He didn't meet her eyes. "We leave at dawn. Alfie made the arrangements. Your father… helped."

"B-but it's too long and too far away!" The words scraped out of her.

His shoulders shifted. "Until I've built something they can't take. Until I can return as a man they can't deny."

"You shouldn't have done it," she said, sharper than she meant. Fear gave her tongue its edge. "They watch you always."

"He was in agony. I had the skill. Why shouldn't porcelain on gold be for anyone who suffers? Why should comfort be a privilege?" His voice was low but fierce.

She stepped nearer. "Because you're exactly the man they want to break. And now they'll drag Father down with you."

His jaw set hard. "That's why I'm leaving. To spare him. To spare you. I just wish—" his voice roughened—"I wish you could come."

Her arms locked around herself. "I can't. He needs me. Deena needs me."

The silence between them pulsed.

At last he turned, and the look in his eyes stole her breath. "You shouldn't have to carry it all alone."

Her throat burned. "I will. For them. But not without you."

They faced each other, words useless, the air alive with what neither dared say. Then she moved, drawn by something unstoppable. He caught her, hands steady on her, and their mouths met—urgent, consuming, a kiss against time itself.

Her cloak slid to the floor. His fingers framed her face, trembled once, then steadied, memorizing her. The kiss deepened, carrying the vow neither dared speak: no exile, no ocean, no distance could unmake this fire.

⫸⫷

OUTSIDE, VIENNA STIRRED. A vendor cart creaked down the lane. A bell from *Stephansdom* tolled, heavy and insistent. Morning was on its way—but not yet. Not for them.

Her gown slipped from her shoulders, pooling around her ankles with a whisper. Candlelight gilded her skin in amber and shadow. She stood barefoot, trembling—but it was not fear. It was certainty. This was the threshold. Once crossed, there would be no going back.

Faivish stilled, as though struck. He let his gaze drink her in, every curve, every trembling breath—not with hunger alone, but with reverence, memorizing her like the gorgeous image could carry her across the sea inside his chest. At last, he stepped forward, lifted her hand between both of his, and kissed it. Not a kiss—a seal.

"You're sure?" His voice rasped low.

"I am." Her eyes held his, steady. "I promise I'll wait."

The words felt like vows. Not said lightly. Not for them. They bound hearts as surely as if a canopy had been raised above them and the blessing spoken aloud.

A sharp breath left him. He pressed his forehead to hers. Whatever oceans lay ahead, she was his, and he hers.

They moved together then. Linen against linen, the whisper of garments loosening, of skin bared and discovered. Thought gave way to touch—the brush of her hair against his jaw, the heat blooming wherever her hands found him. She clutched his shoulders and he kissed her, deeper, until nothing remained but vow, warmth, and the aching sweetness of her mouth.

He drew back just far enough to see her face, flushed and unguarded in the candlelight. Her chest rose unevenly, her shift clinging sheer to her form, revealing and concealing at once. Her tremor undid him—not weakness, but raw trust.

"You're so very perfect," he murmured, and kissed her again.

She rose on her toes, pulling him closer. He lifted her easily and set her on his narrow cot. Her shift slipped higher along her thighs; she made a soft sound that melted into anticipation.

He knelt beside her, breathing hard, tracing a reverent hand up her leg. "May I?"

Maisie nodded, hair spilling wild over his pillow.

He lifted the shift, revealing pale skin inch by inch, until she lay before him, arching ever so slightly in invitation. He bent his head, kissed her, and her breath broke into a sound he knew would haunt him if he lived to be a hundred.

When he moved lower, her hands hesitated at her hips. Her eyes went wide. "I've never—no one has ever…"

He froze, searching her face. "We don't have to."

Slowly, she moved her hands aside. That act alone felt like the greatest gift of his life.

"You're beautiful." The awe in his voice cracked through.

She opened for him, and he worshipped her with kisses— thigh, hip, then deeper—until she cried his name.

Breathless, he rose, stripped himself bare in the candlelight, not ashamed, not boastful—only a man offering everything he was. She touched his skin with trembling fingers and he pressed a kiss into her wrist before laying himself between her thighs.

He kissed her again, slow and deep, and when he entered her—inch by careful inch—he whispered for her to breathe. She gasped, then smiled through tears. "I'm all right."

"I'll never hurt you," he said.

"Then don't stop."

He moved gently, then with growing urgency as she rose to meet him. Her nails marked his back, her body tightening around him until his control faltered.

"I love you," he groaned. "I love you—always—"

She cried out, shattering beneath him, and he followed, trembling with the force of it. He pulled away at the last, spilling against himself, shuddering as he gathered her close.

"I won't risk you," he gasped.

She touched his face, fierce through her tears. "You just did."

"No," he whispered. "When I come back, we'll start a family."

The city moved on beyond the shuttered window. Another bell tolled. Another carriage clattered past. But here, in this dim room, time bent around them.

He kissed her fingers like a vow. "I'll come back. Even if the sea swallows me, I'll crawl back to you."

She laid her palm over his heart. "And I'll always love you. Always."

The candle guttered low. Dawn pressed under the shutters. He buttoned his shirt with trembling hands, bent to kiss her once more, and left the room carrying her name in every heartbeat.

Chapter Ten

THE CITY STILL wore its night quiet when Maisie slipped from the dormitory, Faivish's promise wrapped around her more tightly than her father's old cloak.

A year, he had said. She had said yes.

One year. It sounded small, like something she could hold in her hand. But already it pressed on her chest like a weight.

By the time she turned onto their street, dawn had begun to silver the rooftops. She expected darkness—shutters drawn, her father still at rest, the practice silent. Instead, light leaked in jagged strips through the curtains of the treatment room, unnatural at this hour.

Her pace faltered. At this hour, light?

Inside, the air struck her. Ash clung sharp and bitter in her throat, as though a fire had died choking. Ink spattered across the desk in dried rivulets; chairs were knocked aside as if there'd been a struggle. Papers wrinkled like autumn leaves left too close to a flame. From deeper in the house came voices—low, overlapping, taut as wires pulled to snapping.

Then a name cut through them like a lash:

"Hofstätter!"

Maisie stilled in the shadow of the doorway. Three young men stood in the hall, their coats cut fine, their expressions smug. She knew those faces—the *Burschenschaft* men. One, broad-shouldered, had Hofstätter's same sharp cheekbones, though he would not look her in the eye. They weren't visiting, they were attacking.

A sound rose from the kitchen—not words, but a groan thick with pain.

She pushed past before they could block her way.

"Father! No!" Deena cried.

Maisie followed her sister's voice and found them quickly. Father sat bent in a chair, one trembling hand clutching at his chest, his fingers curled into the fabric as though trying to hold his own heart in place. His other hand braced against the table, nails dug into the wood. "Father?"

But he didn't respond. His breath came jagged, too shallow, each pull like it might be the last. Sweat gleamed along his hairline. At his knee, Deena clung to him, her small face blotched with tears, whispering fragments of comfort that broke apart in her throat.

Beside them stood the Marquess, straight-backed, papers clutched in his fist like a summons. His eyes locked on Maisie's with clipped urgency.

"Miss Morgenschein," he said. "It is time."

Time for what? Maisie's mouth opened, but before the question formed, her father's rasp broke through, raw and thinning, "Leave Vienna and go to London to Rachel. She'll know what to do."

She dropped beside him, knees striking the floorboards. The *Burschenschaft* shadows shifted closer, their nearness answering the question her mind refused to finish. This wasn't illness. It wasn't chance, but rather a punishment for defying them and daring to let Faivish finish what he had earned.

Her father's hand flew to his chest. His groan cracked through her like glass.

"Father," she choked, gripping his wrist, the thin bones hot beneath her palm.

His eyes found hers, dim already, but still fierce with meaning. "Take Deena," he whispered. "Go to Rachel. I thought I'd have more time…"

The words shuddered into silence as he sagged, the Marquess catching his shoulder before he slid from the chair. Deena cried out, her thin wail piercing the air, and Maisie gathered her close, pressing her sister's face into her skirts to shield her from the sight.

Behind them, one of the Burschenschaft stepped fully into the kitchen, his smile wolfish. "Should've left when you had the chance."

The Marquess turned on him, voice steel. "Take another step and I'll have your name delivered to every foreign ministry from here to London."

The *Burschenschaft* men paused, then shifted, and finally withdrew muttering something vicious.

Her father's hand, still warm, slipped from the table and hung there helpless and emptied of its strength. The lamplight blurred; whether from tears or smoke, Maisie could not tell.

She dropped beside him, knees striking the floorboards. The *Burschenschaft* shadows had crept closer. Their boots scraped the floor. One leaned toward the doorway and sneered.

It struck her in a wave: the man who had taught her every stitch, every careful measure, who had held their fragile world together since Mother's death—gone. There would be no voice at her shoulder correcting her grip on the scalpel, no quiet hum of Yiddish lullabies when Deena had fevers. The silence where he had always been was unbearable, pressing against her chest until she could scarcely breathe.

Her heart howled with the injustice of it. That men with crests on their folders, boots polished to a glare, could callously snuff out a life like this. To leave her with a child's sobs and a wrecked practice. She bent her head to Deena's hair, kissed her crown, and promised without words that she would not let her drown in this loss.

But as the room filled with the shuffle of hurried feet and

hushed orders—the Marquess speaking to someone she couldn't see—one thought pierced through the haze of grief, sharp and merciless: *If they take our home and the practice away now, how will I keep Deena safe? And when Faivish comes back—how will he ever find us again?*

When the Marquess returned, his voice low and certain. "You'll go in my carriage and under the protection of my name. Tonight. You'll be in Italy by tomorrow evening. England within the fortnight. I promised I'd protect his daughters and hope you'll protect my only heir."

Maisie looked at him—truly looked. At the man who had stood between them and danger. Who had carried her father's weight without flinching.

"I'll care for your son," she said. "I swear it. I'll do whatever it takes."

Chapter Eleven

London, 1817.

FIVE YEARS HAD passed.

Felix Leafley—though in his heart he was still Faivish Blattner—could never decide if those years had crawled like winter molasses or thundered past like a midsummer storm. All he knew was that it had been five years without her. Five years since hurried farewells under Vienna's heavy skies, since whispered promises made with grief clinging to every word.

Even here, in London's noise and bustle, Maisie's absence lived in him like iron chained to his ribs. He kept his vow—to her, to himself, to every patient—that he would be the best in his craft. But what was skill worth without her? To go on forever without her love felt like a cruelty he could hardly name.

"I've barely enough gold for a week's work," Felix muttered, pushing open the familiar door of his supplier's shop—his friends.

35 Regent Street

Klonimus & Sons, Jewelers

The workshop greeted him with the warm scent of beeswax, wood shavings, and fire-polished metal. It was the smell of things built to last. But before he could brush off the London drizzle from his coat, a voice called from the back.

"Faivish!"

Mrs. Chawa Klonimus filled the doorway, her silhouette broad and comforting, her eyes sharp with kindness. Her voice carried like the scent of fresh bread on a winter morning—something that reached straight into the hollow of him. When she said his name, his *real* name, in Yiddish no less, it was like being folded briefly into the life he'd lost. So warm and soothing to hear his real name for a change. For a moment, his chest loosened.

In this household, laughter always had room for him. At their table, he was counted as family. And yet every kindness pressed against the same hollow—because no warmth, no welcome, could erase the shape Maisie had left behind.

"Faivish, come eat with us upstairs."

"You know he calls himself Felix now, Mama," Raphi said from his bench, amusement tugging his mouth.

"Felix, Faivish, Blattner, Leafley…" Chawa waved her hand, unconcerned. "All the same. But to us—you'll always be Faivish."

The name cut deeper than he let show. He chuckled faintly, but it was forced, the sound thin. *Maisie wouldn't even know me now,* he thought, *not as Felix Leafley.*

Raphi's glance caught the sigh he hadn't meant to let slip. So did Chawa's. They looked at each other quickly, as if he wasn't meant to notice.

He noticed. *They think me a lovesick fool. Maybe I am. But I'll never stop looking for her.*

He forced a smile, hollow as it felt, and bent his head toward the floorboards. But memory rose unbidden: the Morgenschein practice, patients' voices in the hall, evenings lit by lamplight with Maisie's hand brushing his. That was before the *Burschenschaft* had shattered everything, before India, before the silence.

By the time he had clawed his way back across continents, the practice had been gutted—stripped by the university. Their home was gone. Deena vanished. And Maisie… nowhere. Only a gentile potter answered the door, speaking of his kiln as though clay could replace everything Felix had lost.

Now in London, the trail was cold. No one spoke her name as though she had been erased.

Chawa's voice softened. "Eat with us, yes? Warm brisket makes even wandering hearts less restless."

Felix inclined his head. He couldn't explain that no food, no hearth, no family could still that ache. Not yet.

When he settled at Raphi's side, the younger man nudged him with dry humor. "Eat something, for Mama's sake. Spare us both the scolding."

Felix almost smiled for real. The scrape of gold against wood, the measured clink of his tools, steadied him as he worked. Raphi's presence filled the silence—not intrusively, but like ballast against a ship listing too far into a storm.

"She'd finally give up her rugelach recipe if you smiled more often," Raphi teased. His tone was light, but the warmth underneath said what words didn't: *I know where your thoughts have gone. You don't need to say it.*

Felix's jaw tightened. He bent harder into the work, twisting the wire as though precision could keep longing in check. Work had always been his shield. It dulled the ache, gave him discipline. But every curl of gold reminded him of what he should have had—Maisie's laughter in the next room, a life that had been his and hers together.

Raphi watched him quietly, then murmured, "Even good gold can't fill every hollow."

The words caught Felix where his armor was thinnest. He didn't answer. Instead, he pressed the wire flat, steadying his hands though the ache inside threatened to split him open.

"Ikh bin aykh ale zeyer dankbar." I'm very grateful to all of you. The Yiddish surprised him—familiar and foreign at once—yet it came unbidden from his own lips.

"Far gornisht!" It's nothing, Chawa replied with a smile, brushing her apron as she turned toward the narrow stairwell. Her steps creaked upward to the rooms above the shop, leaving the air behind her faintly warmer, scented with bread and cloves.

Though jewels for the Prince Regent glittered on the benches here, the true treasure was upstairs: the Klonimus family table, loud with laughter and soft with prayer, a place where belonging didn't have to be earned.

Raphi chuckled, shaking his head. "She means you're family. You know that, don't you?" His gaze lingered where his mother had stood, fond and certain.

Family. The word throbbed inside Felix. These people were more than friends, just like Alfie—they read the weight in his silences, teased him out of gloom when it was too hard to bear the nagging question of where Maisie was and how she was. On those particularly painful days, the doctors from Harley Street and the Klonimuses stitched him into their own days without question. Thus, over his time in London, he had gathered more than companions: Nick with his surgeon's precision, Andre with his pacifist stubbornness, Wendy with her quiet competence. Together, they had raised a practice at Harley Street that was both refuge and crusade. The Klonimus family had folded him into their search as well, passing letters through their network, scanning Europe for the one face he longed for.

But every night the ache remained. Staying still hadn't made the longing fade; it had only taught him how to carry it. Each day without Maisie felt stolen, as if fate itself were mocking him.

Raphi leaned forward, tapping the half-finished candlestick in Felix's hand. "So—are we finishing this? Or are you polishing wire to some great philosophical end?"

Felix huffed a laugh and set the pliers down. The lamplight trembled across the workbench, shadowing their hands. Upstairs, the smell of brisket thickened, rich and insistent.

"You should go," Felix said, his tone lighter than he felt. "Be with your Laila and little Joseph. It'll be his bedtime soon."

Raphi's grin was easy and affectionate. "Joseph? As if he sleeps before nine. I'll stay as long as you need and then I'll go and read him his favorite story, David and Goliath. There's more gold to press." He picked up the hammer again, his movements sure and unhurried. "Besides, Mama will save us both plates. She always does."

Felix looked up. The corner of his mouth lifted, small but real. "Brooding as always," he said.

And Raphi only smiled wider, as if he knew exactly which ghost still sat at Felix's shoulder, and was determined not to leave him to it.

Raphi raised an eyebrow in mock challenge and brought the hammer down with practiced precision, flattening the next piece of gold wire into a bright, shimmering ribbon. The soft thud, steady and hypnotic, reverberated through the room before he handed the piece to Felix.

Felix fed it into the press, carefully rolling it back and forth. The resulting sheet grew thinner with each pass, until it was delicate enough to catch even the faintest glimmer of light. He cut the sheet into even squares, then rolled one between his fingers. The gold foil crinkled delicately while he shaped the ball between his fingertips.

He pressed the mallet harder than he meant to. Gold was forgiving. People were not. Vienna had taught him that—taught him what it meant to watch someone pay for your mistakes.

"I'll never understand how this becomes so compact with just a mallet," Raphi remarked, handing over the next flattened piece.

"That's what makes gold special and superior to all other metals." Felix didn't look up, his fingers deft as he formed another ball for the wooden case he had carefully sectioned into compartments. It was nearly half-full now, the precise organization of variously sized gold balls a small triumph in itself. He found satisfaction in the systematic nature of the work. "I clean the cavity," he explained, his tone natural, "until only the hard enamel creates an edge. Then I push the gold balls in and compress them with pressure. That's why I have a tiny mallet."

"And it doesn't hurt the patients?" Raphi's gaze narrowed with genuine curiosity.

Felix paused, glancing at him. "You've never had a cavity, have you?"

"No. Have you?"

Felix gave a shrug. "No—not yet."

"Then how do you know it doesn't hurt?" Raphi pressed on, his tone teasing but underpinned with true interest.

"Because I know it would hurt far more if the cavities reached deeper than the hard enamel," Felix replied pointedly, flattening another foil. His next words came slower, quieter. "Once it gets to the pulp, the pain can be excruciating."

Another ball rolled into place within the case. Good. A week's worth of material—for patients who depended on him to preserve their teeth against a lifetime of discomfort, or worse. Felix exhaled, the stakes always heavy on his shoulders, a weight he chose willingly.

"Then I'll stick to my jewels," Raphi said with a wrinkle of his nose, turning his attention to his work.

"You're not just a jeweler." Felix's words broke the rhythm, quiet but resolute as he looked up.

Raphi quirked an eyebrow. "Oh? What am I, then?"

"You're an expert," Felix replied, threading confidence through his tone. "You don't simply craft jewels. You studied geometry and graduated from the University of Edinburgh with honors. The connections between shapes and angles, along with your calculations and sketches for the Royal Service—I've seen what you are capable of. That's why you're one of *the* Crown Jewelers. There's art in precision, Raphi."

Raphi considered this, his normally calm expression softening with something close to gratitude. "I suppose you're more than a dentist, then?"

"Yes," Felix said, surprising himself with the stark honesty of the word. "I am someone who helps. There's good work in preserving what others might discard." His fingers clenched briefly over the handle of the press. "I'm not like the butchers and barbers who don't truly understand teeth, who leave people worse than before." Felix didn't want to say it, but he'd seen what those crooks did: extracting teeth too early or with pieces of the jawbone. They damaged adjacent teeth and caused patients such harm that they were left terrified of ever seeking help again. No, they were not dentists; they were perpetrators of assault on the human body. Despicable.

Raphi nodded, handing over another flattened wire. "And yet," he murmured, "those less skilled often thrive. The dishonest ones profit from chaos. There's no lack of them, not even across the street, making false jewels and taking shortcuts."

"There'll always be those who sell glass beads as pearls. Those who cut corners may get to their goals faster, but don't learn much along the way," Felix said quietly, though his jaw tightened at the thought. "But I admit, they get away with more than they should."

The room stilled. Felix adjusted the press, his movements slower now, as his mind drifted to the man who had gotten away with the most, and who didn't deserve to continue.

Baron von List. His crimes—poison, attempted murder, kidnapping—were numerous. But his punishments were not.

"I'm afraid to ask about Baron von List," Felix said at last, watching for his friend's reaction.

Raphi's expression darkened. "Then don't," he said sharply. "Ask me anything else. He's taking the shortest path to victory and gets away with crimes twice and again." He paused as if the name of the baron smelled bad. "Instead of using glass beads, List is the sort of man to put dung balls on a chain and get the world to admire it as if it were pearls—he's the sort of criminal who dazzles with threats."

"Blindingly so," Felix remembered him well—the patient who had strutted into his chair, muttering that he'd never trust a Jewish dentist. Felix's name had hidden him then, Leafley instead of Blattner, like the camouflage, but List wasn't a natural predator; he was a menace. The memory still made his stomach tighten. Confidentiality kept him from speaking, even if the patient had been Baron von List himself—the same baron who carried his venom from Vienna into London, who cloaked his cruelty in titles and influence.

List had not only unleashed Bailiff Nagy against the Klonimus family—under cover of the Austrian Kaiser's authority—but had made himself a parasite in Parliament, using his noble guest-rights in the Lords to block every measure that hinted at equality for Jews. To him, success was contagion; if a handful of Jewish families prospered in London, others might follow, and the thought of that ambition spreading struck him as the greatest threat of all.

List was dangerous. And Felix hadn't forgotten the ride in the Spanish Riding School back in Vienna, the one who'd said that List was related to Hofstätter. A tightly-wound network of enemies across Europe. At least List hadn't found out about Felix's true identity, his connections to Vienna.

List was busy with the Jews in London. Specifically, to break the Klonimuses, whose commissions from the Prince Regent relied on steady gold, he'd gone for the source. Bands of men—his men—had stripped the mines in Transylvania, trying to starve the family's supply and topple them from favor. If the ore ran dry, the Crown's patience would run out, too.

Felix exhaled slowly, rolling the tension out of his shoulders. Baron von List was a reminder of everything Vienna had taken from him and everything London still demanded. He couldn't go back—not now, not with 87 Harley Street depending on him, not with the Royal Warrant binding them all to their patients and to the Crown. Leaving would be betrayal. He told himself he'd never do such a thing.

He turned to Raphi, his voice even, though something hard pressed against his ribs.

"Your contacts at the docks. Tell me—any word?"

Five years of silence. Five years of hope clung to like glass shards—cutting, but impossible to let go.

Raphi's pause spoke before his mouth did. And then, softly, the blow: "Nothing."

The room seemed to dull at once, candlelight paling, shadows thickening. Felix blinked hard, forcing the sting back, refusing to let it spill here. Not in front of Raphi. A man doesn't bear the wound that hasn't healed. And yet, Maisie's absence still felt as raw as the day she'd been torn from him.

"She's still out there." His voice was low, meant for no one—or perhaps only for himself. His hand tightened on the press until his knuckles blanched. Raphi's hand came down, firm, steadying.

"You'll find her," Raphi said. Simple words but weighted with the kind of loyalty that never mocked hope, even when it hurt.

Felix met his friend's eyes. For a moment, he nearly said the truth—that if words alone could bridge the sea, he'd have been back in Vienna long ago. But Harley Street tethered him, and he couldn't risk undoing everything they'd built. Worse, searching blindly meant passing her in some port or inn, missing her by a day, an hour. Better to stand fast and send the net wide—Raphi's letters, his trade contacts, his quiet inquiries stretching farther than Felix could reach without raising suspicion.

But standing still was its own torment. Every unanswered letter was another lash, every empty ship's list a blade across the hope he refused to release. He was fighting blind, chained by duty, yet still—still—he never stopped turning stones, never stopped pressing forward.

He looked down at the gold in his hands. Cold, unyielding, yet promising something lasting. If he could mold this metal into crowns, bridges, lives rebuilt, then surely—surely—somewhere in the city's shadows lay the answer he was searching for.

And even if tomorrow crushed him again, he would keep searching.

Always.

Chapter Twelve

F OR FIVE YEARS, Maisie had carried this letter like contraband—slipped under hems, hidden in satchels, pressed against her heart on nights when sleep refused her. The creases were soft now, the ink beginning to blur where her fingers had traced the lines too often.

She had read it first on the night her father collapsed. The *Burschenschaft* had come like a storm, and by morning, everything was gone. The university seized his practice, his instruments, even the brass lamp that had always glowed on his desk. A whole lifetime—his skill, his teaching, his pride—stripped bare, as though Vienna could swallow a man whole and erase every trace he had lived.

That night, while the house still smelled of candle smoke and overturned ink, the Marquess had pressed the letter into her hands. His words were clipped, urgent—there had been no time for comfort. His carriage waited in the street, the horses stamping, breath steaming in the cold. She could still feel the roughness of the parchment, the way her fingers trembled as he closed her hand over it. "Read it when you are safe," he'd said. Then the door had slammed, and she and Deena were jolted into the night.

She had clutched the letter ever since. Through border crossings and borrowed rooms, through the endless rehearsals of a life that wasn't hers, she read and reread until Eleanor Spencer's story slid over her like a second skin.

And tonight—here in London—it mattered more than ever.

IT HAD BEEN her father's final request delivered at the hand of the Marquess, who'd be forever tied to her now, the blueprint of a life she had never chosen. This letter felt less like protection than a commandment: the old world erased, a new one imposed.

Dear Miss Morgenschein,

If you are reading this, it means the plan your father and I spoke of in private has come to pass—sooner, and with more cost, than either of us wished.

Forgive me. What I ask is cruel: to step into another woman's life, to take her name as your own, and to let your own vanish from the ledgers of Vienna. Yet it is the only way to keep you and Deena safe—and to save my son, John, from a fate I cannot bear.

You know what Vienna has taken from you. The night your father defended Faivish Blattner against the university's cruelty, I believe he knew the price. When the Burschenschaft came for him, there was no time to send word. I had your name struck from every record "for your protection." It was as if you had never lived there at all.

I have kept the death of my sister Eleanor private. In truth, Eleanor is gone—taken by illness years ago—but in law, she still lives. Her absence from society makes it possible for you to become her. It is the only way to keep John from a guardian appointed by the Chancery who would squander his estate and break his spirit. The papers, the household, the servants—all are arranged.

Upon your arrival in England, you shall take Eleanor's estate. You will not inherit her life, but her absence, her seclusion. That shadow will be your shield. A tutor will be waiting to teach you and Deena to speak and move as Englishwomen, so that no one might suspect your origins.

I know what this costs you. I know you'll lose contact with Faivish, your home, and your father in one cruel sweep. I cannot give those back. But I can give you this: a life beyond the reach of those who would harm you, and the power to protect your sister and my heir.

Hold to this role until the world is kinder. One day, I hope, you may take back your name.

Yours, in trust and necessity,
Charles Stewart Spencer
Marquess of Stonefield

Those had been the Marquess's last words to her, and his plan had been financed by his executor along with the tutor who schooled her and Deena in English vowels, manners, and silences.

Maisie remembered—sharp as broken glass—the night in Vienna when she had glimpsed her father and the Marquess bent over his desk, voices hushed, papers spread before them. She had caught fragments—*your sister Eleanor... the boy... protection*—before the door closed. She had not understood then. But she did now.

Five years earlier, she had rehearsed Eleanor Spencer's story and she'd spoken her name aloud until it no longer caught in her throat. Yet she carried her father's name—her true name—pressed against her in secret, the ghost she could not lay to rest.

And now, London. No longer practice, but reality. The ruse her father had devised, the shadow-life the Marquess had secured—it was no longer a disguise but her future. And as Father had asked her, she'd go to Rachel.

She folded the parchment with deliberate care and slid it deep into her glove, as though tucking her true self safely inside. At her side, John—barely thirteen, eyes already older than his years—stood straight, the invisible weight of his inheritance bending his small shoulders. Deena clutched Maisie's other hand, her grip tight, frightened.

Maisie drew them both closer. "Come on," she whispered.

Her voice came out steadier than she felt. "It's time."

The Pearler residence loomed ahead, its façade all polished stone and symmetry, windows shuttered like watchful eyes. Maisie's steps faltered at the threshold, nerves clawing at the calm she had practiced on the walk over. It wasn't just a house she faced. It was Father's last plan—his way of binding her to a safety he would never live to see.

The lion's-head knocker gleamed, brass polished to a mirror shine. Maisie's gloved hand hovered above it, her reflection wavered in the metal, blurred and uncertain, as if even the house itself demanded: Who are you to enter?

Father's voice pressed against her memory: Trust the Marquess. England will protect you. His faith in this arrangement had been unshakable, and so here she was—five years of obedience behind her, five years of silence pressed down like a stone on her chest. Five years without Faivish.

Would Father have chosen this path if he had known the cost? That his daughter's name would vanish from Vienna's ledgers as if she had never lived there? That the boy who had promised to return in a year would find nothing—no trace of her, no whisper of her existence? If Faivish ever set foot in Vienna again, she was a ghost to him now.

Her grip tightened around Deena's hand until the younger girl glanced up, eyes wide with questions that Maisie could not answer. John, on her other side, shifted his weight. At thirteen, he carried himself with a solemnity that belonged on older shoulders, his gaze fixed straight ahead, jaw tight with duty.

Deena's attention flicked to the knocker, then back to Maisie. She straightened her posture—chin lifted, shoulders squared— with a practiced composure that startled her sister. Sixteen, and already steadier than Maisie felt. Children learned to adapt; perhaps that was her gift. Maisie envied her courage, for her own heart was still waging war inside her chest.

She swallowed hard. Father had wanted the protection of Eleanor Spencer's name. But that protection had cost Maisie her own heart. Every beat of it still whispered of Vienna—of lamp-lit nights and vows spoken in a dormitory where the future had felt certain, if only for a breath.

Her chest tightened. Survival did not care for love, or vows, or what-ifs. Survival demanded silence. And here she stood: five years of silence, five years of hiding.

Once, she had pictured her life as clear as porcelain—her father's practice carried forward, her work at Faivish's side, their lives entwined in purpose and love. That dream now felt like something seen through glass warped with age: faint, unreachable, almost belonging to someone else.

Maisie exhaled slowly, the sigh weighted with everything she had lost but not her courage. She lifted her hand to the knocker.

If only Faivish were here…

But wishes were lost thoughts in the wind. Maisie lifted the knocker and let it fall, once, cleanly. She couldn't stand in what-ifs any longer; John's eyes were on her.

The door opened at once. A butler in ink-dark velvet stood framed by marble and light, his stillness practiced to an art.

"Lady—" Maisie began, the alias catching on her tongue.

"Mrs. Pearler awaits you in the green drawing room, Lady Eleanor Spencer," he said with a slight inclination, as if finishing the sentence she'd struggled to start. A maid slipped forward, deft hands already reaching for their cloaks.

Warmth lifted from the hall like a hush after snow. The entry's black-and-white tiles shone as if they'd been polished between heartbeats; beeswax rode the air, subtle and clean. For a breath, something in Maisie tugged backward—not quite homesickness, but close.

"Shoulders, love," she murmured to Deena, squeezing her fingers. She straightened—quick study, old habit—and Maisie's own spine obliged.

Behind them, the young marquess kept pace in his small, faultless coat. His silence had weight; it matched her own.

The green drawing room earned its name: walls the deep

green of a hawthorn leaf, silk catching the light; chairs swallowing sound; gilt grazing the moldings. Beauty here did not soothe; it arranged. Every symmetry reminded her she was a guest in someone else's order.

Rachel Pearler stood by the tall windows, face tipped to the pale day. Petite, composed, steel wrapped in silk.

"Miss Maisie Morgenschein!" she said warmly, the name precise on her tongue, as if she'd practiced it once and never forgot. Before Maisie could brace herself, Rachel crossed the room and took both her hands. Her eyes were bright with welcome and edged with appraisal. "And you must be Deena." Her glance softened, measured. She turned to the boy. "And the young Marquess—welcome. *Ich freue mich, Ihnen behilflich sein zu können.*"

So she moved between worlds with ease—German, Yiddish, and English, heritage and society—no seams showing.

Maisie's chest tightened—gratitude laced with caution. One weighs help; one never stops.

"*Vielen Dank, dass Sie uns so bald nach unserer Ankunft empfangen,*" Maisie said, formal despite the thrum in her throat. Thank you for welcoming us so soon upon our arrival.

"*Es ist selbstverständlich, Fräulein Morgenschein,*" Rachel replied smoothly. It goes without saying, Miss Morgenschein. "My father wrote that your road from Vienna to Oxfordshire was not kind. I'm glad London has you at last."

Deena sank into a cushioned chair, reticule balanced primly on her lap. John hesitated, then sat beside her, posture too careful for thirteen. Maisie smoothed her skirt and joined them.

Rachel poured tea, hands sure, not a drop spilled. "Your arrival was prepared for with care, Lady—" her gaze touched Maisie's face, knowing—"Miss Morgenschein."

The cup rattled once in Maisie's saucer. *Miss Morgenschein.* A name erased in Vienna, spoken here like a kept secret. For the world, she was Eleanor Spencer. But under Rachel's look, the truth felt close enough to touch—danger and relief in the same breath.

"Please call me Maisie." *I feel like I'm a living lie. All I wanted was a life with Faivish, with Father alive, with Deena safe beside me. And instead... this.*

She lowered her eyes to the rim of her teacup, where the steam blurred her vision. Father had made her promise obedience, but he hadn't seen what it cost her. He hadn't seen her years of silence, her letters unsent, her heart left to guess if Faivish had searched for her and found nothing.

Rachel's voice, low and deliberate, cut through her thoughts. "Your father made it clear why you needed an opportunity," she said, lifting her cup with practiced elegance. "The men who hunted him would not hesitate to hunt you. That is why you had to disappear from one life in order to live another. I know the feeling all too well."

Maisie's breath caught; she couldn't deny it. The *Burschenschaft* had already stolen her father and were the reason Faivish had left Vienna. If they—or someone like them—discovered she lived, Deena would be the next to pay the price. And where else could they go? As long as she looked after John as Eleanor Spencer, she was safe and so was he.

Rachel set her cup down and reached across the space between them, her eyes steady. "I can imagine what's in your heart because I lived in a similar situation. This isn't hiding, my dear. This is about integration. Acceptance. Played correctly, your presence in London will mean survival—not just for you, but for those you love."

Maisie blinked against the sting in her eyes. Survival. It was what she had traded everything for. But oh, the ache of all she had left behind—her father's study still echoing with *Burschenschaft* shouts, Deena's small cry in the night carriage, and Faivish who probably came to look for her and to find she'd never existed...

Acceptance. The word struck hard. Lacking it had cost her Vienna, cost her love. For the past five years, survival hadn't looked like acceptance. It looked like disappearing. Pretending. Eleanor Spencer's careful signature written in her stead.

"I seem to live better in other people's lives than my own, Mrs. Pearler," she murmured, the confession too quiet to be more than a passing thought—yet her hostess had heard.

"First of all, you must call me Rachel. And second, may I make an observation on your disguise?" Rachel asked, her voice slipping into something brisker. "Your papers tell a slightly different story than the one you lived."

Because my life is a lie. Or at least it had been—since Vienna, since the funeral, since her father's warning about Hofstätter's powerful family, including the nephew whose name had been spoken as if it conjured the devil himself: Baron Wolfgang von List. If London society knew who she truly was, the Baron would see to her ruin—and John's estate with it. It certainly had been a lie through the years in Oxfordshire, hidden away, impersonating the little marquess' late aunt.

But Rachel's gaze caught and held Maisie's with a steadiness that felt almost disarming. There was no performance in her manner, no cruelty hidden behind kindness. Only recognition— the look of a woman who had endured and still stood upright. Maisie understood it in an instant. Rachel Pearler was not someone to fear. She was exactly what Father had promised: sharp, loyal, and unwilling to bend. Perhaps even a friend—if Maisie could dare trust herself with one. And now that she had come to London to keep John safe, she might finally have the chance.

"We are survivors," Rachel said softly. "We do what is necessary when the law and society close their doors to us." For a heartbeat her lips pressed flat, a flicker of old pain breaking through her poise. "Our truths may change shape for practicality's sake, but they remain truths nonetheless. You've only borrowed this new name—worn it like a winter coat. As long as it shields you and those children, it has purpose. And purpose matters more than pride."

Maisie nodded—a small motion, but it came from some-where real. Her heart resisted the comfort, but her mind heard the sense in it.

Perhaps I'm not as alone as I thought.

John sat stiffly beside her, his hands folded too tightly in his lap. Maisie remembered the prayer she'd overheard from his lips the night before—that he might never be sent away from her. The memory pressed against her ribs now, tender and raw. His mother was gone, his father little more than a story. And soon a school would claim him, stripping away what little sense of home he had left. He leaned into her arm—just slightly, the instinctive tilt of a child needing anchor. Maisie laid her hand over his, trying to pour steadiness through her palm when inside she felt anything but steady.

Rachel's demeanor softened when it fell on him. "You've been rather brave, young sir. But you must understand—Marquess of Spencer is not an ordinary title, and you are not an ordinary boy. The law will take notice of you. The Court of Chancery will appoint guardians—one for your estates, another for your person. Neither may be of your choosing."

John's mouth pulled tight. "But why can't I just stay with Maisie? She's kind. She keeps me safe." His voice cracked, breaking the word, and Maisie's grip on his hand tightened like a vow.

Deena leaned forward, her wide eyes fierce with urgency. "And if he wants to stay, surely that counts for something?"

Rachel's sigh carried both compassion and resignation. "Not enough, I fear. The guardian of his estate will almost certainly be chosen for influence and wealth. And such men may see you, John, not as a boy to be loved but as property to be managed. The guardian of your person may be different—or the same—but either can bring the other before the Lord Chancellor. And so, it will be argued over you."

"As though I were property?" John's voice trembled with disbelief.

Silence fell, thick and bruising. John's small fingers curled tighter around Maisie's. The memory of his prayer rose again in her mind, and something inside her cracked. She wanted to scoop him into her arms, shield him with her body, cry out against the men who wrote laws without ever hearing a child sob in the dark. Instead, she only held him closer, her defiance pressed into the quiet, unyielding pressure of her hand on his.

"Do try the tea," Rachel offered at last, handing Maisie a porcelain cup ringed with violets. "I dare say it will taste familiar."

The floral scent curled upward, and Maisie's breath caught. The jasmine was the same her father had brought home from Rachel's father's trade—sharp, fragrant, memory-laced. Maisie blinked quickly and raised the cup.

"It's jasmine tea," Rachel said gently. "My father always claimed it was the finest. Yours certainly seemed to agree."

"He did," Maisie replied, her voice steady, though her fingers trembled. The taste was a memory in liquid form—sweet and bitter, like all good things lost.

Rachel leaned back, her expression warm. "I always wished we'd met sooner. My father spoke of yours so often. It's truly a pleasure to meet you at last. And your sister." Her eyes darted to Deena. "She's lovely, you know. Quite the picture of your family. My father said you were the image of your mother as a child and he was inconsolable when she died. She was my father's only living cousin."

Deena flushed and toyed with her sleeve, but Maisie reached over to squeeze her hand. "You are very kind."

"Nonsense." Rachel waved the words away, though her expression softened. "Tell me, how are you settling in? Comfortable in your new home?"

"We've been fortunate," Maisie answered cautiously. "The young marquess inherited a fine house, and for now, we have the means to manage it."

"Then let me tell you how you *must* manage it," Rachel said briskly. She cleared her throat, and a footman appeared with a leather binder. Rachel passed it directly to Maisie.

"My father tells me he knew yours well," Rachel said, turning to the young marquess. "Stonefield was a man of principle. He went to Vienna to speak on behalf of those your universities and guilds would not admit—to give voice where none was wanted. That kind of courage makes enemies. He didn't deserve to leave England as he did."

"No," the boy said quietly. He swallowed hard. "It made my mother sick with grief. She died last winter while I was at school in Kent."

Maisie's hand stilled over the leather binder. There it was again—grief stitched into the boy's posture, into the silence between his words. She looked at Deena, and the familiar guilt returned. Her sister deserved more than this life of pretending to be her companion. Not for lack of comforts—they had more than they ever imagined—but because they had lost their names. Their truth.

And how could fate find them, when they were hiding from it?

"My condolences," Rachel said, her voice a gentle thread. "You're orphaned too young." She didn't rush the moment. Even her silence felt deliberate, gracious. Maisie saw then what made Rachel formidable—not force, but presence.

"Thank you. I shall go to Eton soon," the boy added, as if reciting lines rehearsed alone.

"That is good," Rachel said. "My husband often speaks of his time at Eton. Rare for a Jew to attend, but he passed unnoticed. The friendships he made there shaped his future."

Maisie managed a small smile. She still said nothing, too aware of the line they walked. The house was the marquess' in name, but he had no control. Deena, the companion of a dead woman, had no legal identity. It was all so fragile.

Rachel's gaze didn't waver. She spoke with a steadiness that felt almost like a hand extended across the table. "You and Deena are welcome here—Shabbat, holidays, or simply to rest. Let our fathers' friendship continue with us."

Maisie's throat tightened. "I should like that very much." The words came out quieter than she meant, and she hated how needy they sounded. Five years in Oxfordshire had kept them safe, yes—but safe was not the same as seen.

Rachel smiled, the kind that softened the sharp lines of her face. "Good. Then as your friend"—the word landed deliberately, as though Rachel knew exactly what it cost Maisie to hear it—"let me give you the tools to thrive."

She drew a thick binder across the table. Its leather edges were worn smooth, the pages crammed with notes in several hands. "These will help you inhabit Lady Eleanor Spencer in London. My mother-in-law and I gathered what you'll need—names, timelines, mannerisms. Enough that anyone who might have known Eleanor before she vanished into the country will find no reason to doubt you."

Maisie opened it, the paper crackling faintly under her fingers. Lines of ink. Birth dates. Clubs. Servants' names. The sort of details that made up a life. Her voice felt dry as she read aloud: "Born 1788. So much younger than the Marquess…"

"Yes," Rachel said, her smile thinning. "That marriage was… complicated."

Maisie flipped a page. "She moved to Reading? With her governess?"

Rachel poured tea as she spoke, her hand steady, her tone measured. "She withdrew. Preferred solitude. And no longer cared about the scandals."

A strange chill traced Maisie's ribs. This was the life she must step into—another woman's retreat, another woman's shame.

"She caused a scandal?" The question slipped out, hushed.

Rachel glanced toward John before answering. "She was disappointed in love. Society punished her. She chose to disappear at Greys Court. You'll need to know it well."

Maisie nodded. She hadn't even been there.

"So I am to become Eleanor Spencer." This time, she didn't flinch—though her hands curled into her skirts under the table.

John shifted beside her, brightening with a sudden thought. "My aunt had dogs. Terriers. Mother liked them best." His voice carried a spark Maisie hadn't heard in weeks.

Rachel seized it. "Then learn everything about terriers. It is the small details, Maisie, that anchor a truth."

Maisie's chest pinched. Eleanor Spencer—a name sewn onto her like an ill-fitting gown. She had already abandoned Maisie Morgenschein once. And yet, when she looked at John's eager face, flushed with pride at remembering, she knew she would do it again. For him, she would wear the mask.

Rachel's eyes softened. "As Eleanor, you can stand between him and men who would use him. If you remain Maisie, they'll sweep you both aside."

The words fell into silence. John leaned into her arm, his small fingers knotting into her sleeve, and she laid her hand over his. His whispered prayer from last night returned to her—*Please, let me stay with Maisie.*

Rachel's voice broke the quiet again, gentler now, but pointed. "Do you know Debrett's, John?"

He shook his head.

"It is the great book of titles," Rachel explained. "Every noble family, every estate written down as if in stone. But you will not find a single Jewish name there. Not one." She let that truth settle. "Titles come from land. And land is closed to us, for Jews can't own land. The record is silent—and silence is its own weapon."

John frowned, brow tight. "But the estate is mine."

"Yes," Rachel said softly. "By right, it is. But men like Baron von List are waiting for heirs without protection. The gossips of the ton confirmed the rumors that you may be his next target. Without an unimpeachable name beside you, he can twist the law and take what's yours with you or without. That is why your guardian"—she turned her gaze to Maisie—"must take on another name, a titled relation of yours. So no one dares strip you of what is yours."

Maisie closed her eyes for an instant, steadying the storm inside her. How badly she wanted to reject it, to cling to the truth of her own name, her own heart. To believe she could walk openly as Faivish's chosen so that he could find her and she could be his for life. But John's thin shoulders were bowed under losses no child should bear, and Deena's life was knotted to hers.

She opened her eyes. "I will do everything I can to protect them—under Eleanor's name but with my heart."

"That is what goodness is, Maisie—not the life we wish for, but the life we give so others may keep theirs." Rachel's expression softened. "Does anyone else smell *rugelach*?"

Denna leapt at the opportunity but John mumbled, "What's *rug-leks*?"

"*Rugelach*," Deena corrected with a small laugh. "Delicious buttery pastries filled with nuts and honey paste."

"Go to the back of the hall and see if anyone has brought them out yet," Rachel said.

As their footsteps faded, Rachel's tone shifted, and she leaned forward just slightly. "Now," she said, her voice lower, purposeful. "How can I help you settle in more comfortably here in London?"

Maisie hesitated. She hadn't intended to speak of it—but the question opened something inside. The words came unbidden. "There is someone I need to find," she said, her voice quiet.

Rachel tilted her head, her brow furrowing slightly—not out of judgment, but concern.

"A family member?"

Maisie shook her head. "No."

Rachel didn't press, but her gaze was steady. "A man?"

Maisie nodded once, and that one gesture cost her.

The man. The only one.

Rachel said nothing at first. Then, gently, "I understand."

She reached for a small notepad and quill on the side table.

"Give me his name. The ton has its ways. If he is here, or even rumored to be, we'll find him."

Maisie's hands trembled slightly as she accepted the quill. Her throat tightened. "Thank you," she whispered. "I have had no success finding him as Eleanor in the countryside. Perhaps here, in Town..."

"Yes." Rachel didn't look away. "You deserve more than survival. Let's find your heart a future, too."

Before Maisie could respond, Rachel turned her attention to the next topic. "And your sister? Where will she go to school?"

"I'll teach her," Maisie said quickly. "Everything Father taught me. A nurse." She glanced at the door through which Deena had left with John a minute earlier with a small frown. Everything but the surgical skill and precision she'd once known by heart. That part of her life felt locked behind glass now visible but unreachable.

A sudden yelp startled them both. Maisie turned to see the marquess clutching his jaw, wincing, the half-eaten rugelach in his hand as he re-entered the room. Maisie sighed and placed her cup down. "Not again."

Rachel's brow rose. "Is everything all right?"

Maisie gave a wry smile. "The daughter of a dentist, looking after a boy who clearly needs one—and I can't even find the man I love who could help him."

Rachel tutted and smiled faintly. "We must remedy that. Eton waits for no one, and he can't sit exams with a toothache."

She walked to a small desk near the window, opened a drawer, and produced a card, handing it to Maisie.

Folsham, Collins, Fernando, Leafley
87 Harley Street

Maisie turned it over, her breath catching at the final name. It was odd and yet she couldn't say why.
Leafley.
She swallowed. "Thank you," she said.

Rachel's gaze lingered with a quiet smile. "At the very least, the marquess will be well cared for."

But Maisie heard what Rachel *meant*.

And for the first time in years, something inside her whispered: *Maybe so will I.*

Chapter Thirteen

O N AN ORDINARY afternoon on Harley Street, Felix was sick of the hopelessness of finding Maisie. Plus, the practice was loud today. Voices echoed through the hallway, muffled behind closed doors. Someone coughed down the corridor; someone else fake-laughed too loudly. His next patient wasn't scheduled for another half hour, so Felix slipped into the back kitchen down-stairs and shut the door behind him with the soft finality of someone not wanting to be followed.

It was a plain little room—sturdy oak table, a row of barely chipped mugs, a half-tin of tea that rattled when he picked it up.

He filled the kettle and lit the flame.

One scoop.

And another.

Still not enough. Nothing was enough anymore. *I miss her so much.*

He paused, the tin in his hand.

She used to bring tea to the practice in Vienna—always care-ful not to spill when she balanced the teapot and cups on the tray as she pushed the door from the waiting area to Professor Morgenschein's treatment room open with her back. Once, she'd set the tray down beside him, and he'd said—without quite thinking—that she'd looked perfectly pretty that day.

She'd gone still, just for a second and then smiled.

He added a fourth scoop.

Then a fifth.

The leaves hit the pot with a soft hiss, like something breaking. He missed how her braid came loose by the end of the morning. And that one night, when her braid had come apart under his touch and she'd given herself... if he had known he wouldn't see her again, he would have never let her go. That stupid promise to be back after a year... five now. He'd left her and didn't even know where she was. But sometimes, it was as if he could sense her sadness. Or was it his own broken heart? Either way, every second without Maisie felt too long. The leaves had clumped in the bottom of the pot like dirt. That's fine, he thought. Let it brew bitter. The flame hissed low. He didn't move.

Behind him, the door opened.

"Oh—you're here?" Andre sounded surprised. "Thought you were upstairs."

Felix kept his back to him, still holding the spoon.

Andre stepped closer. "Felix. What is that, tea concentrate? You'll kill someone with that."

"I just want a biscuit," Felix said. He opened the cupboard. Empty. Bent down. Nothing but crumbs in the jar. "Isn't there anything useful in this kitchen?"

"I dare say, we're pretty useful," Andre said.

Before Felix could answer, the door opened again. "Who's talking about useful?" Wendy walked in, tugging off her gloves. "Oh, tea."

She poured herself a cup, took one sip, and gagged. "Ugh. Who made this?"

"It's too strong," Felix muttered.

"Too dark," Andre added.

"Too intense," Felix said, quiet now. He picked up the mug.

He didn't sweeten the tea. Sugar ruined teeth—and masked the bitterness that gave the leaves their strength. This was black tea, from the foot of the Himalaya, the kind he'd drunk in India, meant to be steeped slowly, touched with clove or cardamom. Instead, he'd prepared it without thought about the richness of the brew and it was just like everything these days: rushed, bland, or bitter. It tasted like something he knew too well. Something broken at the start, but swallowed anyway.

He took a sip. It burned his mouth. He drank again. "I'll clean the kettle tonight," he said. "Buy better tea tomorrow."

He moved for the door, but Wendy stepped in his path and nodded in Andre's direction.

Andre's voice was gentler now. "We know you're alone here at night."

"I've always been alone," Felix said. "You've just noticed now because you're not." Felix loathed himself for how that came out. He was happy Andre had his princess, Thea, and Wendy had her Prince Stan, and yet, that made him no less lonely without his Maisie. She wasn't a princess but the queen of his heart, mind, and soul, no less.

Wendy frowned. "That's not true, we always noticed."

He laughed under his breath. It didn't sound amused. "There's nothing you can do, Wendy," he said, unable to mask his sadness.

"I've asked Thea for help," Andre said. "She's trying to help find your Maisie. Nobility have their ways."

"But Maisie isn't nobility," he went on, barely pausing. "That's the problem. No paper trail, no titles, nothing to search. She's unfindable."

"People don't disappear like ghosts, this is not a story in a book," Andre said.

Felix looked down at the tea, swirled what was left in the cup.

"I saw her yesterday," he said softly. "Outside a bakery. It wasn't her, but I followed the woman with a parcel of lemon tarts half a block before I could stop myself. Then again in my sleep." Silence. But sleep didn't come easily on the days he wished he could hold her, which was every day, admittedly. "I don't even know what I'd say if I did find her," he admitted. "Except maybe

I'm sorry for ever leaving her in the first place."

He swallowed the last of the tea, the heat cutting sharply.

"I wish I could stop needing her," he said, not quite looking at either of them. "I really do, but that's impossible. She's a part of me. She has my heart, and it feels like the muscle inside me isn't even pumping without her love nearby. I just can't…" I can't bear the pain of missing her thus. He didn't say it. Not again lest Wendy and Andre pity him, and he hated pity.

No one moved.

Wendy took his empty cup and poured him a fresh one. This time, she stirred in a spoonful of honey without asking.

"Then let's start there," she said. "You're not alone."

He didn't answer.

But he stayed.

"Perhaps there's still hope to find her again." Andre gave a smile of the sort he'd give for a fatal diagnosis and yet didn't have the heart to take the patient's will to fight.

⫸⫷

ACROSS TOWN IN *a different house but the same evening…*

"Don't you want honey in your tea?" Deena's voice broke the quiet, gentle but persistent, like a thread tugging loose.

Maisie didn't answer right away. She sat at the long kitchen table, stirring her tea in slow, idle circles. The spoon clinked against the porcelain.

"Nothing will save it," she said at last, nose wrinkling at the bitter, over-steeped brew. "It's all wrong."

Deena, undeterred, dipped the spoon into the honey pot anyway. "You used to like it sweet."

Maisie didn't look up. "The tea I liked wasn't this kind."

She traced a finger along the edge of the cup. "Back in Vienna, I brought tea to the practice in the mornings. Always something light—rose petal, sometimes jasmine. Rachel's father used to send parcels to us, wrapped in muslin with yellow bows.

The scent would fill the kitchen before I even opened them."

"Was that for Father?"

Maisie nodded. "And for Faivish."

Deena smiled faintly. "He liked rose and jasmine?"

"He liked whatever I brought him." Maisie's voice dipped lower, as if the words were too old to speak aloud.

There'd been a day—one ordinary morning—when she'd tripped slightly as she set the tray down, nearly spilling the cups. Faivish had caught her wrist to steady her and said, "You're perfect." Then he cleared his throat and said, "perfectly pretty today, Maisie."

She hadn't known what to do with the words. She'd just stood there, blushing like a fool, until he looked away. What a fool she was to let him go all those years ago.

She stirred the tea again, slower now.

The memory slid against her ribs.

"What's wrong with it?" Deena asked, watching her.

Maisie hesitated. "Nothing."

Everything.

"You probably don't remember," she said instead. "But in Vienna, we never had tea after dinner. It was a mid-morning habit—just before the sun got too high."

Deena shook her head. "I was little. I remember… playing outside. Not tea."

Maisie smiled faintly. "You used to come back in just before dusk. Always with dirt on your knees and bits of grass in your hair."

Deena tilted her head. "Was that when you started helping Father? With his patients?"

"Yes. He didn't teach me per se. I just learned—watched him, listened. I knew which tools he needed before he asked. How he liked his instruments laid out. I learned to see when he was thinking, and when he needed silence."

Deena studied her. "And were you Faivish's nurse, too?"

The question dropped so softly it shouldn't have hurt. But it did.

Maisie's breath caught—not sharply, but as though the air had thickened. She looked down into her cup. The tea had gone darker than her thoughts.

"Yes," she said. "I brought him tea. And towels. He was always working. Always focused. I'd bring the tray while you were outside, and he'd give me that quiet smile like he hadn't known he was thirsty until I appeared."

She didn't say what else she'd brought him. Or how many times she'd waited until the house quieted and slipped out again.

She could still feel the rough plaster of the courtyard wall beneath her palms. The sharp scent of the rose bush leaning over the rain barrel. And Faivish always waiting for her.

She'd asked him once to teach her how to kiss. He'd laughed softly, then did.

And every time after had felt like the world narrowed to that one stolen kiss between them.

There were moments they hadn't spoken at all. Just the warmth of his fingers lacing through hers in the dark.

"I remember the night we left Vienna," Deena said, her voice a little smaller. "Father wouldn't let me outside. He said there was danger in the streets before you came home."

Maisie nodded, her hand tightening around the cup. "There was."

What she remembered wasn't the violence—not as the first memory of that dreadful night. It was Faivish's face, lit by candlelight in the practice cellar, the fear buried under calm. She remembered how he held her that last time—too tightly, as if letting go would make the world collapse.

And then it had. So terribly even that Father's heart stopped as if he couldn't bear a world so cruel anymore.

She blinked down at her tea. The color was wrong. Flat. Like ink left too long in water.

"You loved him," Deena said.

Maisie didn't look up. "Yes."

"And do you still?"

There was a long pause.

"I don't think love works like that," Maisie said finally. "You don't put it away in a drawer when the war ends or the papers stop printing a name. It doesn't end just because the world moved on." She touched the rim of the cup again. Her fingers were icy. "It stays. Even when it's not allowed to. Even when it doesn't make sense anymore."

Deena reached for the teapot, but Maisie shook her head.

"It won't taste right. Not tonight."

They sat there, the clock ticking softly, the house creaking as it settled into sleep.

"I hope he's alive," Deena said, not looking at her.

Maisie closed her eyes. I hope so too. But she'd learned not to say that part aloud. Hope had a way of unraveling when spoken too often.

"I dream about him sometimes," she admitted. "He's older. Changed. But he looks at me the same. Like I'm still the girl who brought him rose tea in a chipped cup and flushed when he smiled at me."

The fire crackled low.

"I wish you'd gotten to say goodbye," Deena whispered.

Maisie's throat tightened. "I did." But I didn't expect it to be a farewell.

But the worst part was that she hadn't known that the last kiss would be the last. That the next morning, everything would break.

She pressed her hand flat to the table, grounding herself. "I miss her," she said softly. "The girl I was with him. She was brave."

"You still are."

Maisie looked up. Deena was watching her—not as a child, not as the girl she used to tuck in—but as a young woman.

"I don't feel brave," Maisie said.

Deena poured her own cup and drank. "Then let me be brave

for you, just for tonight." Then she reached out and held Maisie's hand.

The firelight flickered across the walls. Outside, the fog pressed thick against the windows. Somewhere in the street, a carriage rattled past, fading quickly into silence.

Maisie looked down at her tea one last time.

She didn't drink it.

"After we left Vienna and came to England so soon after Father's death, I didn't even know where to start." Her fingers tightened around the spoon. "But here... I've started to look for Faivish again." Deena gave a small nod. "The executor of the Marquess's estate has been thorough," Maisie said. "He traced Faivish to Calcutta. That's where the records stop. No notice of his return to Vienna. No ship manifests with his name. Nothing in any hospital rolls, no obituary, no letters."

"And Rachel?" Deena asked softly. "Do you think she might be able to help?"

Maisie investigated her cup, as if the tea might offer an answer. "She might. But without a name, without something more than a memory... I'm not sure she could find anything we haven't already tried." She drew a slow breath. "It's like chasing fog."

$$\sim\!\!\bullet\!\!\sim$$

Chapter Fourteen

The next day, 87 Harley Street...

LATE MORNING SUNLIGHT poured through the tall windows, spilling across the polished wood floor and catching on the brass fittings of the chair. Felix adjusted the mouth mirror one last time, tilting it until the light slid exactly where he wanted it. Shadows could hide infection. Shadows could ruin trust.

He stepped back, letting his gaze take in the room as a patient might: the linen drape smoothed crisp and neat, a roll at the headrest laced with lavender and chamomile. Not ornament—defense. Frightened children breathed easier when the air carried something soft. On the tray beside it waited clove oil in a stoppered vial, a scent sharp as memory, and his favorite burnisher gleamed like a promise. The gold pellets lay in their case, each one shaped by his own hand the night before. Tiny spheres of permanence. Gold yielded where it must and held where it mattered. If only hearts could do the same.

The hallway gave a faint groan, and he looked up.

"Still fighting with the light, Felix?" Alfie's voice came before he did, warm and teasing, like friendship carried on creaking boards.

He appeared in the doorway a moment later, a satchel slung across his shoulder, his grin boyish despite the faint scar on his cheek. "I brought more calendula salve."

Felix let the corner of his mouth lift. "You know I keep it

ready."

"And yet you'd have set the room three times over if I'd let you," Alfie said, stepping in, his apothecary's bag thumping against the table. "I swear, you've been polishing since breakfast."

"Precision matters," Felix replied, but the cloth was already in his hand, sweeping over the tray again though it needed no more.

Alfie folded his arms, watching him with the patience of someone long used to this ritual. "It's not every day the Crown Jewelers send word. You could almost fool me into thinking you're nervous."

Felix dipped his chin, though he didn't quite deny it. "Rachel Pearler wrote herself. Said the boy was delicate. Said his guardian might be his aunt. That was all."

Alfie's brow rose. "Rachel Pearler doesn't write letters for trifles. Her firm cuts the stones that princes wear on their fingers. If she says 'delicate,' she means the ton is already sniffing around."

Felix's gaze fell back to the tools, to the glinting gold. "Delicate is a polite word. Children like that aren't left alone—they're turned into currency. She didn't say who's circling."

Alfie's grin slipped. His voice dropped low. "List?"

The name burned in the air like a hot iron.

Felix's jaw worked until it hurt. "Who else? He's sniffing at Parliament again. Whispering that foreign heirs don't belong, that Jewish guardians can't be trusted. A boy like this—alone—" His fingers closed hard around the case of gold pellets, as though he might crush the threat with his hand. "He'd be easy prey."

Alfie's silence was answer enough.

Alfie let the words hang a moment, then he let out a breath that could scatter the heaviness with it. "You'll do well. You always do. That's why people trust you. Still—it also means the boy's terrified, and no one else has the patience to see him through." He set a small box on the desk. "New salts. Lemon, faint enough not to fight the lavender."

"Thank you," Felix murmured, taking the box and setting it

neatly aside. "If the air smells safe, maybe he won't dread the clove so much."

Alfie watched him for a beat, lips twitching. "You're preparing like he's the Prince Regent himself."

Felix shook his head. "He's only thirteen. And he's lost both parents. That's enough reason to give him every dignity I can."

Alfie's grin softened into something quieter. "You've too much kindness in you. I hope the world gives you a fraction of it back. You patch people up with gold as if you can mend the whole world."

Felix turned a small pellet in his fingers, letting it catch the light before placing it back in the row. "Gold doesn't ask questions. It just fills the cracks and holds them together. If only more men were made of it."

Alfie chuckled. "Always the philosopher."

The clock ticked, its steady beat tightening the room. Felix glanced at it. "They'll be here soon."

Alfie swung his satchel back over his shoulder, pausing at the door. "Don't forget to charge them properly. Just because half of Mayfair's servants get free fillings from you doesn't mean the practice can live on goodwill."

"I don't charge for easing pain."

"You should."

Felix's eyes lifted, calm but firm. "I charge the ones who can afford not to feel it."

Alfie shook his head, smiling despite himself. "Noble man. I'll be at the dispensary if you need me. And don't let the boy bite you."

Felix almost smiled. "He won't."

When the door clicked shut, the room seemed to exhale. Felix adjusted the neck roll one final time, his hand lingering there before he drew it back. Soon a boy would sit in that chair— heart heavy, mouth aching—and for a little while, Felix could make one small corner of his life better.

He didn't know what face would meet him when the door

opened, but he already knew it wouldn't matter. Not to the boy. Not to the work. And not to the ghost of a woman who had once steadied the lamp for him, her hand warm on his shoulder. A touch he still carried, five years on.

That was enough.

JUST AS THE carriage jolted over the stones of Harley Street, Maisie glanced at the boy opposite her. John sat very straight for his age, though the swing of his small boots against the floor betrayed him. Deena's soft humming drifted up, threading through the clatter of hooves.

John tipped his head, studying her with mild suspicion. "What is that tune you're always humming?"

Deena only shrugged, her gaze fixed on the window. "Just a song Father used to sing to me at bedtime."

Maisie looked up from the gloves in her lap. Her voice softened before she could stop it. "Not only bedtime, Deena. He sang it with Mother for you, too, when you were too little to remember."

The carriage seemed to quiet around them, as though even the horses slowed to listen. Maisie's throat tightened—she hadn't meant to let it slip, hadn't meant to open that door. The memory of those voices—her parents, twined together—rose inside her, both balm and blade. She forced her gaze back to her gloves, steadying her hands for Deena's sake.

Deena's reflection blurred in the glass. Her lips pressed together, as though holding the tune inside. Maisie longed to reach over, smooth her sister's hair the way their mother once had. Instead, she allowed the silence to linger, anchoring them to shared memories of the dear past.

When the wheels slowed to a halt, Maisie lifted her chin. She smoothed the blue wool of her pelisse across her lap, armor for the day ahead. Deena's humming had returned, quieter now, the old Viennese lullaby rising and falling without words. Maisie closed her eyes briefly, letting the sound settle around them like candlelight. The ache in her heart sharpened, but she didn't want to worry her sister and gave a warm smile. Children carried the past forward—not as chains, but as echoes. That was why she must keep them safe.

John shifted, peering out at the house before them. His careful posture melted a little, replaced by the plain worry of a boy about to sit in a dentist's chair.

"Will it hurt terribly?" His voice was small, but steady.

Maisie leaned forward, her tone calm, warm. "Dentists trusted by the Crown Jeweler are the best in London. Whatever you feel, it will pass quickly. If we leave it, though, the pain will grow worse—especially once you're at Eton and won't have me to give you cloves."

He considered this like an adult weighing testimony, his brow furrowed. After a moment, he gave a small, solemn nod. "If you think so."

"I know so." Maisie reached across, touching his wrist lightly. "Our father was a dentist. He treated your father for many years. You'll be well looked after., Rachel promised this one's the best."

The boy blinked, surprise softening the edge of his fear. "I didn't know my father was your father's patient, I thought he was only his friend."

Maisie held his gaze, her hand warm over his. "Now you do." She gave a wistful smile. "You weren't there. You were always in England." Maisie took a careful breath, hoping she hadn't unsettled him. She'd seen many children freeze in fear at the sight of the chair. "And your father was always grateful for the gold that kept his teeth from hurting."

"It will look like I ate a girl's necklace." He grimaced. "It will show when I laugh. What will the other boys at Eton say?"

"That you're precious. Not everyone can afford proper gold fillings. It shows you come from refined stock and shouldn't be trifled with."

"I shall command respect then?"

"As marquess, you'll know just what to say—if you listen to your heart." She reached out, steadying the fall of his cravat with a sisterly care that faltered at the edges of something deeper. She was not his mother; she could never be. And yet here she was, filling a silence that should have been hers to speak into. "You are braver than you think, John. Whatever they see in your mouth, let it stand as proof of courage—of facing what's imperfect, and making it your strength."

"How am I doing it?"

"You're taking something that causes you pain and making it strong again." Maisie gave his hand a gentle squeeze.

"You make it sound like the dentist will build a dam in his mouth," Deena said.

I hope not.

"How do you know this dentist is as good as your father was?" the boy asked again. "Are you not coming inside to meet him?"

Maisie glanced out the window at the elegant row of buildings. The door had a fanlight; the brick facade was stately and symmetrical, with wrought iron railings and high windows. Just as Rachel had described—a hub of refined expertise. *I need to find my Faivish. He's somewhere in the world...*

"You don't need me. The doctors here have a Royal Warrant. There's no one better in England." Maisie glanced again at the polished brass plate by the door—her pulse stuttered. Something about the serif of the lettering, the precise spacing, the faint lavender wafting from within... A memory stirred. A trick of hope, perhaps. She looked away quickly lest her vulnerable heart let the tears come again in front of the children. Not this time.

John seemed more settled. When Deena slipped from the coach to guide him inside, he turned back. "So you're truly not coming with us?" he asked, his small hand on the doorframe.

Maisie shook her head with a regretful but firm smile. "Not today. I have another matter—one that cannot wait. You'll be in the best hands with Deena. She can speak on my behalf."

At the step, Deena turned, her bonnet shadowing little of her face. For a fleeting moment, Maisie caught her breath. Deena looked so composed, so English, her gown fitted to perfection and her bearing already that of a young lady. It was hard to reconcile this careful companion with the child who once ran wild through the Vienna streets with baskets of apples and berries, hair streaming loose. A pang of loss tugged at her, bittersweet and sudden. "I hope you find him," Deena said softly, her voice steady with more understanding than her years should hold.

Maisie's hand tightened imperceptibly on her skirts. Her lips lifted in a faint smile that didn't quite reach her eyes. "Thank you, Deena," she said quietly.

The moment stretched between them until Deena gave a nod and extended her hand to the boy. She led him away while Maisie leaned back against the seat, her fingers tracing the window frame.

Outside, London moved as it always did—but Maisie didn't seem to play any part of it. Not without *him*.

Without Faivish, time ticked forward, but life itself remained still.

She waited until they had gone inside, then tapped the roof for the driver. As the carriage pulled away, the tune Deena had hummed—*Tumbalalaika*—rose again, softly, from Maisie's lips.

A single note, then another—no words, only the song. Like a fragment of a life that had once been hers.

The pain in her soul flared sharp and hot, but she let it burn through, steadying her chin as she breathed into the rhythm of the wheels: *"Tumbala, tumbala, tumbalalaika."*

Vienna lay far behind her, but Faivish's smile still glowed in memory—bright, clever, unforgettable.

She did not look back. She did not falter.

She sang not to soothe, but to steel herself. A vow carried on melody.

And she would keep singing until she found the man who could mend what had broken in her—just as he had once mended others.

✦

Chapter Fifteen

OH, THAT BOY'S *teeth*.

The thought came as Wendy bustled out with her usual efficiency, leaving Felix alone to ready the instruments. Gold foil, burnishers, hours of work. His fingers flexed in anticipation of the ache. The tray already gleamed, but he wiped it again, habit more than need.

The boy had shuffled in with an air of obligation, not fear, his hands folded loosely across his middle. Felix liked that—it meant less trembling, fewer flinches. But it wasn't the boy who unsettled him.

It was the girl.

Fifteen, perhaps sixteen. She moved with the watchful care of someone older, as though every step had been measured in advance. And she was humming.

Felix kept his eyes on the instruments, but the sound threaded through the room, soft, persistent. Not quite a tune for a child, not quite a prayer. Something else. Something that reached under his ribs.

Maisie.

He tried to ignore the thought, jaw tightening as he arranged the mirror just so. The boy's molars. That was what mattered. The work.

But the girl hummed again, and the lilt of it snagged him.

That rise, that fall. He knew it too well.

It can't be. She isn't here.

He hadn't slept the night before—hadn't in years when her dreams came too vividly. Vienna bled into London in those hours, and he woke with her name lodged in his throat. Perhaps this was the echo of another sleepless night. Perhaps he was losing his mind.

He set down the last tool, aligning it with meticulous care. Everything in order. Everything ready.

And then he glanced up.

Just a profile, caught in the slant of afternoon light. The line of a cheek. The neat tuck of hair.

His breath hitched.

For one raw second, he saw her. Maisie, standing where she always had—steadying the light, watching him work, the air between them charged with everything they hadn't dared speak.

He blinked, and the illusion broke. Only a girl remained, a stranger with careful hands and a humming voice.

Felix turned back to the gold, his face blank, his chest aching. He told himself it was absurd—sad, even—that he saw her everywhere. In shop windows, in shadows, in the reflection of his own glass. But that was his life now.

Always searching and missing her.

The curve of the cheek. The neatness of her hair.

Stop it.

Felix dragged his gaze back to the boy in the chair. He was seeing Maisie everywhere these days—in the sheen of a shop window, the break of a stone wall, even the folds of his own coat. If he wasn't careful, he'd start imagining Wendy in her likeness next.

Absurd. Sad. But it was the truth of his life now.

The boy looked up at him with quiet unease, and Felix softened his voice, coaxing.

"Now, open again for me. A bit wider... that's it."

They worked in near silence. Each time the boy flinched even only slightly, Felix stopped, let him breathe, then continued. Patience was its own medicine. Wendy caught his look and wordlessly passed him the finer scraper, her expression matter-of-fact—like two of them could coax trust back into a child who had every reason to withhold it.

"You may rinse now," Felix murmured, tipping his chin toward the basin.

The boy accepted the glass from Wendy's hand. Sage-scented water gleamed as he tilted it carefully, spitting into porcelain with the neatness of someone already trained to mask mistakes.

Felix should have kept his eyes on the patient. He knew that. But across the room, the girl sat with a book unmoved in her lap. Her gaze wasn't on the page.

She was watching him.

His hands, perhaps? The steadiness or care?

The moment he looked her way, she ducked back behind the cover, but too late—he'd seen it. And still, at the edges of his hearing, that low humming circled him like smoke.

"When am I finished with the scraping?" the boy asked, voice muffled as Wendy dabbed his mouth with a cloth.

Felix eased the tool aside. "It will take a while longer," he said gently. "These teeth must have troubled you for months. Has no one taken you before?"

The boy hesitated, then gave a half-shrug. "I don't remember my father. My mother was ill, and the servants were—" He cut himself off, color flaring in his cheeks. Too much spoken.

"She died last year," the girl said quickly. Her voice was even, but her lips pressed tight, as though sealing back the grief that wanted out. The look on her face—a ripple of pain contained, then gone—stilled something deep in Felix's chest.

Wendy, practical as ever, broke the hush. "Is this your sister?" she asked, nodding toward the girl.

The boy opened his mouth to answer, but Felix was already fitting gauze into his cheek, sparing him the words.

Wendy returned to her tray. Felix bent over the work again.

But his mind wasn't on the teeth.

That girl. That song. The uncanny thread of memory winding through her presence.

It was nothing, of course. It had to be nothing.

And yet—why did it feel as though a shadow from his past had just walked into his treatment room?

❖

Chapter Sixteen

Maisie sat stiffly in the corner of the rattling carriage, her gloved hands tight around the reticule, as though she might spill the future she'd once imagined and hadn't stopped chasing since. With Deena escorting the little Marquess to the dentist, Maisie had a few stolen hours to continue her search.

London's streets blurred past the glass, faces flickering by—anonymous, hurried, forgettable. Soot filmed the brick facades, a dull gray crust left by winter. She barely noticed. Her mind tugged toward one destination, one last thread she refused to let go of.

The carriage drew up to a narrow shop, the wooden sign above creaking faintly in the wind:

Rams and Son, Booksellers and Newsmen
Periodicals and Archives Acquired and Catalogued

Her boots struck the stoop with a soft click, skirts whispering over the worn wood. She didn't pause, though the air hummed with gossip about frost and failing crops. None of it mattered. None of her newspaper adverts calling for a Faivish Blattner had brought a single answer.

Inside, the familiar perfume of paper and ink wrapped around her, heavy as memory. The counter overflowed with ledgers and broadsheets. A fire muttered in the hearth, half-hearted but enough to thaw the chill.

The clerk behind the desk, spectacles sliding down his nose, looked up mid-scratch of his pen.

"Good morning, ma'am," he said, inclining his head. "What may I help you find?"

Maisie's voice surprised her by sounding steady. "I've come to search your archives. Newspapers, if you please."

He tilted his head. "From where, exactly?"

"Vienna. France. India, if possible. The past year or two. In English, French, or German." She knew how absurd it sounded—like trying to summon love out of a ledger. But if Faivish's name had surfaced anywhere, she couldn't afford not to look.

The clerk rose with unexpected briskness and gestured her through the aisles. Leather bindings and dust pressed close around them until they reached a long table at the back, flanked by two rickety chairs. He motioned to the precarious stacks.

"These should suit. Ring if you need me."

Maisie sat, smoothed her skirts, and opened the first volume. The air ticked with paper and clockwork. Time seemed to thin itself into silence.

Her eyes skimmed headlines—opera notices, political columns, the marvels of steam engines, scandals of duchesses. Page after page, name after name. Never his.

Faivish Blattner. Dr. Blattner. F. Blattner. She whispered his name in her mind a hundred ways, hoping to see it inked here.

Just not in the obituaries. Please, oh please, not there.

Her fingers trembled as she turned the pages. He was clever—too clever to leave a trail if he wanted to vanish. But what if he hadn't wanted her to find him? That fear bit deeper than all the rest.

Another sheet. Another disappointment. A name close—so close—but not him. Her shoulders sagged, the knot in her stomach tightening.

The fire hissed in the grate, smoke scratching faintly at the air. Maisie blinked hard, willing the blur in her eyes away.

No one was coming to rescue her from this endless hunt. But

she could still search. She could try.

Memory tugged her back—Vienna, her father's quiet practice. Faivish bent the rules for a friend. She, clumsy with instruments, cheeks burning. He had smiled—patient, warm—so certain of her. He had risked everything. She had risked her heart.

Now, only echoes. Only the rustle of pages in a London bookshop.

And still, she turned another.

⟫⟫⟫⟪⟪⟪

THAT EVENING, BACK at 87 Harley Street, the apothecary's back room breathed of mint and myrrh. Tooth-powder dusted the lips of glass jars, each labeled in Alfie's slanted hand. Felix eased the final cork into place and smoothed a paper slip flat with his thumbnail: *Charcoal & Sage*. Beside him, Alfie twisted a square of muslin into a neat parcel for the front counter. The boy's carriage had come and gone—polite, brisk—leaving a return appointment and a silence that pressed.

"Too tight," Alfie muttered, not looking up. "You'll crease the paper and my shelves will look like a butcher keeps them."

"I'm a dentist," Felix said, dry. "You knew the hazard when you asked for help."

"I asked for help before you alphabetized my stock. Astringents can't live beside cooling herbs—my tinctures will get ideas."

Felix lifted a brow. "You're welcome."

Only then did he realize he still wore his coat, patient cards peeking from the inner pocket, bills folded in his fist. It was easier here—among rows of jars and Alfie's reliable complaints—than in the quiet practice where the room felt larger after each patient left.

Especially today, when he'd caught himself searching a girl's face for the shadow of someone he'd sworn he'd stopped seeing everywhere.

Footsteps clattered on the stairs. Both men turned as the door pushed wide.

"Raphi," Alfie said, surprise folding into a grin.

Felix straightened. Raphi Klonimus slipped in with urgency at his heels, coat collar damp, breath thin from the cold. He didn't greet them. He set a stack of letters and folded sheets on the worktable; the edges wore the grime of travel and being read too often.

"Everything my contacts in Vienna could pull," Raphi said. "About Maisie Morgenschein."

Felix's stomach knotted. His hands went careful and still. For years, every inquiry had ended in a clean, echoing nothing—as if the world had swallowed her name. Now paper sat between them, heavy as proof.

Alfie edged back, eyes flicking toward Felix.

"She vanished from the official record in 1813," Raphi went on, softer. "Just before you returned from India. There's the synagogue notice for her father a few days after you left—then the trail dies. No employment. No address."

Felix's breath hitched. "That isn't possible."

"I thought the same." Raphi unfolded a page. "Translation says the post confirms her name was stricken from the resident registry. I asked why."

Silence settled.

"No answer."

Alfie splayed a hand over his face. "So someone scrubbed it—on purpose?"

"I don't know. Rot, fear, or order from above—it reads the same." Raphi met Felix's eyes. "They erased her."

Felix stepped back until the counter found his spine. He swallowed once, then again. "So I can't find her."

"I'm sorry."

Felix nodded. The cold that had been pacing his chest lay down and stayed. Impossibility wasn't a reason to stop, only a weight to lift.

Raphi cleared his throat. "And that's not the worst of it."

Felix blinked. "What now?"

"My contact in *Bistrița*—Northern Transylvania—says Baron von List's men are raiding gold shipments again. And Wendy said Prince Stan's family has soldiers there."

Alfie stiffened. "The Carpathian routes."

"Disguised as banditry, too regular to be chance. Klonimus reserves are down. The Crown-Jeweler network will strain. And you, Felix—your gold for restorations dries up if this keeps happening."

Alfie swallowed. "If the Royal Warrant is questioned—if supply fails—"

"I won't treat the charity cases," Felix said. "Or keep standards for the titled ones."

"And that," Raphi said, "is the point. Discredit the Jewish jewelers who supply the Jewish doctor, undercut trust on Harley Street, and Parliament nods along while List calls it service to the Crown."

Felix's jaw set. It was never only medicine with men like that. It was power, and the boy at the center of today's case made the perfect lever.

No one spoke. In the quiet, Alfie's hand landed heavy and warm on Felix's shoulder.

"You saved my smile," Alfie said. "When no one else would risk their place."

Felix gave a small, rough sound. "The rules weren't right. That's all."

"No," Alfie said, "some men live to make right things impossible. That's where we don't stop."

"Nor will we," Raphi added. "My brothers stand with you. So do the Pearlers. We'll keep the gold moving. You keep the mouths mended. No one's taking your Warrant while we can breathe."

Felix looked down at the nearest letter, the ink feathered by strange hands. He slid one page toward himself and squared its corners, the old habit of a man who needed one true line to work from.

"All right." He spoke low and steady but the air didn't feel as though it filled his chest entirely. "Then we begin."

❖

Chapter Seventeen

THE NEXT DAY, on Regent Street, not far from the dazzling jeweler shop at number 35, the bell above the tailor's door gave a quick, cheery jingle as Maisie ushered John and Deena inside. Damp air clung to her hem, London's drizzle following them in, but it was quickly swallowed by the sharper scents of the shop—wet wool mixed with starch, cedar, and a trace of pipe smoke. Bolts of fabric stood like silent statues in greys and navy, the tailor's long measuring tape draped across his neck like a medal.

When the clerk appeared at once with a folded uniform, he ushered John onto a low wooden platform in front of a looking glass. Maisie smoothed his lapel, coaxing his scowl into something closer to patience as the stiff collar dug at his throat.

"This itches," John muttered.

"It will soften. Hold still," she said, tugging gently at the sleeve. "Your first day at Eton, you'll want it to sit just so."

Behind her, Deena perched on the windowsill, chin propped in her hand as she watched carriages splash past. "You sound as if you've been to Eton yourself."

Maisie gave a low laugh. "No. But I've known many men who went to similar establishments if not the one. Their mothers always said the collar looked worse than it was."

John tilted his head. "Where did you learn all this—tailoring, posture, the way you tell me not to itch?"

Her hands stilled at the buttons. The question was innocent, but the edge of truth in it pricked sharp. She pressed the fabric smooth before answering lightly: "Oh, here and there. One learns when one must."

Maisie fastened the last button and brushed a speck of lint from his sleeve. "There," she murmured. "Much better. Stand tall. See?"

John looked down at the crisp line of the jacket, then back up at her. His small brow furrowed, as if he were studying more than the fit of his coat.

"You always fix things for me," he said, quiet but certain. "Like my collar. Like when I stumble." His gaze lingered on her face. "You look after me as if you were… more than just an aunt."

Maisie's breath caught, but she only smiled, smoothing his lapel one more time.

"But you're not married, are you?" John asked suddenly, his voice a little louder, braver now. "Do you even want to be? Married—or in love?"

Her lips parted, but before she could speak, the tailor swept in with a throat-clearing flourish, stepping between them as though she were nothing more than an attendant.

"Stand straighter, my lord," he intoned. "Yes, fine shoulders—you'll cut a figure at Eton."

John puffed his chest, but his eyes darted to Maisie. She smiled for him, a steadying one, though resentment prickled like effervescent water from the springs in the Alps. Invisible again.

On a side table, a newspaper lay folded. The tailor, catching John's glance, picked it up as though it were a scepter. "Have you read the morning's report, my lord? Most edifying. A noble man has come to London with the purest intention: to preserve order in the kingdom."

John tilted his head. "Preserve it from what?"

"From chaos," the tailor replied briskly. "From the flood of foreign influence. A Prussian baron, no less, with the courage to address Parliament itself."

Deena's voice cut in, sly with curiosity. "Is he to clean the Thames, then? Or sweep the muck from the streets?"

The tailor didn't so much as glance her way. His eyes stayed fixed on John. "Not the streets, miss. The spirit of England itself. Baron Wolfgang von List. A man determined to prevent dangerous reform."

Maisie's stomach tightened. The name was a match struck inside her—Rachel's whispered warnings from Vienna flared at once.

John's brows knitted. "Dangerous? What reform?"

The tailor pricked his sleeve with a needle. John yelped.

"Hold still," the man chided. "Why, Jewish emancipation, of course. The Crown grants them more rights here than anywhere else already. They keep shops, earn money. What next? To let them study at university? To open the professions? After that"—he sniffed—"why not women, too?"

John rubbed his arm where the needle had stabbed. "Why not? They'd have to earn it first. Show good grades, I suppose."

The next prick was deliberate—sharp enough to make him flinch again. Maisie darted forward, steadying him with both hands. Her voice was even, but her grip lingered longer than was proper, a shield between boy and man.

"Careful," she said. But her gaze had already fallen to the newspaper.

The black letters leapt at her:

The Jew is not of our stock, nor of our soil. He is other. To elevate him is to abase the Englishman. Better a mongrel hound at one's hearth than a Hebrew in the halls of Parliament.

Maisie's face stayed serene, her practiced mask. Inside, her skin burned.

Her eyes dropped again.

Woman, at least, is fashioned to nurture. But why do we need the Jew? To admit him to our universities is to sully the minds of England's sons. To tolerate difference is weakness; to honor plurality, treason.

The words blurred. She swallowed hard. She could not let her hand tremble, not here, not with John watching.

John wrinkled his brow. "That sounds… cruel."

Maisie gently squeezed his arm again, her tone airy, calm, the voice of a lady who must not disagree. "It is not for us to dispute Parliament, *nephew*." She let the word hang but she hid behind John as much as he hid behind her. They were family and responsible for one another, regardless of whether they were related by blood or not.

The tailor gave a grunt of approval, tugging John's collar into place, pleased with her supposed agreement—oblivious to the fire smoldering in her chest.

But Maisie's thoughts were elsewhere—on Rachel's warning, on Faivish, on the tide that seemed to rise higher with every passing day, threatening to wash them all away.

And on the vow she had whispered into her own silence more times than she could count: *she would never abandon John.*

The tailor bowed himself out, muttering about delivery dates, leaving them briefly alone. John tugged irritably at his collar, cheeks flushed from the pinpricks of the needle.

Maisie exhaled slowly, smoothing her skirts as though pressing calm back into her bones. The words from the newspaper still echoed, sharp as vinegar, but she would not let them show. Not here.

Deena slid down from the windowsill, eyes blazing. "He spoke as though you weren't even in the room," she whispered in Yiddish, too soft for John to catch. "As though women and—" She bit the rest off, her teeth closing around the danger.

Maisie's glance cut quick and warning, but her smile to John was gentle, as if none of it had touched her. "Your collar sits perfectly now. You'll look quite the young gentleman."

John studied her, suspicion clouding his young face. "Why didn't you answer me?"

She blinked. "Answer you?"

"When I asked if you wanted to marry. Or to be in love."

The words landed like a splinter under skin—small, piercing, impossible to ignore. Maisie bent low, fingertips brushing the lapel of his jacket, her voice lowered into a half-whisper meant for him alone.

"Love in marriage," she said softly, "is like smoothing the planks of a table. It makes the surface easier to live with. But it doesn't make the table stronger."

Deena tilted her head. "So what does?"

Maisie's gaze lingered on her sister, then returned to John. Her voice gentled further.

"Trust," she said. "That's the nails. It keeps everything together when the weather turns. When the wood begins to warp, without trust, even the finest timber will break apart."

John's brow furrowed as though he were engraving the thought into memory. After a long pause, he asked quietly, "Do we have that? The nails?"

Her throat ached. How could she tell him about the hollow carved inside her—the name she had buried, the man she had promised to wait for? And yet, what did any of that matter? This boy was hers to protect. Whatever the law said. Whatever the tailor or Parliament whispered.

Maisie laid her palm gently on his shoulder, steady as a vow. "We do," she said. "We are family now. We hold."

Deena's lashes lowered quickly, but not before Maisie saw the glimmer in her eyes. She turned her head, pretending sudden interest in the bolts of fabric stacked neatly against the wall.

The bell above the door jingled. The tailor returned, bowing stiffly as he offered the parcel wrapped in brown paper.

"Your nephew will be a credit to Eton, madam," he said.

Nephew. The word pierced her, another hidden needle. Maisie accepted the parcel with serene grace, thanking him with the practiced voice of a lady who had never been anything but. Inside, her chest burned.

Stepping into the street again, the city rushed back—carriage wheels clattering, hawkers calling through the drizzle, the air thick with coal smoke. Across the way, a jeweler's sign swung faintly in the damp breeze.

Maisie tightened her hand on John's shoulder. He would not see the venom she had read. He would not know that Parliament debated whether he was even worthy of belonging. Let the Baron sneer in Westminster. Let the tailor nod in smug agreement. John would never doubt. Not while she lived.

He had trust. He had nails. And he had her.

FELIX WIPED HIS hands on a towel as he came down the narrow staircase, the smell of cloves still clinging to his sleeves. The front door thudded shut, the last trace of a purple silk coat vanishing into the street. Pale knuckles had drawn it closed—Baron von List.

Felix's stomach twisted. The Baron left nothing behind but the sour echo of his voice, clipped and polished to civility, yet steeped in scorn. He came often enough that passersby might mistake them for acquaintances, perhaps even allies. Felix knew better. To deny him treatment would be to hand him the very scandal he wanted: proof that Harley Street's doctors turned away nobles. Their hard-won reputation could shatter in a week. So they endured his charade of ailments, holding their dignity while he hunted for ways to ruin them.

Down the hall, Alfie emerged from the apothecary, rolling his sleeves, his apron blotched from tinctures. Nick stepped from his surgery room with Wendy close behind, tucking her nurse's cap into place. Andre appeared from the far end, coat buttoned, eyes sharp. They were all drawn by the same thing—the aftertaste of

List's visit.

"What did he want this time?" Nick asked, though the answer was obvious.

"Valerian for his nerves," Alfie muttered, his lip curling.

Andre crossed his arms. "He's staking us out. Like a rat with a monocle."

"Says he has unfinished business and will get to the bottom of it soon," Alfie said as he narrowed his eyes.

Felix leaned back against the wall, folding his arms across his chest. "Not a rat," he said. "A fox. Watching its prey before the strike."

"So you remember Vienna, too?" Alfie asked.

"What happened in Vienna that I don't know about?" Andre asked, since he and Nick had been at the same university, and Wendy had already started to learn alongside Nick. They all took a step toward Felix. "Tell us!"

"I didn't connect it at first, forgot for a while…" Felix looked at Alfie, whose mien had gone dark, which confirmed Felix's worst suspicion. "There was an afternoon when Alfie tended to the horse at the Spanish Riding School, and one of those horses belonged to the nephew of Rector Hofstätter."

"Baron Wolfgang von List," Nick more groaned than spoke the words.

"He has unfinished business?" Wendy asked. "But why?"

"His son attacked Felix that night and got me instead," Alfie explained.

"Alfie defended me," Felix added.

"They would have killed you!" Alfie said. "They didn't want Felix to graduate at the top of our class."

"Altenburg and Hofstätter, titled and well-connected students were vying for the top spot, and I took the spot even though the exams were anonymous," Felix explained. Scoundrels from the *Burschenschaft*.

"So a Jew outranked the titled students. Meritocracy. Everything List stands against." Nick cast one of those protective glances at Wendy, like he usually did when he felt the need to protect his younger sister, even though she was all grown up. Yet, they were all List's targets for one reason or another. And thus, they were all in danger.

"It's List's cause and he's brought it with him all the way from Königsberg in Prussia to London via Vienna," Alfie said with a tone that could have announced the end of the world.

His words settled, heavy. Then he added, quieter: "Raphi Klonimus says he's gathering more names. Old officers from the campaigns, men of rank and purse. They're printing his words in the papers now, calling themselves defenders of order."

Nick's jaw tightened. "So that's the cause. To tear down the Crown Jewelers—strip trade from the Klonimus family, choke the gold coming out of Transylvania. Weaken the suppliers, and anyone who dares stand beside them. Which means us."

Wendy's brow furrowed. "And because the Klonimus name is tied to the Crown, List counts their allies as fair game." She glanced at Felix, her voice low but certain. "It isn't only hatred of Jews. It's power. He wants the estates, the routes, everything— until his name eclipses the rest."

Andre's arms folded tighter. "I can't believe he's still skating along the edge of legality."

Felix's reply came measured, though his throat felt tight. "You may be assured he'll press further. Men like him always do."

Nick turned, studying him. "Are you well, Felix?"

Felix didn't answer immediately. His eyes stayed fixed on the door where List had vanished, as if some part of him still tracked the man's shadow.

Wendy crossed her arms, her tone decisive. "We shouldn't leave him here alone at night."

Alfie cut in, softer now. "You're the only one who stays— because you've no wife to pull you home."

Felix gave a dry laugh, though it thinned before it reached his eyes. "I don't mind being here." What he wanted to say was: *It's Maisie I miss. She's my wife in every way that matters. What if she comes looking—and I'm not here to be found?*

"That's not what I meant," Alfie said, his voice edged with memory. "He won't kill us. We're tied to aristocracy—it doesn't serve him. But you…"

Felix caught the weight beneath the words. He was the easiest target. The one left alone under the roof of Harley Street. He forced his jaw to stay firm.

Wendy tilted her head. "Any closer to finding her?"

Of course, it was Wendy—always seeing into the heart of her friends. It wasn't a secret among them: Felix missed Maisie more than breath itself. His jaw worked, but no words came. At last, he was alone.

They all knew how he'd searched. Letters to synagogues across Europe. Notices in every newspaper that would print them. Inquiries to clerks who might know if she'd married under another name. Each silence cut deeper than the last. If she were married, she lived under another man's roof—an agony too sharp to dwell on. If she is dead… he couldn't let the thought take shape.

Nick laid a hand briefly on his shoulder. "You don't have to leave to prove anything. But we see it, Felix. What you carry."

Felix gave a faint, bitter smile. "I didn't lose her. I let her go, believing she'd wait. I built a life she could come back to—just not in Vienna. And now… I can't find her."

The silence that followed was not heavy but whole, the kind that comes when brotherhood doesn't need words.

Andre moved toward the back door. "I'll lock up. If you need anything, send word—I'll come back from Cloverdale House."

Felix knew they would. They always did—stand with him, guard him as if he were breakable. But he didn't want their pity. He didn't want to be the brokenhearted stray tucked under the roof of 87 Harley Street.

He wanted Maisie. To carry her name beneath a canopy, to give their children the names his parents had borne, to prove that his vow had been more than a boy's desperate promise. He had earned money—more than most of them—but what was gold without a family to guard it for? Without Maisie, he was hibernating, wings folded tight against his ribs. To find her would mean breathing again, experiencing the full span of life once more.

Alfie's voice cut into the quiet. "I'll leave the valerian in the top drawer under the counter. If List comes sniffing, it'll keep the charade alive."

The others drifted out one by one, their boots echoing hollowly down the hall.

Felix stayed.

The lamp above him flickered, then steadied, casting a weak circle of light that trembled around his still form. The corridor smelled of mint from Alfie's tinctures and smoke from the candle stubs, but beneath it all was the ache he couldn't air aloud.

He stood alone, ringed by silence and the ghosts of words he had never spoken. Every unspoken vow clung in the air—sharp, sweet, unbearable—like the lingering perfume of something beautiful already burned.

And in the quiet, the only thought that came was the cruelest one of all:

Even if he found her now, after all these years, would she still be his?

"WHAT YOU SAID about love and holding together... did you mean me, too?" John sat at the dining table with one leg swinging under the bench. He had a pencil in his hand but wasn't drawing anymore. His gaze kept flicking toward her.

Maisie looked up, surprised.

In her mind, before she could answer, the question turned itself over like a stone in a river.

What if I found him? What if I saw Faivish again, tomorrow,

or the next day? What would I do?

She didn't have to imagine long because she knew. First, she would throw herself into his arms. Then, she'd kiss him, long and fierce, until the world disappeared. Until Vienna didn't feel so far behind them, and London wasn't so cold. They'd speak the old words. Maybe even sing again. There would be a chuppah to wed under—some simple white cloth. They'd find two chairs. Two witnesses. Her hands in his.

Her father, if he were still alive, would bless them.

But the warmth that bloomed in her chest didn't spread. It stayed tight and hollow. A dream she could picture in exquisite detail—but one she didn't trust to stay.

She blinked, clearing it. "What do you mean?" she asked John.

John didn't look at her. He resumed tracing circles with his pencil on the edge of the paper. "I mean if you married him, he'd be here, wouldn't he? Like… like a father for me?"

Maisie's mouth went dry.

She hadn't thought of it like that. Not in words. But of course—if Faivish came back, if she found him, if love could stretch across everything and reach again—they would be a family. What would Faivish say to her changed circumstances?

"I suppose we would," she said softly. "Yes."

She bit the inside of her cheek, watching him. She didn't know what he'd say. Whether it would be too much. Whether the idea of a father would push him away.

A moment passed.

Then John spoke, very softly. "I've never had a father who was here." His fingers stopped drawing. "I'd like to have one."

Maisie didn't trust herself to answer. She just reached across the table and let her fingers rest lightly on the edge of his paper, close enough to be felt, but not so close as to press.

One day, she thought. If love can find its way back. If Faivish is out there… I'll bring him home.

Behind her, Deena came in with the wind still clinging to her shawl. She carried a few scraps of paper and a dusting of flour down one sleeve. "I took the letters to the post."

Maisie turned, her thread still looped through the needle. "Which letters?"

Deena was already at the hearth, dusting her hands. "The ones on your escritoire. You sealed them, so I assumed they were ready."

Maisie's heart thudded once. "Even the one with no address?"

Deena gave a small shrug. "It said something about a missing person. Just capital letters, I think?" She paused.

"Initials." Maisie spoke without taking a new breath. "I hadn't meant to send that one."

"I thought you did," Deena said, more gently now. "It was sealed."

"I sealed it so I wouldn't keep reading it," Maisie said, setting the shirt aside. Her voice was too even. "It was for Faivish."

Deena stilled. "You didn't write his name. You don't know where he is."

"No. I wouldn't." Maisie walked to the edge of the table and placed her palms flat. The air between them shifted. "That's why I never ask anyone. Never write to anyone official. I don't even use his name when I speak."

Deena said nothing, but her face sobered.

"You know what they are doing," Maisie continued quietly. "Clerks copying synagogue records. Sifting through shipping manifests. Keeping books on where Jews live, what they own."

"List is in London now, Rachel said," Deena added. "Buying off printers. Paying boys to sit in Jewish shops and report who comes and goes."

Maisie nodded. "If I put Faivish's name on a letter and it lands in the wrong hands…" She trailed off. "He could be in danger."

"But you don't know where he is." Deena said and Maisie knew what that meant. I don't even know if he's alive and has returned from India.

Maisie looked down at the table, her fingers brushing a thread someone had missed.

The silence thickened. The fire cracked low. Outside, the same rough voice called again, some street name twisted into an order, half-sung, half-cursed.

Maisie turned back to John with a pained smile. *I'd like to be a real family with Faivish here, too.*

"You didn't mean to send it," Deena said, as if mourning the deed.

"No," Maisie murmured. "But it's gone now."

Love meant not shouting his name to the world, even if it ached to keep it hidden. Love meant staying quiet, staying careful.

Because even far apart, she would not be the one who endangered him. Not her Faivish.

Hope could ache. But it could not betray.

Chapter Eighteen

A FTER THE OTHERS had gone, Felix remained at the practice. He gathered the last of the damp towels and dropped them into the wicker basket, fingers brushing the worn weave as though tidying could quiet his mind. The air still carried the day's mix of camphor and lavender soap—a scent that clung to his sleeves even as he closed the door behind him, shutting out the phantom echo of patients' voices.

The corridor was hushed, the wall sconce throwing a single ring of flickering gold across the floorboards. Felix tugged free his cravat, the knot loosening with a sigh that seemed to reach his bones, then started down the narrow stairs. The boards creaked underfoot, the sound oddly loud in the empty building.

At the bottom, he paused. Through the glass-paned door, he saw light still glowing from Alfie's apothecary. Odd. Alfie never lingered now that his wife Bea was waiting at home. Curiosity quickened his step.

The apothecary smelled of earth and herbs, its rows of jars catching the lamplight. Behind the counter, Alfie bent over a box, his movements too quick, too restless to be orderly.

"Alfie?" Felix called softly.

Alfie jolted upright, nearly upsetting the box. "Oh—Felix."

"I thought everyone had gone," Felix replied, moving closer. "What are you doing here? Bea will be wondering."

Alfie's gaze darted toward the back corner. "I heard something earlier, near the barrels. A squeak. Thought it was gone, but it's back."

Felix frowned. "A rat? We can't have one here."

Another sound broke the quiet. This time, Felix heard it, too—a faint, plaintive squeak.

Alfie raised the lantern from the counter, its yellow circle spilling across the crates. Both men crouched low, listening.

"There," Felix murmured.

A small shape shivered in the shadows. Not a rat. Felix leaned closer, breath catching. "It's a dog."

Alfie shifted a plank and gently lifted the bundle. A puppy— golden-furred, damp, trembling—blinked against the sudden light. Its ears flopped weakly, its tiny body no heavier than a loaf of bread.

Felix's hands moved instinctively, steadying it against his chest. "It's freezing," he whispered, rubbing her back. The little body gave a thin, wavering whine that cut straight through his ribs.

"It needs warmth," Alfie said. "And food."

Together, they hurried into the kitchen. Alfie rummaged through the linen chest and pulled out an old wool blanket Nick had once left behind for his dog, Chromius. He handed it over. "Wrap it up. I'll see if there's anything she can manage to swallow."

Felix folded the blanket around the pup. It sagged against his chest, so light he could barely feel its weight as the poor puppy's breath trembled against his palm.

Alfie bent to the pantry, muttering to himself as he searched jars and tins. Felix stayed still, the kitchen lamp throwing a warm ring of light across the pup's damp fur. In that circle of glow, it struck him how empty the house would be once the others went home. Alfie had Bea. Nick had Pippa. Andre had Thea. Wendy had Stan.

And him? Only this tiny life pressed against his heart.

Alfie returned with a small porcelain bowl, half filled with warm milk, and set it on the counter beside a pipette and muslin cloth—an apothecary's idea of a nursery. He gave Felix a quick nod before slipping away to return home to Bea.

Alone again, Felix carried the pup and the makeshift nursery upstairs to the treatment room. He laid it gently on the desk and rubbed its back until a faint squeak broke the silence. She stirred, weak legs pawing at the air. *Aha, it's a female.*

Felix smiled. "Hungry, little one?"

He dipped the pipette into the milk, tested a drop on his wrist to make sure it wasn't too hot, then touched it to her mouth. She sniffed once and latched on, lapping with desperate eagerness. Milk dribbled down her nose. Felix wiped it away with the cloth, shaking his head, the sound almost a laugh. "Messy but determined."

A SQUEAKY YIP startled him into another smile. "Quite the voice for someone so small." His hand found the soft patch of fur between her ears. She tipped into his palm, her tiny body dangling over his hand. "Looks like it's just you and me now," he murmured, rubbing behind her ear. "I've been rather lost, too." The pup yawned wide, her pink tongue curling. Felix's chest ached at the sight. "Too young to be left behind," he whispered. He glanced toward the darkened street, then back at her—so small, but alive, stubbornly alive. "Well. You could stay with me. I'm not much, but I could use someone to keep me company."

Setting her carefully on the desk, he pulled down a heavy volume, *Dentition of Mammals*, thumbing until he found the page. He peered into her mouth—tiny white buds just breaking the gum.

"Three weeks. Maybe four. Just a baby." She blinked up at him, snuffling as if in reply.

He let out a soft breath, remembering. "I was twenty-three when I first felt lost. At least I still had Alfie." His smile tugged weak but real as the pup curled into his palm, releasing a sigh so delicate it barely stirred the air.

For a long moment he sat there—man, puppy, lamplight, the silence wrapped around them like a fragile promise. "You'll be all right," he whispered. "I'll see to it." His thumb brushed her fur once more. "Shall we choose a name for you?"

Chapter Nineteen

T HE HOUSE WAS quiet save for the soft tick of the clock on the mantel. Maisie sat alone at her escritoire, the candle guttering low, wax sliding in uneven ridges. The shadows didn't just lean in—they crowded close, nosy things, as if they meant to read along. Her quill scratched, stuttered, a blot of ink blooming where her hand shook. Not from weariness. From the weight of words she would never send.

She wrote as though he might still hear her—no, not hear, but feel—the drag of ink, the spill of thought, as if paper could be a bridge. But she did not know where he was. Did not even know if he breathed, or if her letter, should it be found, might betray him.

And still, she wrote. Because silence frightened her more than danger. Because if she stopped, the words would rot inside her, and she would rot with them.

My dearest Faivish,

There are nights I close my eyes and whisper your name into the stillness, as though the darkness itself might carry my words across the miles to you. In my heart, I am already your wife. And yet—I tremble to write such a thing, for I fear I am unworthy of the honor of loving you.

You left to prove your heart was true, and I let you go. Even

*on the night when we sealed our promises—when I gave you all
that I was and all I could ever be—I faltered. I ran. Not from
you, never from you, but from a world that would not let me
keep what was mine.*

*What if you believe I did not keep faith? What if you think
I broke the vow written in my very soul? How could I, when you
carry my heart still? It beats only for it remembers your hands,
your voice, your touch.*

*I do not know if these words will ever find you. But if they
should, know this: whether you are near or lost to me forever, I
am yours. Entirely. Eternally.*

—Maisie

She folded the letter slowly, smoothing the paper with her
fingertips, careful as though the ink might smudge or the words
dissolve. Her hands lingered on the crease before tucking it into
the small carved box at the back of her escritoire. She didn't need
to open it to know it was already full.

There were so many already.

Letters. Pleas. Confessions. Pages that would never travel
farther than her trembling fingers. She didn't know where he was.
Didn't know if her words might place him in danger—or if they
would ever be read at all.

So, she kept writing.

And hiding and hoping. Because the only thing more unbearable than silence was the thought of forgetting how to speak to
him.

Later, when morning had pressed its grey light against the
windows and the rustle of freshly ironed newsprint stirred the still
air of the Spencer breakfast room, Maisie sat at the table with a
stiff neck and a heart no less splintered than the night before. She
held the paper upright, not to read it, but to hide behind it. The
faint scent of ink clung to her fingertips, mingled with ink and
regret.

When she'd told the butler once that the papers didn't need

to be ironed, he'd only replied, "Don't let your fingers get ink-stained, madam."

She hadn't bothered arguing again. Not after the second time.

It wasn't the crumpled paper that made her hands go still. It was the headline.

Baron von List proposes halt to Jewish emancipation; generously offers guardianship to orphaned aristocrats.

Her stomach tightened. Not just from the words—but from how calmly they sat beneath the masthead, like it was simply a policy shift, a clever bit of social engineering. The article discussed List's generosity: *Guardianship. Schooling. Proper thought.* As if this man wasn't slowly coaxing Europe toward a future far more dangerous than anyone cared to admit.

Her gaze snagged on that word—*proper.*

A chill spread through her chest, slow and invasive. It wasn't enough to argue in Parliament anymore. Now he would shape children. Mold their minds before they were old enough to question. Until contempt for people like her was not a belief but a reflex.

She could almost hear Rachel's voice, low and urgent: *He dresses it up in polish and reason. That's how he gets in.*

The door flew open. Quick footsteps. A voice already mid-sentence.

"I'm famished!"

John barreled in and collapsed into a chair with all the subtlety of a thunderclap.

Maisie didn't look up right away. She lowered the paper slowly, one brow rising. "Good morning to you, too."

He paused, sheepish, toast already halfway to his mouth. "Good morning," he mumbled around a grin, grabbing for the butter and wielding the knife like a child soldiering through a battlefield.

"You missed dinner," she said, folding the paper with care and setting it aside. "There was soup waiting for you after the treatment yesterday."

"Wasn't supposed to eat for a few hours." He shrugged, then added around a bite, "I fell asleep."

She chuckled, the sound catching a little in her throat. But before she could say more, Deena swept in—composed as ever, though the glint in her eyes betrayed her amusement.

"He has to go back again, you know," she said, leaning in to kiss Maisie's cheek.

Maisie tipped her head into the touch. Deena's hand found hers and gave it a quiet, grounding squeeze. It was a ritual they never spoke of but always kept.

"Why?" Maisie asked, glancing between the two of them, curiosity pricking at her.

Deena only arched both brows and reached for the teapot. A non-answer.

Maisie crossed the room and bent toward John. He didn't protest—just opened his mouth with the air of someone used to being examined, or perhaps too tired to resist.

She leaned in. "Hmm." Then stepped back. "Very good. He's going to make gold cast inlays for the larger cavities."

John squinted up at her. "Why do you know so much about teeth?"

Before she could answer, Deena beat her to it. "Our father was a dentist," she said, casually, pouring her tea. "She worked in the practice. I played outside."

"You grew up with a dentist? That's vile!" John wrinkled his nose.

"The most renowned in Vienna," Maisie added with pride. But her smile didn't quite reach her eyes. She pressed her lips together, an old habit.

John didn't notice. "Did this one do good work on me then?"

"Very good," Maisie said, though her eyes flicked quickly to Deena and back again. "Did you stay with him the entire time?"

Deena set her teacup down with a small clink. "Yes. Just as you instructed."

"And does it feel very smooth?" she asked John, her voice

easy, casual almost—but the way she watched him was not.

"What?" he said, nearly sputtering his milk.

Maisie didn't press further. She only watched. Closely. No flinching between bites. No grimace when he swallowed hot toast, chased by cold milk. The discomfort he used to show at meals was—gone. As if it had never been. *Very good work indeed.*

"Deena," Maisie said suddenly, her tone sharper now, "did anything strike you as unusual while you were there?"

"No," Deena replied, sipping her tea. "The tiny hammer was annoying, but I hummed a song to tune it out."

"A song?" John said. "It was like bees buzzing in my ears!"

"So when did he say you must return?" Maisie asked.

John seemed to feel for his teeth with his tongue as he spoke, his words muffled as if still chewing. "In a day. To insert another piece of gold. He explained it—something about wax and casting—Deena's humming distracted me."

"Yes, yes, a gold cast inlay?" Maisie asked, the question escaping more sharply than intended. Her hand tightened on the table. The other hovered mid-air, fingers trembling just enough to catch Deena's eye.

That technique. Rare. Precise. Passed down by only one man.

Her father.

And Faivish had learned it from him.

But so had others. Too many others.

This probably doesn't mean anything.

Maisie's hand slipped from the chair. Her fingers curled into her skirt.

"What song did you hum?" she asked.

"Tumbalalaika," Deena answered.

The breath caught in Maisie's throat. Faivish had known that song. Had loved it. Had once paused mid-sentence, just to listen.

"And he didn't react?" she pressed. Faivish would have known it.

"No." A pause. "Not truly."

Maisie traced the rim of her teacup. Around and around. The

paper beside her plate blurred. Tension crept behind her eyes, pressure building where the light touched too bright.

That technique—it had a fingerprint. A signature. Invisible to most. Clear as a name, to her.

Her father would have smiled.

But her stomach twisted. She knew better than to hope to find Faivish in London. She had combed registries. Asked every contact. Not one clue. Faivish might be in Vienna. But there was no sign of him in London. He was lost somewhere between here and India.

She swallowed hard, forcing down the lump that had risen in her throat.

Wouldn't he have found her? Wouldn't he have searched?

But after the riot, she hadn't dared to leave word with any-one—not when every knock could've meant danger. She had fled with only what she could carry. No goodbyes. No explanations. No safety in trust.

After five years, could there still be hope?

She wasn't even herself anymore. Not really. Certainly not Maisie Morgenschein. Just Lady Eleanor Spencer now. Wrapped in titles. Hidden behind the safety of a name no one would think to ask for.

He couldn't find her. Even if he'd come close. But there had been no letters. No messages. No one asking. Not even a whisper. Cruel symmetry. She hadn't been there when he returned. And now she was here, and he was nowhere.

Her lungs fought to draw air. Each breath felt like it took more effort than it should. She pressed her hand lightly to her bodice, fingertips seeking something—anything—that might steady her.

But there was nothing. Not even an anchor or a touchstone. Just silk, bone stays, and emptiness.

What if he went back? What if he waited... and I didn't?

Across the table, Deena and John let the staff clear their plates. The clink of porcelain—so faint, so ordinary—yet scraped along her nerves.

Maisie lifted her gaze.

"I'm going to visit Rachel today," she said evenly, as if she hadn't just come undone inside her own skin.

Harley Street, around the same time...

THE ROOM WAS still dark when Felix woke with a jolt. His breath snagged in his throat, chest rising too fast, heart kicking like it was mid-chase. For a long moment, he lay still, eyes pinned to the ceiling beams, sweat cooling in the hollow of his back. Rain tapped at the windows. Inside him, heat still pulsed, low and stubborn.

It was her. Not a dream. Not fantasy. Maisie. The curve of her mouth under his. The hollow of her throat, warm against his lips. The way she laughed—so close to yielding. His body ached with it, sharp and specific, remembering the weight of her. Her breath. Her hands.

A sound escaped him—low, raw. He rolled over, pulled the pillow over his head. Pointless. Her imprint stayed.

He wanted her.

Not shadows and fragments.

Maisie.

The press of her hips against his. The shudder of her limbs around him. The cry that broke from her when everything inside them tightened, then came undone.

Felix exhaled through his teeth and pressed both fists into the mattress, even more than his hips.

Maisie.

He could still feel her hands at the nape of his neck, the slow curl of her fingers in his hair. Her shift, slipping under his palms like water. He remembered her sounds, her breath, the rhythm she fell into. His body did not forget.

From the corner of the room, the puppy stirred.

"Sorry I woke you, little one," Felix said softly.

She stretched, small and unbothered, paws spreading wide as she yawned. The noise was so small, so trusting, it pricked something deep in his chest.

He bit his lip, hard enough to sting. The next image came anyway.

Her breast in his mouth—warm, giving. The tight pull of her nipple under his tongue.

He swallowed. The tension stayed. His skin hot, drawn tight. His body refused calm. Pressing into the mattress only deepened the ache.

Her scent drifted through his memory—lavender, and something deeper, earthy, unmistakably hers.

He had caught it yesterday. A flicker in the air as someone passed.

Felix sat up, shoved the pillow aside. The sheets clung to him, damp and twisted. He raked a hand through his hair, jaw clenched. The tension gripped him low and sharp, impossible to shake.

He had left her. For honor and a chance of a better future. The irony wasn't lost on him. And every day since had opened another hollow inside his chest.

The puppy turned in Chromius' old basket near the hearth, tail tucked beneath her chin.

Felix rose. Slowly. He braced his weight on his knees, then stood. Dressed. The wool of his breeches scraped over damp skin.

He couldn't stay here.

Maisie.

She had once been home. She still was.

And somewhere—just beyond reach—she breathed.

He dragged a hand through his hair, his fingers catching in the damp strands.

"Little one," he murmured, reaching down to stroke the puppy's back. "Do you want to go for a walk?"

His voice was steady now. Or close enough.

Nothing could change the past. All he could do was remember.

And remembering? That was both his greatest torment and the only solace left.

I have to find her.

Chapter Twenty

THE MORNING AIR hit Felix like a clean slate. The street still held onto the dark, the dawn reluctant to warm its edges. He pulled his coat tighter with one hand, the other holding the pup close beneath the fold.

He hummed without thinking, a tune that came and went like breath. Vienna. He'd heard it a hundred times growing up, but the words had long since scattered. That unsettled him more than he liked. What else had he forgotten, or left behind without meaning to?

Maisie came to his mind. Always her, waiting behind stray thoughts.

The puppy stirred a little, curling tighter into the warmth of his chest. Her small body breathed in a rhythm that calmed his own, as if she understood this was a fragile sort of morning.

When he stepped onto the cobbled path, his boots brushed against slick patches where dew clung to the stones. The city hadn't quite woken. There was a hush to it—not silence exactly, but that in-between quiet just before life picked up again.

He turned toward the small patch of grass near the practice— the one sunlight reached first. The melody he'd been humming returned, stubborn and unfinished. Somewhere, bells rang the hour. Seven. Softer here than at *Karlskirche*, but the echo pulled at something inside him all the same.

He crouched beside the puppy and placed her gently on the grass. One hand stayed close, palm hovering near her back.

She blinked at the world, tilting her head, ears flopping slightly. Then she looked up at him, wide-eyed, uncertain.

"Don't you need to do anything here?"

Tentatively, she scraped the toe of his boot with a whimper, like she wanted permission.

But nothing came out.

"Think of rain."

With her big brown eyes, she just stared up at him.

"River bends. Waterfalls. Ocean waves?"

Nothing.

"Well, I can hardly show you what to do!"

She bent down and picked up her tiny front paws, one at a time, as if to tell him that the wet grass was pricking her delicate soles.

"A small creek, perhaps? Or drops trickling from leaves?"

She squealed and clumsily came to the tip of his boot and scraped it.

Felix chuckled lightly, the sound low but kind. "Alright, I'll carry you," he said, scooping her up again. "But you have to tell me when it's time to find a patch of grass, please." She settled almost instantly, her face burying itself against the warmth of his chest beneath his open coat.

"You know, one day, when you're much bigger, you'll have to do things on the grass, alright? And then we'll run together."

He smiled faintly at the idea. A gentleman wouldn't, of course—but he'd never been one. Not in the way that counted. Thus, he could run and exercise as much as he wanted—where else could the pent-up energy go otherwise?

He took a breath, filling his lungs with the crisp air. "Just at the birth of a new day, the air is freshest. And if we wake up before six o'clock, it's the *vata* time in Ayurveda. I learned about this in India. It's far away, but it was worth going." He hesitated, voice quieter. "Coming back was the hard part. I lost someone very dear while I was away." His fingers brushed the pup's tiny back, holding her closer. "In fact, I came home to find her name gone. Her place swept clean."

Like she'd never been real.

But this wasn't something to burden a little creature with. She barely filled the crook of his arm. He kept walking. "So, what I'm trying to teach you is that rising early aligns with the rhythms of the world. Helps you breathe clearer. Think straighter."

The puppy didn't stir.

"One day, when you don't need to nap after every meal, you'll run early in the morning with me, alright?"

He paused, catching himself.

"You're just a baby, though, aren't you?"

So had he been—when he thought skill alone could excuse what he'd done. When he used the gold-in-porcelain on Alfie without asking. As if excellence meant permission. As if being right was enough.

The street stretched ahead, empty but for the long cast of his shadow. He let his feet choose the way.

Once the puppy slept again, her breath came warm against his chest, a delicate weight tucked beneath his coat. Felix kept walking, each step measured, the cold brushing his face, loosening the restless knots that hadn't left him since he woke.

"I'll teach you to run really fast with me one day," he murmured, glancing down at the tiny dog. She'd slipped back into sleep, her face slack with dreams, her paws limp in the makeshift muslin swaddle he'd tied awkwardly but snugly against his chest.

The city had begun to shift. A carriage rattled past, its driver perched high, baskets piled behind him. The scent of warm bread followed in its wake, rich and tempting in the crisp morning air. Felix passed two men in black hats, their steps clipped, their conversation hushed. Above, a window blinked with light—fires lit, kettles stirred, households easing into the day.

His pace held steady as he turned onto Mansfield Road toward Piccadilly. The wind caught a loose thread of his cravat, but he let it tug. His gaze stayed on the sleeping pup. She gave off a soft warmth, steadying him in a way nothing else had in weeks.

Regent Street curved ahead, quiet and broad, its facades touched by early light. He didn't count buildings—he never had to. Number 35 waited near the bend, its stone exterior still steeped in shadows, the large window blanketed in the stillness of a day not yet begun.

Felix stopped. His eyes traced the sign above the door, familiar down to the hairline cracks in the wood. Something loosened inside him—something that had been drawn tight since the night before. He looked down. The puppy's nose twitched.

"Come and say hello to my friends, little one," Felix whispered, voice softer than the breeze. He shifted her gently, making sure she stayed tucked and warm, then stepped toward the alley beside the shop. Gravel crunched underfoot, the sound oddly steadying in the quiet.

The scent of toast and fried eggs drifted down from above, edged with honey. He smiled faintly. Breakfast time.

Inside the workshop, slanting light from the high windows fell across worn benches, catching on bits of scattered metal and half-finished chains. Order made out of chaos. Felix stepped through the door, the wood giving a quiet creak beneath his boots.

Only Pavel was there, Chawa's husband and the father of the six Klonimus brothers—shoulders broad, eyes narrowed in concentration, one hand holding a sliver of metal, the other guiding a chisel with precision.

He didn't look up right away. "What are you doing here so early?" Gruff, yes—but not unkind. Never with him.

Felix shifted slightly, the movement drawing Pavel's attention. "I found something," he said. "Thought I'd show you all."

Pavel's eyes dropped to the tiny bundle as Felix loosened his coat. The puppy blinked once in sleep, unbothered.

"A *nishumela*," Pavel murmured. The word curved softly off his tongue, old and full of affection—*a little soul.*

Felix smiled. It settled low in his chest, the kind of warmth he hadn't felt in days. Not just the word, but the way Pavel said it—like it mattered.

The older man chuckled under his breath and wiped his hands on his apron. "The children are upstairs eating," he said, though his gaze lingered on the puppy a moment longer.

Felix adjusted the wrap as she stirred, her nose nuzzling closer for warmth. "Thank you," he said, stepping past the bench toward the narrow stairs in the corner.

They creaked as he climbed, the wood shifting under each step. The stairwell curved just enough to crowd him, the banister brushing his shoulder. With every turn, the smell of warm bread and strong coffee thickened, layered with the soft murmur of a house at ease.

At the top, he didn't have to look for the dining room. He'd been here often enough to move as if he belonged. Then the noise met him—laughter, clinking cutlery, voices overlapping. Morning in full swing.

The Klonimuses, as usual, took up every inch of space at the long table, plates crowded with half-eaten food, mugs passed hand to hand. Gideon was laughing. Someone else was arguing about butter. Little Joseph, balanced dangerously on his chair, was wide-eyed and trying to keep up with the noise.

Felix paused at the threshold but the puppy wriggled in his arms.

"A puppy?!" Joseph shrieked, his pitch soaring above the room. His chair screeched back, and he launched himself toward Felix, arms already reaching.

"Yes! Truly?" came a lilting voice from the far side of the table.

Rosie, Gideon's wife, leaned forward with careful eagerness, one hand braced on the swell of her belly as if to anchor herself. She didn't rise, but she didn't need to—the glow about her said everything. It softened her face, making her already luminous smile shine brighter. "Bring her closer, Felix, if you please."

He stepped fully into the room, his mouth tugging into a smile as the ripple of delight spread around the table. The puppy yawned toward the noise, blinking slowly and bleary, her tiny paws stretching wide as she sniffed at the unfamiliar air. Joseph was practically buzzing beside him, teetering on the balls of his feet.

Felix crouched slightly, sheltering the little creature behind one hand. "She's just waking up," he told Joseph gently. "Give her a moment. She's a little shy still."

"What's her name?" Joseph breathed, eyes round as saucers. He rocked back and forth, squeezing his hands against his chest like he might burst from holding in too much wonder. "She's so small!"

"Little one," Felix said.

"That's not a name," Gideon replied dryly. "That's an observation."

But even he couldn't quite keep the affection from his face as he leaned in for a better look.

Rosie let out a soft laugh, her fingers tapping the rim of her plate. "Wherever did you find her, Felix? She's no bigger than a teacup."

"She was in a crate at the apothecary," he said, rising again and shifting the puppy higher against his chest. "Alfie and I found her there."

"So she found you," Raphi said from further down the table.

Felix looked up, caught the warmth behind his friend's eyes.

"She must have a perfect nose then," Raphi added, the meaning behind it clear. They were all his friends—the Klonimus brothers and everyone who came with them. But Raphi had once lost Laila. Had clawed his way back from that kind of absence. He understood.

Felix didn't answer right away.

Maybe he needed to stop hiding. Maybe it was time to be found. By Maisie, of course.

Felix's fingers brushed lightly over the pup's head. Her ears flopped with the movement, and her head lolled once more against his coat. "She's thin," he said, quieter now. "But I've fed her. She'll be alright. She just needs some care."

Rosie glanced at Gideon, and the look they shared was quiet and sure, the kind only couples fluent in each other could pull off. She turned back to Felix.

"A *nishumela*, indeed," she said softly, echoing Pavel's words. Her French accent smoothed the syllables into something almost musical.

Her eyes lingered on Felix as he adjusted the muslin around the puppy again. He didn't notice—he was focused on keeping her warm—but it was the sort of gesture that lingered. Quiet. Endearing. The kind people remembered.

"She's a soul of sweetness, this one. Look at these eyes! Such trust, such light." Raphi traced a finger down the pup's delicate nose while she barked softly, a sound more chirrup than growl.

"How about Goldie? A soul wrapped in golden fur," Gideon said.

"Says the Crown Jeweler who works with gold?" Felix arched a brow.

"So do you, the dentist who works with gold," Raphi's retort caused the others in the room to break out in laughter.

Felix turned to Raphi, curiosity piqued, his gaze settling on his friend. "You have that speculative expression again. Pray, do not subject us to one of your whimsical names."

"Whimsical, is it?" Raphi sat upright, feigning affront written all over his face. He scratched beneath the puppy's chin, his tone softening as he spoke. "Her name's clear, Felix. It came to me this very moment. Lilly."

Felix blinked. "Lilly?"

"Yes." Raphi's dark eyes met his, brimming with a sincerity that Felix, for all his stoicism, could not dismiss. "Lilly, like the flower. Pure. Bright. Cherished." He hesitated, stroking the pup's soft ears, his voice quieter now. "It calls to me. Like a *nishama*… a soul. Something too good for this world, but here just the same."

"How very symbolic," Gideon said. Even he must have caught on that Raphi nudged Felix with another double meaning.

But he was right. Lilly was perfect in so many ways.

Beside Raphi, stacked neatly at the edge of the table, was a bundle of letters tied with thin cord.

"I picked these up at the meeting with the Rabbi this morning," Raphi said, brushing a hand across the bundle. "Mostly the usual. Lost fortunes, missing persons, half-written names. Just initials in most. Nothing from Vienna. Nothing in German."

Felix knew the sort, handwritten pleas, inquiries, hopes folded into cream-colored paper.

He paused, touching one envelope that bore a faint smudge near the seal. "This one looked like it might've been kissed," he added, voice lighter than the words deserved.

"Someone missing someone, I suppose."

Felix's gaze dropped to it. His fingers twitched. There was something about the way the ink bloomed just slightly where the name should be but only letters appeared. Someone's initials. A softness to the fold. He didn't reach. Didn't dare. But his breath caught.

It could have been her. Could have been.

Not with those initials though. Not in English.

But the puppy gave a soft, startled squeak and wobbled into Joseph's lap, kicking Felix's thigh in the scramble. The boy laughed, delighted.

Felix blinked down, refocusing.

When he glanced back, Raphi had already swept the stack into his satchel, the knot in the twine tugged tight. "They'll go to the committee at the synagogue," he said, voice light again. "Perhaps someone else will recognize a name of a missing relative."

For a moment, neither spoke. The children played softly, the pup tumbling over Joseph's hand to curl against his leg. Felix cleared his throat, absurdly feeling the faintest tightness in his chest.

Could Lilly be the messenger he needed? Had she found him, and would she open his path toward the family he'd always hoped to have?

He wanted Maisie here. In this room. With his friends. With this silly puppy tucked under her arm. He wanted her to laugh at Raphi's dramatics, to raise a brow at Gideon's dry wit, to sit beside him and take his hand like no time had passed at all.

Oh, Maisie, where are you?

"Well," Felix said briskly, clasping his hands again. "If you must saddle the puppy with sentimentality, Lilly shall do as well as any other name."

Raphi grinned up at him, triumphant. "Sentimentality is the lifeblood of good names, Felix. Remember this when you next despair over my wisdom."

Felix smiled but said nothing, instead crouching beside Joseph and the puppy, letting his fingers trace lightly over her silken fur.

Lilly. A name as simple as breath and soft as morning.

The pup blinked up at him, her small pink tongue darting once over her nose before she curled tighter against Joseph's side, her trust absolute.

And for the first time in too long, Felix felt something shift inside him. A hush beneath the ache. A murmur that hope, perhaps, had not left him entirely.

Even if her name had nearly been under his hand. Even if it had slipped past him in silence, folded into a bundle of the nearly lost.

If only he could find Maisie.

Chapter Twenty-One

THE KLONIMUS' WORKSHOP had taken on a thicker kind of quiet—the kind that settled once the brothers arrived. They moved with purpose, sleeves shoved up, tools in hand. No fanfare. Just the slow clink of metal, the thud of wood against wood. The day had begun.

Felix paced the floor. The same three boards underfoot gave a faint groan with every turn. He didn't change his route. Let them speak.

Above the hearth, the brass clock ticked with the patience of someone watching him waste time. Each second, a door closes.

"I just wanted to ask about your inquiries before I leave," he said, shifting Lilly against his chest. "First patient's at nine."

"I know," Raphi said. "I waited." He nodded toward the nearest chair. "Sit down."

Felix stayed where he was. He didn't need to hear the words. Raphi's voice had already dropped—low, careful. Bad news wore that tone like a coat.

He rubbed the bridge of his nose. "There's no central record. No registry. A woman can disappear here just by avoiding the synagogue. And if she doesn't marry under our rites, she leaves no trace. Parish books list only heads of household. Governesses? Companions? They don't exist unless someone names them."

He looked up, jaw tight. "Maisie wouldn't hide from me."

"Not from you," Raphi said, his voice even. "From men like List, and there are plenty like him, from the law. If she needed to run, she'd leave pieces behind. Enough to start over."

He tapped the table twice. "She wouldn't need much. Change one letter—Maisie becomes Mary. Morgenschein becomes Morning. Shine. To the world, she's a distant cousin, or a nursemaid. The kind of woman who stays polite, keeps quiet, and doesn't belong to anyone."

Felix's gaze dropped to the pages on the table—letter after letter, address after address. None of them was written in her hand. None of them hers.

Ghosts on paper. The phrase landed hard.

Raphi kept going. "You have to ask the one question you don't want to. What if she doesn't want to be found? After the riot, would you have left a message behind? I wouldn't. Not when a knock at the door could end everything."

Felix blinked. His eyes stung.

He remembered the broken windows. The blood. How silence had become the only response when his parents were beaten to death and when Alfie…

Raphi leaned forward, quicker now. "If she's staying with someone, she's off the map. But the map isn't where we'll find her. We look in the ledgers that run alongside: tailors, coachmakers, booksellers, apothecaries. She may be gone from the records that count names—but not from the ones that count coin."

Felix looked up. "Then we trace the transactions. Not the people. She touched the world—she left fingerprints."

"We'll need access," Raphi said. "Most won't let us in."

"I'll find a way."

"Then we search for the shape of her life. That's all we've got."

Felix stilled. Let it settle in his chest. He held light little Lilly in his arms, her tiny breath steady against his ribs. If Maisie had chosen to vanish—if she'd stepped sideways into another name— he'd still find her.

He turned to Raphi fully.

Raphi's hand landed on his shoulder. Solid. Kind. Too much.

"She's not listed in Vienna," Felix said, voice steady now. "Or London. Or Paris. Not in Prague. Or Edinburgh. Or—" He stopped himself. "She's somewhere else. Just out of reach."

He exhaled. Deep. Measured.

"We keep looking."

Five years.

Hiding. Waiting. Or worse—trapped somewhere, needing him.

Felix's jaw worked as the thought twisted in deeper. *If she's in trouble… if she's alone and thinks I gave up…*

Raphi's voice cut in, tentative. "Are you sure it's not time to let go?"

Felix jerked back, the touch like a heat wave. "You think I haven't asked myself that?" His voice came out too fast, too raw. "You think I don't know how insane this sounds? Every sane part of me—every logical scrap—says I should've stopped ages ago. And still…" He broke off, the sentence splintering. "Still, I wake up with her name in my mouth." *And of her in my heart.*

He gave a brittle laugh. "I'm going to be the mad dentist of London. The man who's asked every soul from Budapest to Dublin if they've seen the woman who once smiled at him like he was the only man alive."

Raphi didn't speak. His mouth tightened; fingers tapped once, then stilled. The silence settled in—not empty, but full. That kind of silence only old friends could hold between them, when nothing said *was* still something.

"I've looked everywhere," Raphi said at last, voice low. "What else can I do?"

Felix's shoulders tensed. "Nothing," he said too sharply. "No one can." He exhaled, but it didn't loosen anything inside him. "I know it sounds absurd. Every day, I fill hollows with gold. I patch teeth. I mend things. And still—" He pressed his palm to his chest. "There's this place in me that nothing touches."

Raphi ran a hand through his hair, the movement slow. "If you haven't found her name," he said, choosing his words with care, "then she's changed it. And you know what that means."

Felix turned too fast. "Of course I do." He slammed his fist against the table. The sound rang out—dull, heavy—bone against wood.

Pain was registered, but only as a background sensation.

"You think I haven't pictured it? That she married someone else? That she's living some quiet, safe life under another name in another city—one I'll never set foot in?" He inhaled, shaky now. "I still love her. I'd love her in a thousand versions of the world. Even if she forgot me."

Raphi stared down, knuckles white on the chair's edge.

"You're breaking yourself," he said. "Why not… stop chasing? Live the life you've built."

Felix raised his head. There was no heat in his voice now. Only truth. "She *is* my life."

He stepped closer. "Maisie's the part of me that breathes. That works. That hopes." He paused. "If Laila had vanished—no trace, no goodbye—would you have stopped?"

Raphi's throat moved with a swallow. His face shifted, just enough.

"No," he said finally. Barely above a whisper. "Never."

Felix nodded once. "Then don't ask me to."

The words fell between them. Soft. Final. Like dust settling over a gold foil sheet—quiet, but unmistakable.

Raphi turned away. But Felix stayed, facing the scattered tools, the bent wire, the cold cup of tea. The room didn't feel empty. It felt stalled—like a breath held too long.

The world might keep moving. But he would wait, always, for her.

ABOUT A TWENTY minute walk away, sunlight spilled across the drawing room just off Green Park. Maisie had asked to see her friend Rachel Pearler—no grand purpose, only a restless pull she didn't bother to question. She'd run down every practical lead, sent notes to every newspaper that might have taken interest, and now her search for Faivish clung to a thread grown thin with wear. Every day without news tightened her.

She was starting to come apart.

The butler opened the door. Maisie adjusted her grip on Deena's smaller hand, steadying them both. John bounded in ahead, all elbows and energy, already at ease. Maisie paused at the threshold.

The chambers inside smelled of lemon tart and ripe apples. Warmth met her like a shawl pulled from the oven—but she didn't step forward. The sounds beyond the foyer—silver on porcelain, voices overlapping—slowed her. Too much comfort that wasn't meant for her.

She wasn't here to visit and didn't want tea. She wanted time to collapse into something she could name.

"This way, madam," the butler said, bowing. She followed, skirts sweeping softly over polished wood. She had imagined the usual parlor—Rachel cross-legged on the settee, Deena curled at her feet, cold tea forgotten. But they passed down a different hall.

The drawing room opened wide.

Sunlight flared against burgundy damask walls. Crystals swung from a chandelier overhead, scattering color across the white-draped table like a dropped handful of gems. And then— music.

Low at first. A fiddle, a singer, a man at the pianoforte. The notes curled through the room—slow and lush, pulling at the edges of things.

Maisie stopped in the doorway.

The sound swelled, close enough to touch. It filled her chest, leaving less room to breathe.

She had come looking for a distraction. But the music didn't clear her thoughts—it pressed against them. Thick and ornate.

She didn't want beauty but stillness. A quiet space large enough to hold his voice but anywhere she turned these days, she thought of Faivish. She could almost feel him. *Am I going mad?*

By the fireplace sat Eve Pearler, Rachel's mother-in-law, whom Maisie had only met once in passing. But even at a glance, Eve commanded a room the way some women wore diamonds—calmly, deliberately, without apology. She sat straight-backed in a high-back chair, her posture untouched by comfort, surveying the room like it belonged to her simply because no one had challenged her claim.

Children sprawled at her feet, tumbling over pillows. Little Maia, Rachel's daughter, waved at John, who had already plopped down cross-legged at the front. He looked entirely at home. Eager. Unbothered. As though Maisie weren't standing frozen behind him, her chest tight with unease.

"Over here!" Rachel called, her voice warm as always. A footman appeared and adjusted a chair. Maisie moved reluctantly, tugging Deena's hand until the girl wriggled onto a footstool beside her.

Rachel leaned in, her voice pitched low beneath the string's hum. "They're from Warsaw," she said. "Traveling musicians. Eve arranged it."

Of course, she had. Eve Pearler had a way of making generosity feel like a binding contract. Maisie had heard the whispers: Eve was sunlight. Everything grew around her—but stand too close and you'd burn.

Maisie wasn't here to be scorched. She needed quiet, not attention.

"They played at the new synagogue, too," Rachel added.

Maisie nodded. Polite. Tight. Her hands rested carefully in her lap, fingers still. She didn't clench them, but the effort cost her. Every courteous smile felt like a betrayal—of urgency, of longing, of Faivish.

Rachel's smile didn't waver. "Most in London haven't heard

anything like this."

The next piece began—slower, aching. The fiddle keened. The voice followed, heavy with memory.

Maisie's pulse thudded behind her eyes.

She'd always hated these Yiddish laments. Not the language, not the notes—but the surrender in them. Heartbreak set to melody. She didn't understand why people turned their sorrow into song and offered it up like incense. Around her, handkerchiefs appeared—Rachel, Eve, even Deena swayed softly, caught in the current.

Maisie kept her eyes on her skirt. Gray wool. Pressed. Every pleat perfectly sharp. Each note pressed in harder. The lump in her throat rose too quickly.

Lately, it took nothing at all to cry. And the reason—always—circled back to him. Faivish. If she gave in here, in Rachel's drawing room, in Eve's curated spectacle, she might not know how to stop.

How many nights had she stared at the ceiling, wondering if he still remembered her laugh? If his voice had changed? If he was breathing free air? Or if she'd been chasing a shadow all this time, while life pushed forward without her.

She reached for her handkerchief.

Rachel took her hand. Gave it a quiet squeeze. A nod that said, *Yes, we share the weight.*

But her tears weren't Maisie's.

The music stopped. Maisie's head snapped up.

Her breath caught when the fiddle fell silent. A flute took its place, playing a low and eerie melody. Then the fiddler stepped forward. Maisie's chest pulled tight. Then came the first unmistakable notes.

Tumbalalaika.

Deena clapped softly. "Maisie," she whispered, eyes wide. "Isn't it wonderful?"

Maisie nodded faintly. She couldn't speak. The song pierced too close, too familiar, as if the past had found her here in this glittering room, refusing to let her pretend.

She leaned toward Rachel. "Do you know this, too?"

Rachel nodded, eyes still on the musicians. "Everyone does. They play it at *simchas*." Celebrations.

But this wasn't one. Everything around her faded—the damask walls, the rainbows, the hush of polite admiration. All she heard was the melody. Every note was a plea. A memory. A wound. Every note was Faivish.

❧

Chapter Twenty-Two

AFTER THE LAST song, the musicians slipped away for tea—their bows tucked, eyes bright with relief. Maisie exhaled, relief blooming through the tight coil in her stomach. She'd asked them about Faivish. They hadn't known. And so, she lingered at Rachel's elegant home with a heavy heart.

The drawing room had emptied into stillness. Deena and John drifted off, drawn toward the smaller parlor where rugelach and warm milk waited like a salve. The hushed quiet that settled between Rachel and Maisie became cavernous.

Rachel sat forward, her shoulders soft. A breath of breeze drifted through the open window, sending the sheer curtains floating, landing lightly across the room.

"And you've gone through everything in the archives?" she asked at last, voice gentle.

Maisie drew in a slow breath, crossing her arms over her midriff as though she could catch herself from falling apart. The question pricked, as if Rachel didn't trust she'd done enough. She had burned through ledger after ledger, hoping for a flicker of proof, but only found dead ends.

"The old broadsheets?"

"Yes," Maisie said, voice thin, tighter than she meant. "In French. In Prussian."

Rachel hesitated. "What about those single-print leaflets?"

"Yes. Everything." Her own voice betrayed her—strained, raw. She'd scoured every record of births, deaths, marriages, and notices. Every name but his name had answered her in silence.

"I've left no stone unturned. He's nowhere."

Rachel turned her gaze away and smoothed the fabric of her gown. Silk shifting under fingertips. After a moment, she offered a whisper: "Maybe… he doesn't want to be found."

The words landed like icicles against Maisie's ribcage. Her breath froze. She'd refused even to let herself think it. "Why ever not?" she managed, throat tight.

Rachel didn't answer with words. Instead, her brow arched—the same cool gesture her mother-in-law made when disagreement glided too close to argument.

Heat rose across Maisie's face, anger coiling under dread. The thought that he might have turned away from her—rather than the other way around—felt intolerable.

She forced out a hollow laugh. "Maybe he's content—in India?"

The words tasted sharp in her mouth.

Rachel's features eased. "My brother-in-law, Benjamin Klonimus, was in India once. He said the Jewish communities there are small, but alive. Thriving, even."

Maisie leaned forward, voice lower still. "Would Faivish search for me, do you think?"

Rachel shut her eyes for a breath. "Perhaps," she said, and Maisie could hear restraint in her tone. "But…"

That trailing off—meaning pulsed there. Final.

Maisie's chest felt too tight to breathe.

Before she could say more, Deena entered the frame, pale morning backing her up. "Maisie, it's time to go."

Her skirts felt heavy as she rose. She smoothed the folds—an automatic gesture, a shield over the tremor that ran through her.

They moved into the hall. Rachel followed her with watchful quiet.

"Has the dentist helped the marquess?" she asked.

Maisie stopped. The question felt simple. But her mind was tangled in one man she'd never found. "He has," she said eventually. Her voice found itself. "Very much. He's... skilled. Perhaps more than expected."

Rachel's expression softened further. "They say that of Harley Street doctors. Gentlefolk queue for them—some of the highest in the land."

Maisie's breath clipped. *Queue of patients.* The idea snagged memories—her father's waiting area filled with women every Tuesday and Thursday when Faivish was there. For a heartbeat, something wild dared to hope.

But fear followed: if the dentist learned from Faivish... then he might carry his name. And if he carried it, others would know.

Her fingers clenched around Deena's hand behind her skirts. She managed to smile, smooth and small.

Deena tugged at her. "You promised the bookshop next."

They moved on. Their path led them from the Pearlers' house, down the street, toward Pall Mall. But the name haunted her step.

Harley Street dentist. Skilled. Known. Not yet familiar, though Deena said not familiar at all.

The carriage rocked with a lazy rhythm, wheels murmuring over the uneven cobbles. Maisie adjusted her gloves, tugging at the fingers to keep her hands steady. John slouched beside her— all elbows, knees, and shoes still too large for him.

"You'll eat fewer sweets now, I hope," Maisie said, her tone light but pointed.

"But I thought you liked it when I smiled." He grinned wide—a flash of new gold gleaming at the back of his mouth.

Maisie's lips twitched, but she kept her voice even. "At Eton, you'll be on your own. I'm trusting you."

"No more chocolates?" John asked.

"No." She paused. "But I'll send letters. I'll bring you home for the holidays. I'll always be just a note away."

Deena leaned forward, her arm resting against Maisie's.

"We'll be there when you need us."

John straightened a little. "I suppose that's better than chocolates."

Maisie nodded. A warm ache unfurled behind her smile. "Good."

The carriage began to slow.

"Did you get John's uniforms?" Maisie asked.

"They'll be ready this afternoon," Deena replied.

"I'll fetch them. I want to stop by the archives again."

John looked up. "You're not coming to the dentist?"

"You'll be fine with Deena. Dr. Leafley is said to be… extraordinarily skilled. I'll meet him after."

The words landed awkwardly. They echoed too many times—*skilled*, always *skilled*. The same word patients once used for her father and Faivish, spoken with reverence and something close to wonder.

As they stepped down, Maisie caught Deena's arm. "One moment."

"Yes?"

"You've seen the dentist?"

"Certainly."

Maisie's throat tightened. "Is he old?"

Deena wrinkled her nose. "Not as old as Father. Not young either. Somewhere in between."

Maisie's thoughts turned back to the boy with steady hands and eyes too serious for his age. Faivish had been young. Too young for all he knew. But five years could soften or sharpen. They left marks on the body, on the soul.

"And?" she asked.

Deena tilted her head. "Handsome, if you like that sort of thing. Broad across the shoulders. Too big."

Maisie's breath caught. *Too big.*

Her heart leapt—then fell. Faivish had been sharp-edged, his strength compact and precise, like a drawn blade. Not broad. And he had been unmistakably theirs.

If this man shared their faith, someone would've said something. A name. A trace. A whisper in the congregation.

Deena and John went in, and the door to 87 Harley Street clicked shut behind them.

Maisie lingered on the step, torn. Every instinct told her to demand an introduction, to walk in and see this man with her own eyes. But another, darker voice warned her of Hofstätter, of List—men who had power to erase. If her father had gone into hiding, if Faivish had been forced to change his name as she had to survive, then her knocking at the wrong door could undo everything. Drawing too much attention was to risk more than just disappointment. It was to gamble with his safety. No, she needed more certainty before she could speak his name to strangers.

She pressed her palm to the carriage door. One look could undo her. One look could reveal him—or destroy the fragile hope she still clutched.

Maisie climbed inside. The door shut. The wheels turned. She closed her eyes.

Not young. Not a Jewish name. Too big.

But still, her pulse would not settle. But something in her refused to believe it. Not yet. She would fetch the uniforms. Visit the archives. Keep searching.

Faivish is out there. I know it.

THE ORNATE LETTERING above the newspaper archive door caught the morning light like a memory catching fire. Felix barely glanced at it. With Alfie trailing behind and little Lilly tucked under one arm, he stepped into the quiet, familiar hush of the building. The scent greeted him before anything else—dusty paper, old ink, and something brittle as parchment left too long in the sun. It wrapped around him like an old thought half-remembered. He almost sneezed, caught it just in time, unwilling to break the fragile stillness.

The room breathed in soft rhythms—murmured voices, the scratch of pens, chairs creaking with thoughtful weight. A symphony of routine, playing just beneath notice.

"Honestly, she'll never learn," Alfie muttered. His voice carried low but unmistakable. "You're babying Lilly to no end. She thinks your arm is a featherbed."

Felix looked down at the golden puff nestled beneath his coat. Lilly blinked up at him, her tiny paws drawn to her chest, breathing slowly with trust. "She is home," he said quietly. "She'll learn. Just… not today."

Alfie scoffed under his breath. "She'd learn faster if you let her walk more than five feet. You'll be scraping off boot mess before long."

Felix didn't answer. He was already at the main desk, his fingers tapping lightly against the counter. "The criminal reports from Middlesex. Last month," he said, nodding to the clerk. He'd already scoured the shipping manifests, dock logs, and registries. Each lead vanished into smoke.

The clerk nodded distractedly and disappeared through a side door.

Felix let his gaze drift.

And then—something. Or someone.

A shape first. The edge of a profile. A line of nose, a sweep of cheekbone. Hair pinned beneath a broad, modern hat. Not the kind Maisie ever wore. Too bold, too of-the-moment. And yet—

Something about the tilt of her head. The grace in the way she leaned in to speak. The poise that threaded through her shoulders like confidence set to music. It didn't match what he knew… but it pulled at what he remembered.

His chest tightened. It couldn't be her.

Or could it?

She turned slightly, murmuring something to the clerk. He couldn't hear. Her back was to him now, posture elegant, the curve of her spine like a brushstroke. Nothing about her said

Maisie. But everything in his blood did.

The rush was immediate. Heat, hope, ache—a chorus too loud to silence.

"Felix." Alfie's voice broke through, dry and pointed. "You're staring like you've seen a mirage. Want me to take Lilly outside while you try to remember how to breathe?"

"No," Felix said quickly, blinking hard as if to shake loose the spell. "This won't take long."

But by the time he looked again, she was gone. Only the swish of a hem remained, vanishing behind the door at the rear of the archive.

He moved instinctively, Lilly held tight against his chest, pushing through the hush of paper and whispers. A cart blocked his way. He swerved, catching the edge of a stacked tower of books that tumbled down in a chaotic spill. The crash rang out— sharp, discordant. Lilly let out a startled yip. Felix cursed under his breath.

Heads turned. Silence deepened, judgment thick in the air.

And still—she was nowhere.

He turned sharply, eyes landing on the nearest clerk. "The woman who just went into the back room. Please—I need to speak with her."

The clerk barely blinked. "That section is restricted."

"It's important." Felix leaned forward, voice taut with urgency. "Just a moment."

The clerk gave a tight-lipped smile, the sort that didn't reach the eyes. "Only distinguished patrons are permitted access."

It wasn't the words, but the weight behind them—coated in disdain, sharpened by scrutiny.

Felix held the clerk's gaze, his jaw tightening. He knew this look. Knew the slow, silent dissection: dark hair, sharper cheekbones, the faint lilt of an accent too foreign for comfort. Not quite belonging. Never quite invited in.

Before he could speak, Alfie appeared beside him, easy as breath.

"The gent's with me," he said, slipping a coin across the desk without breaking stride. "Loyal patron, through and through."

The coin clicked softly, landing with the weight of practiced diplomacy. Alfie's smile made it a jest, a game, nothing serious—just enough to smooth over the friction.

Felix said nothing, swallowing the heat that rose in his throat. He hated needing the gesture. Hated what it meant. But the rope was lowered, the gate unlatched.

The clerk hesitated, then leaned in, voice dropping. "That was Lady Spencer. Sister to the late Marquess of Stonefield."

Felix stilled.

Lady Spencer.

The name glittered like cut crystal—delicate, cold, and painfully unfamiliar. It didn't fit.

And yet.

He almost asked nothing more, but the clerk went on, lowering his voice further. "Odd request, though. She asked for the *Wiener Zeitung for 1812*. Who wants to read old news from Vienna? Said she wanted 1813 and 1814, too."

The words struck him like a fist. Vienna. The year everything had unraveled. Her father's practice raided, Maisie vanished. His breath caught, though he forced his face still.

He gave a faint nod as the clerk stepped away.

Maisie might have changed her name, but sister to a marquess? That wasn't just a disguise. That was a reinvention. *Impossible.*

Alfie watched him, one brow lifted. "Not quite the reunion you were hoping for, eh?"

Felix didn't answer. His thoughts looped, one over the next, spiraling like smoke in the still air. His heart hadn't caught up. Not yet.

But had he imagined it? The resemblance and the flicker of something familiar?

Had longing conjured a mirage indeed? Or had fate delivered one more *almost*? It didn't matter. Whether it was Maisie or not, the moment had hooked itself into him like a barb. And it wouldn't let go of him.

Chapter Twenty-Three

THE CARRIAGE WHEELS rattled over the gravel, each clack crisp in the cool autumn air. Maisie watched John's lean form beside her—his hands tucked under his thighs, posture too steady for thirteen years. Still, the way his boots shifted and tapped betrayed a nervous energy she couldn't quite smooth.

"Maisie," he spoke, pitched with uncertainty, "do you think they'll have pudding every Sunday at Eton?"

She tucked a lock of hair behind her ear and let a soft smile touch her lips. "I should think so. Their cook must be practiced. Maybe even lemon tart."

John's brow furrowed, as if weighing the gravity of a lemon tart on the fate of the world. "Do you think I'll like lemon tart? We didn't have it—Mother didn't care for lemon."

Maisie brushed the thought aside gently. "If you don't," she started slowly, "there'll always be bread and butter. That you do like."

John's slight nod held something stronger—she sensed courage blooming in him. His head tilted, wide-eyed with the next question. "Do you think the other boys get letters and sweets from their mums? If they do, can I send you letters?"

Deena snorted from across the carriage. "We're not sending you sweets," she said, tone firm but fond. "You'll ruin your teeth."

Maisie leaned in, bristling with maternal warmth. "She might be right. But yes—you can write. I promise I'll always write back."

Deena's eyes softened. "Me too," she added quietly, and Maisie caught that tug of familial companionship with such simple elegance.

John's half-smile came slowly. His fidget eased. Maisie glimpsed Deena's playful eye roll, but the softness in her smile couldn't be hidden.

"We're each other's family," Maisie said. She stretched out her hands, and John clambered closer to rest a gentle hug against her shoulder. "Might as well behave like one."

They crested a rise. Eton's sprawl unfolded below: golden stone buildings rising quietly, the river glinting as if tied with light itself.

That must be your dormitory, Maisie thought, shading her eyes. The rows of identical windows looked like puzzle pieces, waiting to be solved. "That building with all the windows—your dorms, I think."

John pressed his nose to the glass. "It's huge," he breathed. "Bigger than our entire townhouse."

Deena's attention had drifted, her gaze fixed on a group of older boys scurrying across the quad—their shirts already smattered with grass.

"Strong and handsome, don't you think?" Maisie teased, leaning into gentle mischief.

Deena wrinkled her nose, lips twitching as though choosing her words carefully. "They're seventeen, nearly men," she said, voice edged with matronly concern. "They're being groomed for governance."

MAISIE BIT BACK a laugh. "Already? Parliament? I suppose those grass stains must be signs of diplomatic experience."

But Deena wasn't playing along. Her gaze stayed fixed on the older boys outside, a quiet curiosity flickering across her face.

Maisie followed her line of sight—more thoughtfully now—but her focus shifted back to John, to the boy sitting beside her trying so hard to appear unshaken.

When they arrived, Maisie was careful not to linger. Good-byes, she'd learned, should be steady. No hesitation or lingering glances. Just enough warmth to hold onto, but not so much that it pulls the child back.

The headmaster met them with polite reserve, his words practiced, his handshake brief. Maisie crouched to John's level, smoothing the lapel of his uniform jacket as she met his eyes.

"Write every week," she said softly, steadying her voice. "The post here is reliable. And if you need anything, anything at all, we'll send it straight away."

John's lips twitched. "And if what I need is to come home?"

Maisie swallowed around the lump in her throat. "Then I'll come and fetch you with pastries from the French patisserie. Friday mornings, without fail."

Not challah, of course. Something else that meant home.

He gave a quick nod, straightening again, his young face set with resolve. But as Maisie rose to leave, he faltered. His feet edged toward the great oak doors—and then, with a sudden turn, he was back at her side.

He threw his arms around her waist, tight, unexpected.

Maisie gasped softly as she caught him, folding him close. Her hand settled over his small back, warm and steady. He smelled of honey soap and fresh linen.

She held him as long as he let her—a moment stitched into memory—and then, without a word, he stepped back.

And just like that, he let go.

She stood a moment longer, one hand resting where he'd held her, her eyes fixed on the doorway that had swallowed him whole. The smudge of soil on her gown was the only sign he'd been there at all.

Chapter Twenty-Four

LATER THAT AFTERNOON, summer light slanted through the glass-paned windows of the Pearlers' parlor, casting dappled warmth across the room. Maisie clutched her teacup with both hands—less for the drink, more for the heat it gave her.

"I tried," she murmured, the words brittle as old silver. "I wrote to every person I could remember in Vienna. I asked the East India Company. They said no Faivish Blattner ever returned to England. No one knows where he is."

Rachel paused mid-stir—her spoon tinkling in the cup—her voice soft as gauze and bright as diamonds. "Maisie… might something dreadful have happened? Could he not have reached India—or something gone wrong on the voyage home?"

The words landed with cold weight. Maisie blinked once, swallowing hard against the knot tightening inside her.

Don't imagine it. Don't name it. Oh, please be alive.

"I've thought of it," she confessed, voice so low it felt tangled in the tablecloth. "Then I tried not to. There were storms that year… I remember a merchant ship lost off Bombay."

Rachel didn't answer with words. Instead, she pressed a fresh cup into Maisie's trembling hands. The rings on her fingers glinted when the porcelain moved between them.

Maisie stared down. The surface of the tea quivered. Fear didn't roar—it just waited, like a weight gathering in her bones.

What if he's gone? Buried under foreign earth, buried from all memory?

Her fingers shook. The liquid rippled. She set the cup down to stop the tremors from showing.

"What if," she said eventually, voice rough and slow, "he doesn't want to be found anymore? What if he's married now—has a wife, a child?"

Rachel blinked, eyes gathering something more profound than her surprise.

"Would he be able to?" she asked, carefully, as if her words might shatter something.

Maisie didn't answer. Instead, she saw him again in her mind: the mischief in his dark eyes, the way light kissed his skin, his laugh pulling her in like gravity itself. They had a bond—but that did nothing to stop him from falling into another's arms if given the chance.

Fear trickled up behind her ribs. She could see the child: inquisitive eyes like his, a silent mother watching, wise and soft with settled strength, orchestrating a household. The sketch formed so clearly it made her whole being spin—before it ghosted away like a nightmare.

"He was mine," she whispered. Not possessed, simply... loved me. Whole. Her voice caught there. "He'd touch my sleeve. Not my hand—just the cloth. Something in him needed that. I'd feel it... He'd pretend surprise, then that crooked smile... I—" She laughed, breathless. "I'd forget the rest of the world." She exhaled. "He adored me. Every look. Every breath."

And later that night... he showed her.

Her lips shook; the next breath was sharp. "If he smiles that way at another woman... if he whispers her name like he spoke mine—" Her gaze dropped to the cooling tea. Words nearly escaped.

"Then maybe it was all a dream." But her heart recoiled from the silence beyond waking. *A life touched by his love—even if dreamed—is better than one without it.*

Rachel didn't speak. Just set her spoon down with a soft click.

"You didn't dream it."

Maisie shook her head. It didn't steady anything.

Rachel leaned forward. "Would you want to know? Even if he had married another?" The question settled between them like fog.

Maisie didn't answer. *If I saw him—just once—I'd know without asking.*

Finally, she spoke. "I think… I'd want to know everything. Even if it breaks me."

Rachel's eyes softened, but then she reached for the folded *Bristol Gazette* on the side table. "Then you must also know this." She smoothed the paper, voice tightening. "Read."

Maisie bent closer. The words spilled like acid across the page:

Summary Punishment.—At Bristol, two Jews, much reduced in appearance, were discovered in the stables of the White Hart Inn, seeking scraps where honest labour could not be had. Their conduct was judged a trespass upon the property of the house, and they were chastised with severity by those present. Their hands were bound together, and the correction proved so sharp that the unfortunate fellows did not long survive. The spectacle, while deemed a just warning to others inclined to dishonesty, left the townspeople with the disagreeable duty of restoring order to the yard.

The words made Maisie's skin prickle. She pressed a hand to her chest. "They write it as though it were a joke."

Rachel's jaw tightened. "That's the point. The law does not always defend us, Maisie. The law sometimes joins the mob—or hides behind laughter. And Baron von List—he applauds these humiliations, encourages them. He is already celebrated on the continent for showing the world how—what was the phrase?— 'deplorable' Jews are."

Maisie drew from her reticule a few folded slips, ink smudged from travel. "I've looked, too. German papers, Prussian ones.

They mention him as if he were a reformer, a champion of purity. But every paragraph is stained. Every 'reform' means another way to make us small. I cannot put a notice for Faivish in such places. If he hides, it may be from men like List."

Rachel's gaze softened, though her eyes gleamed with something fierce. "You've done more than most. You've read. You've searched. You've carried the risk yourself. But you see now—it's not just whether Faivish is lost. It's whether he hides from danger that would devour him if he were found."

Maisie folded the scraps tight in her palm, as if ink itself might shield him. "Then I must walk the knife's edge. To search, but not too loudly. To hope, but not too openly."

The parlor seemed to hush around them, the summer air suddenly heavy. The world beyond them had teeth, and Baron von List was sharpening them.

Rachel leaned closer, her voice dropping. "We know what men like Baron von List can do behind closed doors. He has power, paper, and coin. He can strip a doctor of patients, denounce his remedies as poison, whisper in the ears of parliamentarians eager to believe him. He can ruin a man without ever dirtying his hands. And all the while, the press will cheer, or—worse—turn it into entertainment."

Silence pressed in, heavy as an anvil.

Maisie clutched her teacup tighter, willing its heat to seep into her bones. This wasn't just about storms at sea or marriage vows broken by time. It was about enemies who never rested—enemies with ink and law and resources at their disposal. Enemies who could erase a man like Faivish as easily as scratching his name from a ledger.

And she wondered if her hope of finding him was already too fragile to survive, or if she was truly more useful as Eleanor Spencer than as Maisie Morgenschein.

IT WAS WELL past dusk when Felix and Raphi turned the corner toward Green Park, the cobbles crunching beneath their boots.

The evening air held a damp chill—not sharp, but enough to find its way under the collar of Felix's coat and curl in his lungs. He shifted his satchel higher on his shoulder, trying to ignore the ache in his chest.

"So, listen," Raphi said, light but focused, "I'll deliver these diamonds to Fave Pearler. While we're there, we can ask Rachel a few quiet questions. She may know someone who can help us find Maisie."

"She still has those kinds of connections?" Felix asked.

"Through her father's business, yes," Raphi said. "Docks, shipping ledgers, foreign correspondents. Every name that passes through. If I found no Maisie Morgenschein in England, perhaps her contacts can."

Felix's throat tightened. He kept his eyes ahead, on the soft glow spilling from the tall windows of the Pearler home.

They passed through the curve at Green Park's edge, the city softened by lamplight. The Pearler house rose before them—tall, elegant, lit with the golden shimmer of Shabbat candles.

Felix stopped. "I'm not invited," he said quietly.

Raphi was already bounding up the steps. "You're family."

"No," Felix said. "Not tonight. It's *Shabbos*. I can't… I won't intrude."

Raphi turned, sighed. "Come. You know them."

Felix took a step back. "If I ever find her again," he murmured, "I won't miss a single Shabbos. Not one. I'd hold on to every second."

Raphi hesitated, nodded. "Alright."

He knocked once, confidently. A moment later, warmth and laughter spilled out from the open door, and Felix caught the smoke of burned candles and freshly-baked challah before it all closed again.

He turned away.

The street behind the Pearlers' home curved softly into the

dark edges of Green Park. The house glowed behind him, the light beautiful but distant. Untouchable.

He passed beneath one window, glancing up.

She might have stood at a window like that once. In Vienna. In Paris. Or just down the street.

Maisie.

Even now, just her name stirred him. After all this time, after all the silence. It still ached.

He walked slowly, boots scuffing over the gravel. The truth pressed in with each step—he didn't want to be seen. Not with the streaks of silver in his hair. Not with a name he hardly used anymore.

Faivish had belonged to her. Felix was what remained. But he'd always be hers with all his heart.

And if she had forgotten him—or worse, if someone had told her he wasn't worth remembering—then maybe that was best.

But even so, he couldn't stop the quiet, impossible hope that somewhere, somehow, she hadn't.

Chapter Twenty-Five

INSIDE THE PEARLERS' house, Shabbat candles flickered along the damask walls, their flames casting soft, restless shadows across the dining room. Maisie followed Rachel through the double doors into the study, her gloved hands clasped tightly at her waist. Deena was somewhere else in the house, gently distracted. The table in the dining room lay waiting—silver catching the candlelight, wine glowing like garnet in its glass.

At the far end of the study, Fave Pearler stood near the desk, his fingers idly brushing the velvet rim of a jeweler's tray. Another man stood beside him—taller, broad across the shoulders, his dark hair polished to a sheen under the chandelier. Both had their backs to the door.

"These are remarkable," Fave said, lifting a stone between thumb and forefinger, turning it until it flashed.

"Each is one carat exactly," the man beside him replied, his voice measured, precise. "All twelve delivered, ready for you to set."

Rachel stepped forward, her smile quick and warm. "Good evening, Raphi. *Git Shabbos.*" She kissed him on each cheek with the ease of someone long familiar. "How are you tonight?"

"Well, Rachel. *Git Shabbos.* And you are radiant, as always."

Rachel laughed, slipping her arm through Fave's. "You flatter me just like your brothers do." She turned, her gaze landing on

Maisie. "Have you met my dear friend?"

Maisie stepped forward, curtsying with the poise she had practiced so many times—elegant, correct, entirely automatic.

And in that movement, she felt it—the slip into *Lady Spencer*. The cool, deliberate courtesy of a role she had worn like armor before. Not the girl from Vienna. Not Faivish's Maisie. A woman several years older, an aunt at the edge of aristocracy.

Rachel's eyes flicked. A brief furrow crossed her brow, gone almost as quickly as it came. Her voice rose smoothly: "Allow me to introduce Mr. Raphael Klonimus to Lady Eleanor Spencer, aunt to the Marquess of Stonefield. Raphi is a dear friend, and his brother married Fave's sister."

The lie slid into the room without resistance.

Raphi turned, bowing low. When he took her hand and brushed her knuckles with his lips, Maisie felt it—a pause, subtle but sharp. As if he'd seen something he shouldn't have, or recognized more than he meant to admit. His eyes lingered, just long enough to catch her breath.

"From Oxfordshire," she said evenly, the words falling into place like pieces of a part she had long rehearsed.

Raphi straightened. "Lovely countryside. A pleasure."

Behind him, Fave and Rachel shared a glance—fleeting, sad, and not lost on her.

Yes. She was playing a role. And no one could know otherwise.

If Faivish truly was in danger, her real name helped no one. Better to stay hidden. To become Eleanor Spencer when she must. Someone who could pass unnoticed. Someone who might watch, protect, and perhaps—even if it tore her apart—help him, if only she could find him.

Maisie's throat tightened. The ache returned beneath her ribs—the same old ache that surfaced whenever the woman she pretended to be brushed against the woman she truly was.

I'm not here as a Jew, she reminded herself, lifting her chin. *I'm here for a reason.*

It had been indulgent, sitting with Deena and Rachel, letting the mask slip, laughing as if she were safe among her own. But that was an illusion too easily shattered. Jews endured by silence, by caution. A careless word could be overheard, repeated, twisted—and a whisper was all it took to unravel a life. Even here, in London, even in the houses of those who claimed friendship, trust was a ration to be measured, never freely given.

The gentile shell she wore felt closer than it ever had—what once shielded her now pressed like a hand against her throat. She crossed to the table, setting her palms lightly on its edge, and tried to find a steady breath.

"Would you like me to ask Mr. Klonimus about his connections?" Rachel's voice was soft, pitched for Maisie's ears alone.

Maisie's head snapped up. "No." The word came too sharp, too quick.

Rachel's expression smoothed as if Maisie had merely declined another helping of soup. "He's family," she murmured, gentle but insistent. "One of the most trusted."

Maisie folded her arms across her bodice. It wasn't defiance—it was armor. "No risks," she said, eyes locked on the tidy stitches of the tablecloth. "Nobody can know."

Rachel let out a slow breath and turned to her husband, her expression unreadable.

"Is there anything I might do for you?" Raphi Klonimus asked. His voice carried warmth, measured and calm, the voice of a man long accustomed to standing beside the Pearlers, never beneath them. His coat was bottle-green, the color catching the lamplight, though Maisie hardly noticed. It was his bearing that struck her—at ease, as if there was nothing in him that needed to be hidden.

But I do.

The ache pressed harder against her sternum. People like that—people she could sit with and speak to without weighing each syllable—belonged to another life. A life she no longer had. Rachel was the only one she still allowed herself, and even that closeness she held at a cautious distance.

She would guard what remained: her love, her sister, John at any cost.

Rachel's warning from earlier days drifted back to her. List making speeches in Parliament, stoking fear and suspicion. His boasts at parties about taking guardianship of orphaned heirs—boys with names, with fortunes, but no one strong enough to shield them.

What if he meant John?

The thought struck deep. The ache sharpened into something cold and steady.

If Faivish was gone, if she must wear this mask forever—so be it. But John would not fall into List's grasp. Not while she still drew breath.

She would keep watch—silent, unseen if she must—until the boy was old enough to stand against the world himself.

Without another word, Maisie turned from the table. Her skirts whispered across the polished floor as she crossed to the window. She pressed her fingertips to the glass, the cool pane grounding her as her eyes sought the night.

Darkness had deepened—the last wash of twilight fading into blue-black. Streetlamps along Green Park flickered, casting faint halos that kissed the edges of the clipped hedges. Beyond the garden gate, a stir of movement caught her eye.

The Pearler children had long since gone upstairs. Deena would be among them, perhaps chasing the little ones in the nursery or curled in the library with a book too heavy for her lap. *Deena, perched between child and woman.* Old enough to notice everything. Young enough to pretend she hadn't.

Maisie's chest tightened. The weight was hers to bear now for both of them.

Her gaze slipped back to the garden.

And then—she saw him.

A lone figure moved along the shadows of the park. His stride is unhurried. His posture is upright. The lamplight touched the line of his coat—dark, plain—and glanced off the curve of his shoulder as he paused.

Something about the stillness of him rang inside her, that quiet loneliness she knew so well. She was rarely without company—Deena's laughter, Rachel's welcome—but loneliness had nothing to do with company. It was the hollow echo of a heart searching for its other half.

Maisie leaned closer, palm flat against the glass. Breath slipped unbidden from her lips.

Not again.

It couldn't be.

Her eyes strained against the dark. The man lingered near the hedgerow, past the iron gate. His features lost to shadow, his distance impossible.

Tall. Dark hair. Straight-backed. Nothing remarkable—yet—

Her heart fluttered once, twice, then stumbled into a restless beat. Something in him tugged at her with quiet insistence.

Don't be foolish.

She had seen him before—everywhere. In the blur of carriage windows, in the angle of a stranger's shoulders, in dreams so real she woke certain his breath was still warm against her cheek. Her mind conjured him whenever it pleased, and tonight was no different. It couldn't be.

Still, her eyes clung to him.

The hedgerow shivered. Leaves stirred, restless. She blinked hard. Lamplight fractured across a thin veil of droplets.

Rain.

Her fingertips pressed harder against the glass. "Not again," she whispered.

England rained like Vienna had, but here it carried no sweetness. The Oxfordshire rain had smelled of meadows and turned the fields lush and forgiving. London rain collected in gutters, thickened into mud, and penned her in. No newspapers. No archives. No quiet alleys to chase his ghost.

Behind her, the stairs creaked.

Deena slipped into the room, her voice already softened with the finality of adulthood. "It's raining," she sighed. "I don't want to walk home."

"You can take our carriage," Rachel said at once, rising from her chair.

But Maisie didn't move. Didn't turn.

The man had not stirred—

Until he did.

Slowly, he glanced upward, as if greeting the rain with the kind of patience only solitude allowed. Then, in one unhurried motion, he reached to lift his collar and began to walk.

Something about him pulled at her.

A strange weight pressed behind her ribs.

She exhaled, forced herself to look away.

"Yes," Maisie said, finally stepping back from the window. "Let's go."

She didn't say *home.* Not out loud. The townhouse wasn't quite that—not truly. Perhaps it never had been.

But Maisie was pulled toward the door that faced the street. Her chest tightened; it felt like the room had shrunk around her. She needed to get out—out where the air was raw, even if it was wet and filthy. Her palms grew damp as she pressed them to the wood. If she stayed another moment, she would choke. She needed air. Now.

RAIN. AGAIN.

Of course.

Felix tugged his coat closer and tipped his head toward the sky. The clouds had thickened fast, swallowing the last scraps of light, and now the air carried that heavy scent—wet stone, soot, something faintly green beneath it, like grass pressed into mud.

He'd told himself he would wait ten minutes. Fifteen at the most, while Raphi delivered the parcel. But the minutes had stretched. Too many.

Too long.

Lilly would need to be let out soon. Last time he'd lingered, she'd left a puddle right in the middle of his bedroom rug. The apology had come with wide eyes and a head nudged against his boot—more than enough to win him over. Still, he owed her better.

"I'll tell him I'm going," Felix muttered, stepping toward the door. Best to let Raphi know not to hurry.

He rapped three times, brisk against polished wood. Almost at once, the butler appeared—a tall man, silver hair gleaming, his expression softened by years of careful courtesy.

"Dr. Leafley," he said with recognition. "Good evening. Has anyone called you?"

Felix inclined his head. "Good evening, James. I've not come on a call. I was waiting for Raphael Klonimus."

James stepped back with a quiet sweep of his arm. "Then you needn't stand in the rain. Come in, sir."

Felix crossed the threshold, the tiled floor catching droplets from his coat. His boots left dark tracks on the black-and-white marble.

"I didn't realize you'd been waiting outside," James said.

"I'm not anymore," Felix replied dryly, his gaze falling to the damp trail at his feet. "I only meant to tell him I was leaving. My puppy's likely pacing by now."

James's mouth tugged wryly. "So you've a dog now? Feeling lonely, Doctor?"

Felix let out a small smile, nothing more. "Would you mind telling him I've gone? Just wish him good night for me."

James gave a butler's nod—half an answer, half an evasion. Then: "You're soaked, sir. Allow me to fetch a carriage. You'll reach your puppy faster that way."

Felix inclined his head. "Thank you."

He waited, water pooling beneath his soles. The Pearlers' home stood around him—quietly grand, every detail deliberate.

He'd known of them for years, by reputation and by brief professional encounters. Wealth had not hardened them. They were spoken of kindly, even by those with little.

Maisie would have liked them and trusted them.

If life had bent another way, he might have brought her here—stepped into a dining room like this with her hand looped in his arm. The thought landed sharp, too sharp, and he brushed it aside like rain off his sleeve. Yet some of it clung, soaked through.

He was steadying himself when Raphi came striding down the corridor.

"Forgive me," Raphi said, clapping his shoulder. "That took longer than I meant. They've guests. I left as soon as I could."

Felix gave a dry half-smile. "I told you—it wasn't for me to intrude."

Raphi tilted his head, eyes alight with curiosity. "An odd lady, their guest. Lady Eleanor Spencer. Sister of the old Marquess of Stonefield. The one who vanished on the Continent."

Felix blinked—*the boy. The marquess is only a child.* But confidentiality bound him. "I've heard the name," he said evenly.

"She looks younger than her reputation suggests," Raphi went on. "Much younger. Something about her struck me as… unusual."

Before Felix could answer, James returned, holding a black umbrella with measured dignity. "The Pearlers' phaeton and driver can see you home, Doctor. The landau is engaged with other guests."

Raphi accepted the umbrella with a nod of thanks, the offer closing the moment.

But Felix was still caught by Raphi's words. "What do you mean—odd?"

Raphi shrugged into his coat. "She didn't seem like an aristocratic spinster. She could be one of us."

Felix turned sharply. "One of us? What are you saying?"

"She's young. Pretty. But… warm. Too young for the history

they've given her. There's a vulnerability in her face, a softness. She reminded me of Rachel. Or even Laila."

Felix almost laughed, though it came rough in his throat. "You think an aristocrat could resemble your wife or your sister-in-law?"

Raphi gave him a level look. "You know what I mean. She didn't seem… removed. She felt like someone who could belong at a table with us. Like family."

Felix shook his head as the butler held the door for them. He stepped into the damp air, letting the rain spatter against his face before slipping under the umbrella.

Like family? No. That couldn't be. Aristocratic women were shaped by distance—by closed doors, by cool glances across polished drawing rooms. Not by Shabbat tables. Not by song and easy laughter.

And yet exceptions existed. He'd known them. And that's what unsettled him.

Warmth in her gaze. From Oxfordshire. Lady Spencer.

The one from the bookshop?

Rain blurred his lashes. He blinked hard.

Impossible.

And yet—the ache in his chest stirred. The same ache that never truly left. The one that whispered: *what if?*

He said nothing more. But the questions clung to him, heavier than the rain sliding down his coat.

MAISIE'S TEMPLES THROBBED, each beat sharp, hammering against her skull.

The drawing room pressed in on her—too warm, too full. Laughter drifted down the corridor, ribbons of sound that tangled and thickened until they cloyed in the air. Silver gleamed, skirts rustled over polished floors, and the scent of roast duck wound itself with peonies. An elegant tableau. It should have soothed.

Instead, it smothered.

She slipped closer to the French doors, her fingers biting into the delicate clasp of her reticule. Beyond the glass, the garden glowed, gilded by lantern light. Beauty. Safety. She should have drawn comfort from it. She should have smiled.

But her chest refused. Her lungs caught on the air.

A breath snagged, slight, invisible to anyone else—but her body knew. A warning, sharp and sure, before her mind would admit it.

Where was Deena?

The voices around her blurred, every word oddly rehearsed, brittle as porcelain. As if she'd wandered into a play where the script itself hummed with menace.

Her eyes darted to the front door. The one that led to the street.

Out. She had to get out.

"Deena?" Her voice carried a low, too-taut tone. "Are you ready to depart?"

Her shoulders ached with tension. She turned back, caught her reflection in a polished wall sconce. Her cheeks were drained of color, her lashes trembling like she was waiting—

Waiting for something.

Or someone.

Foolishness.

She was safe here. Rachel's house. The Pearlers' warmth. Safety. Yet still, her breath came shallow, her chest tightening with every tick of the clock.

And then—a sound. Deena's giggle, bright and careless, spilled down the hall. Relief and irritation tangled in Maisie's throat.

Deena came toward her, radiant in blue satin, arms full of cards and wrapped sweets. "Oh, hullo," she called, cheerfully. "You wouldn't believe the pantry in this place—it's twice the size of ours."

Maisie didn't return the smile. She reached for her sister's hand, her grip firm. "Let's go."

Deena blinked, startled. "What? Now?"

Rachel appeared from the corner, a wineglass in hand, her expression warm but puzzled. "Oh no, my dear, are you quite certain you won't stay for supper?"

Maisie shook her head. "No. I—" Her fan slipped in her damp palm, fingers slick. A chill traced her spine, cold against the heat at her temples. "I need air."

Rachel moved closer, concern softening her brow. "You look flushed. Shall I fetch you a cordial? Or some tea?"

"No," Maisie whispered. "Thank you, but no. Only… my nerves."

She tried to smile. It wavered and fell short.

Rachel's nod was gentle, her hand making a small parting gesture. "Then at least let me send a footman and an umbrella to see you to the carriage. It's raining again."

But Maisie barely heard. She'd already turned.

The foyer stretched before her—polished parquet beneath the chandelier, crown molding carved in elegant swirls. She noticed everything and nothing at once: the faint clatter of cutlery somewhere distant, a clock marking time overhead, the shift of stillness near the double doors.

Three men stood there.

She recognized the Pearlers' butler at once, tall, his sideburns neat, one gloved hand resting lightly against the frame.

The others—

Maisie's fingers slipped. Her reticule struck the floor with a sharp, echoing crack.

The sound swallowed every other.

One of the men turned.

It couldn't be.

But it was.

His coat was dark, rain-slicked, the collar turned up. His boots left wet prints on the marble. And beneath the brim of his hat— shadow caught the line of his cheek, the cut of his mouth.

The world tilted. She couldn't breathe.

He straightened. His eyes found hers.

Those eyes.

Storm-dark. Beloved. Too known to mistake.

Her lips parted, no sound escaping. He didn't look away. Held her gaze for a breath. Then another.

Maisie moved forward, slow, unsteady, her pulse pounding.

And then—he spoke.

Her name. Soft. As though it had been locked in his chest for months. "Maisie."

Her knees threatened to give way.

From somewhere behind came Deena's voice, light, inconsequential, a thread of ordinary sound. Around them, the house stirred—glass, footsteps, conversation—but all of it blurred.

There was only this moment.

Her breath caught, but not from nerves.

It was him.

Alive.

Here.

Her lips trembled.

My Faivish.

Chapter Twenty-Six

FELIX'S PULSE ECHOED in his ears as loud as a cannon, but he couldn't move. Couldn't breathe. Not when she stood in front of him, silent, rigid. Every instinct screamed that if he reached for her, she might vanish like smoke.

Maisie. Here.

Her name beat against his ribs like a furious drum. She hadn't aged—no, that wasn't it. She had changed, ripened. The sharp-boned beauty he remembered had given way to something softer, richer. More dangerous to his heart. Her eyes—those impossible, whisky-dark eyes—met his at last.

Still, she said nothing.

The butler hovered. The footman offered her his arm. The rain drummed like a thousand hoofbeats behind him, but inside the house, everything fell into a still, aching hush.

"Lady Spencer," the footman repeated.

Felix flinched. That name again.

His throat worked. "Maisie," he said, low, not quite trusting himself. The sound scraped out of him, raw. "It's… you."

Her lips parted.

He waited another moment. Two. The silence carved him open.

Raphi's voice rose behind him, a hesitant murmur trying to stitch the moment back together. "Yes, Lady Spencer. Of course.

She's the aunt of the Marquess of Stonefield."

No. That wasn't right.

His fists curled at his sides from the punishing restraint it took not to reach for her. Not to touch her. To demand: Where have you been?

How could she have allowed so much time to pass?

"Maisie?" was all that came out. He wanted to say more— *Why didn't you write? Why are you pretending you don't know me?* But the words clogged in his throat. "My Maisie!"

James stepped forward, ever dutiful. "Lady Spencer, the landau is ready."

And still, she said nothing.

The click of Mrs. Rachel Pearler's heels sounded down the corridor. "What is the matter?"

Felix couldn't speak. His ears rang with her silence.

Maisie—Lady Spencer—just ogled him as if he were a stranger. As if he hadn't once touched her hair with reverence, hadn't kissed the hollow of her throat like it held his every hope.

What could it mean, this name she wore like armor?

Please, no. It couldn't be what Alfie had wondered. Or Raphi. Or every awful thought he'd tried to shove down. Had she found someone else?

He'd been hers. Hadn't she once been his?

"I…" He swallowed. "You don't recognize me?"

The butler shifted. The footman's arm hovered, forgotten.

Raphi made a sound—a soft, sorry breath.

But Maisie only blinked.

And then, finally, she said the words. "Faivish?"

Felix swayed. The ring of his true name in her mouth—half-prayer, half-wound—nearly dropped him to his knees.

She turned to the footman and took his arm.

And just like that—she was gone.

The silence she left in her wake was total.

He stared at the empty space she'd occupied, the place where his entire world had just stood. For a heartbeat, he could almost believe he had imagined her.

And then he turned, slowly, the way a man might walk away from a grave.

ONCE.

Twice.

The world tilted.

Two lives collided.

The moment the rain hit her face, Maisie thought she might collapse. Her skirts tangled around her ankles as she fled across the slick stones, heart hammering, the thundering rain swallowing her breath. The air was thick, syrupy, too dense to draw into her lungs.

I don't know how not to be Lady Spencer in front of those people—and his Maisie at the same time.

Her hands shook as she clutched the footman's arm—not with poise, but with the desperation of someone whose knees might give way at any moment. He guided her swiftly beneath the tilted umbrella, but every step dragged her further from *him*.

She didn't look back.

She didn't dare.

If she saw his face again, she would never leave.

The title echoed in her skull: *Lady Spencer.*

Tonight it felt like a curse.

The landau door yawned open. She nearly stumbled on the hem of her wet skirts as she climbed in, breath coming too fast. The door shut with a sharp clap that reverberated in the silence, sealing her away.

Alone, Maisie bent forward, pressing her hands to her mouth. A sob wrenched free before she could stop it. Hot tears streaked down her cheeks, burning against the cold.

It was him.

All the years she had told herself she had done the right thing, that Faivish had long since forgotten her, collapsed in a single instant. He had stood there, drenched and stricken, as if her absence had carved hollows into him too.

She had pretended not to know him—because if she had spoken, if she had acknowledged him in front of all those people, her world would have shattered. She would have fallen at his feet.

Maisie had built her life out of silence. Out of obedience. Out of the armor of *Lady Spencer*.

But her heart had never changed course.

The carriage jolted as the driver mounted the box. Rain lashed at the windows. Maisie wiped her cheeks with the back of her hand, like a child, though the tears kept coming.

She did not know how to live as Lady Spencer while still belonging to the man who had once kissed her into believing in forever. And she did not know—would never know—whether he could forgive her for vanishing into another name, another life.

Her fingers dug into the velvet seat, clutching at it as though it were the only thing keeping her upright.

FELIX COULDN'T MOVE fast enough.

There was no protocol for this. No medical training or apprenticeship could have prepared him. No way to steady his hands or slow his pulse when everything inside him screamed she was slipping away—and this time, forever.

"Doctor Leafley?" someone called.

His head snapped up.

It was the girl from the practice—the tall one with wary eyes and careful hands. She stood in the entryway now, dripping wet beneath a dark cloak. Her voice trembled slightly, but something in the timbre—the very notes she'd hummed at the practice—hit him like a strike to the chest.

Tumbalalaika. That was the tune! He'd heard her humming it while tending the little marquess.

His heart seized. He cocked his head.

No—surely not.

But—

His throat constricted. "Deena Morgenschein?" he rasped.

The hallway froze.

The girl smiled brightly. Rachel Pearler stiffened. Raphi's brows shot up.

Fave turned, confused. "What did you say?"

But it was the girl's face that betrayed her. Her eyes widened. She gasped—and her hands flew to her mouth. "I didn't recognize you!"

Felix's breath caught. *Neither did I.* She was so grown compared to the child Maisie had once dragged through Vienna's streets.

No time to think, but no time to lose.

He turned on his heel.

The door still gaped open—the butler hadn't yet closed it. Outside, the world gleamed slick and gold beneath the gaslamps, rain falling like a thousand pins on stone.

He looked toward the carriage where Maisie had fled. The driver had just opened the landau's door.

And she was inside.

Lady Spencer.

No.

My Maisie.

"Maisie!" Felix shouted, his voice breaking as he ran.

His boots skidded across wet cobblestones, slick leaves clinging to the soles. He caught himself on a pillar, pushed off again, heart pounding like a drumbeat that belonged to another life— their life.

Voices rose behind him, a ripple of speculation and awe.

"Is it her?"

"They've found each other?"

"She was here all this time?"

Hushed, reverent. As though speaking too loudly might shatter the miracle unfolding before them.

But to Felix, they were echoes. Indistinct. Meaningless.

Only her.

He sprinted toward the carriage. Every instinct, every cell of him knew where he belonged—with her.

The landau gleamed in the dark, rain sliding down its windows like tears. The driver turned, startled, but Felix didn't slow.

He tore the door open.

And there she was.

Not composed like in the hall. Not a stranger standing stiffly.

She was curled slightly into herself, her cloak damp, curls loose around her cheeks, tears carving tracks down her face.

His breath caught.

"Maisie," he whispered, softer now—a broken benediction. He could say nothing else.

He loved the ring of her name—especially now, with her looking at him through tears, with those warm, whisky-dark eyes.

She gasped. Her lips trembled.

She's crying. She remembers me.

And he climbed in—without invitation, without pause—and slammed the door shut behind him, sealing them together.

For one long heartbeat, there was only their breathing—loud, ragged. The steady drum of rain. The fragile space between them.

And then Felix reached for her hand. Because how could he not?

"FAIVISH." HER VOICE faltered the instant it left her lips.

His name was a lifeline and a wound, tangled in memory and longing. She said it because she always had. Because she'd always reached straight for him.

Tears fell freely—hot, aching, unstoppable—as if her body had waited years for permission. The cabin was dim, rain streaking silver across the glass, but all she saw was him.

He didn't sit across from her. No, he was kneeling at an angle—on the wet, wooden floor of the landau. His movements were unsteady but sure, like a man whose soul had already chosen. One hand hovered between them, hesitant, but with the other, he cupped her cheek with exquisite gentleness.

He kissed her cold hand. "Maisie," he rasped.

The pain in his voice tore through her. A hush bloomed inside her. She didn't dare look at him—because if she did, everything she'd held together might shatter.

She couldn't find him, so she built her life protecting people like Deena and the boy, ultimately burying her own identity. But this wasn't how she imagined their reunion. Not in a carriage. Not with half the Pearlers watching. Not trembling, unspeakably fragile.

But Faivish was here. Flesh and breath and water—staring at her as if she had never stopped belonging to him.

"Are you still my Maisie?" he asked.

The words struck like lightning—raw, desperate, stripped to the bone.

She blinked. "What?"

"Lady Spencer?" he forced out, his jaw tight. "Did you… marry?" His eyes, rimmed red from rain and something deeper, searched hers.

She couldn't breathe under the scrutiny of that gaze. "No one is supposed to know who I am," she whispered, her voice breaking. "It's too dangerous. For Deena, too. And I'm responsible for the boy."

"The Marquess of Stonefield?" His posture shifted, rigid. His hands dropped. He jerked back. "Your responsibility. Your stepson?" He swallowed hard.

Maisie stared, baffled by his recoil. A question she hadn't anticipated shadowed his face.

"Faivish—" she reached for him, but he caught her wrist.

His lips brushed her hand as he breathed and pressed her

fingers to his cheek, "Say my name again. I've lived in silence long enough."

She did. Soft, pleading. "Faivish."

It broke something open in him. He pushed himself upright, the lantern light catching on soaked wool clinging to the strength of his chest and arms.

Maisie's gaze clung to him. She'd waited five years for this moment and dreamed of it. Imagined it.

He kissed her hand again, lingering—like a man drawing the last drop of water before crossing the burning desert.

"I've been searching for you for so long," she whispered. She didn't even know in what language—Yiddish, German, English— it didn't matter. It came from her heart.

His eyes closed. "And I for you. Every day. In every face."

For a breath, the past dissolved. It was just them.

Then—a knock.

The door opened. Rain and light rushed in, and there stood Deena, cloak drawn tight. Her eyes flicked between them, widening with dawning understanding.

She studied him—the student she once knew, transformed into this man. The West-End cut broad across his shoulders. Hair swept back, darker. A shadow of beard. Hands bearing both fine nicks and the steadiness of a surgeon.

"Faivish Blattner," she said at last, wonder breaking into a smile. "You've changed!"

"And you've grown," he answered softly, his eyes catching hers before flicking back to Maisie.

Behind Deena, Maisie saw the open doorway: Rachel, Raphi, Fave, even James the butler—standing in the rain. Watching. Waiting.

"Go with him," Deena said, her voice low and sure. "I'll stay here with Rachel. You have much to talk about."

Maisie glanced past her. Rachel nodded—slow, warm—the kind of gesture that gave all permission.

And just like that, the door closed again.

The hush returned. Then the wheels moved. The carriage rocked gently forward.

They were alone. Wet and wounded. But together. And at last, nothing stood between their words.

EVERYTHING ELSE FELL away—the rain, the carriage, the years of silence.

Maisie could scarcely breathe. His coat dripped onto the velvet floor, but he didn't seem to notice. He held her gaze as if she might dissolve if he blinked.

"Faivish," she whispered, trembling. Saying his name felt like daring herself to exist again. His eyes burned with the same intensity she remembered—but deeper now, layered with hope and pain. "I thought I'd imagined you," she said in a rush. "I thought I'd gone mad. But you're here. You're real."

"Of course I am." His voice was raw, scraped across stone. "You vanished. I searched everywhere—Vienna, Graz. And everywhere from there to here. There wasn't a trace. Not of Maisie Morgenschein. Not of your father. Not even Deena."

Her mouth trembled. "Because I couldn't be her anymore. I had to disappear. I became someone else."

His next question cut her like a blade. "When did you get married?" The word sounded strangled, bitter.

Maisie's disbelief cracked high, almost childish. "No—never." Her hands rose to his face, sure and instinctive, her touch the homecoming she'd starved for. "The Marquess gave us false papers. We lived in his late sister's name to keep John, his heir, safe. It was survival. Only that. Never betrayal."

"All these years..." His voice broke. "I thought maybe you didn't want me to find you."

She shook her head fiercely. "You. Always you. But the children, the inheritance, the danger—it was bigger than us. If anyone had known…" Her voice faltered. "I built a life without you only so I wouldn't shatter, missing your kiss. But I never married. I never stopped being yours."

Something in him seemed to shift. He leaned in, closing the last fragile distance.

The first kiss came clumsily, too fast—noses bumping, hands fumbling. But she smiled into it, and it steadied, deepened, became true.

And as Maisie melted against him, the storm inside her went still. Her fists curled into his coat, not to cling, but because letting go had never been so easy. She breathed him in—wet wool, cloves, the scent that had always meant safety.

His arms wrapped around her, firm and steady. For the first time in five years, she stopped guarding her heart. She wasn't Lady Spencer or the bearer of burdens. She was simply Maisie. And she was home.

"I've always loved only you," she whispered against his lips. "I promised myself I would never give that vow to anyone else."

His eyes widened. "We were never—"

"We were," she cut in, steady now. "We never stopped honoring that night, did we?"

His throat worked. "Never."

Tears blurred her vision. "I wrote to you but couldn't send them," she admitted, voice cracking. "I didn't know where. I didn't even know if you were alive. So I told myself it would hurt less without goodbye. But it didn't."

He brushed a damp curl from her temple. His hand lingered. "No," he whispered. "It didn't."

They stayed like that, foreheads nearly touching, the world hushed but for the creak of wheels and the tap of rain.

The second kiss was different. The first had been desperation. This one was reverent. Careful. A memory made real again.

His lips touched hers like a question.

She answered with a sigh, tilting her head, her hand sliding to the back of his neck. His damp curls clung to her fingers. She leaned closer.

The kiss deepened. Breath tangled. Heat bloomed. He tasted like rain and longing.

And peace.

When at last they broke apart, Maisie rested her forehead against his. "I thought I'd forgotten what it felt like," she whispered. "But I never did."

His gaze was steady, searching her face. "Neither did I."

The carriage rocked gently.

"You've changed," he said, wonder in his voice.

"So have you." She brushed his cheek. "Older. Stronger. Still mine."

Maisie looked down at their hands, now twined together. Her glove was damp from his touch, her fingers still trembling.

"I was so afraid," she said, loathing the admission, "that if I let myself dream of you, it would break me."

He kissed her knuckles. "Then let's stop dreaming."

Finally, Maisie believed she could wake—and still be whole.

FELIX WAS BREATHLESS and unsteady, yet unshakably certain. He held her when she leaned into him, her touch never faltering. Her hands—slender, steady, familiar—rested against his cheeks like they had always belonged there. Felix couldn't move. Didn't dare. He watched her lashes flutter, the damp curve of her mouth, the rise and fall of her chest with every ragged breath. She was real, here, and still his.

The years had been too long, the loss too sharp. But now, in this gently swaying carriage, she sat before him—alive, fierce, more heartbreakingly beautiful than memory had ever allowed.

"I thought I would never see you again," he said, quieter than he meant, voice hoarse.

Maisie's eyes lifted to his. "I used to whisper your name into my pillow at night."

He closed his eyes. The image—her, far away, whispering his name into darkness—nearly broke him. "Maisie, I feared you were dead."

"I could have been if the Marquess hadn't saved us from the *Burschenschaft* mob," she said. "But Deena and I got out. Papa… he didn't."

Felix reached for her hand. She let him take it. "I wish I had been there for you," he murmured.

"You were doing as he asked, weren't you? You went to India for your profession, for the skills you promised to build. And I—" her voice caught and steadied again. "I did what I had to do. For Deena. For the boy."

"And I came back for you, but you weren't anywhere to be found." He searched her face. "What about the little Marquess now?"

She nodded, slowly. "He has no one else. No mother, no real relatives. If anyone cast doubt on my guardianship of his estate… he could lose everything. His fortune. His future."

Felix's jaw tightened. "You carried all that alone?"

"I had no choice. If anyone discovered the truth about me—about who I really am—it would be dangerous for all of us. A Jewish, unmarried woman raising a marquess? They'd call me a deceiver. They'd say I'd stolen an inheritance. They could take him away in a heartbeat."

He was quiet for a beat, then said, "But you're not alone anymore."

Maisie blinked against fresh tears. "I've tried to be strong, but I'm so tired, Faivish. There's always the fear someone will come and take it all away."

"Then let them come," he said. His voice steadied, like an oath. "I'll be standing beside you when they do."

She laughed—low, incredulous—and then kissed him.

No hesitation.

She leaned into him with all the trust and need she'd hoarded for years, and her mouth found his like it had always known the way. He kissed her back, steady and sure, his hands rising to cradle her face.

When she pulled away, her voice was barely a whisper. "Tell me we're not dreaming."

He rested his forehead against hers. "If we are, I don't want to wake."

She smiled—and it was the most fragile, radiant thing he had ever seen.

"Will you come with me?" he asked suddenly.

Her brow creased. "Where?"

"Anywhere. Back to the practice. To the coast. To the end of the world if need be."

Her breath tangled somewhere between heart and mouth. "I can't leave Deena and the boy."

"I'm not asking you to."

She held his gaze. "You'd take us all?"

"I've never wanted less than everything with you. If that means everyone," he shrugged, "why not?"

The carriage slowed. The world waited outside. But neither of them moved.

And when he kissed her again, it wasn't desperation.

It was certain.

The wheels groaned, the carriage moved forward, and to her astonishment, Maisie wasn't running. She was exactly where she belonged—in Faivish's arms, with the entire world waiting outside.

✦

Chapter Twenty-Seven

MAISIE FELT IT before she could name it. A warmth unfurling under her skin, slow as morning light creeping through shutters after a night too long. Felix's mouth moved against hers—steady, tender—less a kiss than a vow whispered in touch. Her hand found his shoulder, fingers clenching in the damp wool of his coat. He steadied her, solid, unyielding. Somehow, she exhaled and her lungs let go of the fear.

He drew back only enough to see her. His voice scraped low. "I'm not afraid anymore. With you, I can be Faivish Blattner or Felix Leafley and still face whatever hunts me."

Her lips pulled into a shaky smile. "Nor am I. But I must be what John needs."

The carriage swayed, rain smearing the glass. Inside, there was only heat, breath, the thud of his heart close to hers. He was kneeling still, hair plastered in damp curls, collar skewed, jaw roughened. She had never loved him more because he was here. Now.

Her fingers tugged carefully at the top button of his coat.

"You're drenched," she murmured. "You'll fall ill."

His mouth tilted. "Scolding me again, Fräulein Morgenschein?"

Her laugh slipped out, soft, frayed at the edges. His joined it. The sound curled between them.

She pulled at his lapel. "Come sit."

He groaned as he rose, knees stiff from the floor, and sank beside her. Their legs touched. She did not move.

The silence stretched—fragile, humming.

"I've changed," she said at last, her voice a hush. "I've seen cruelties I couldn't have dreamed of."

"So have I." He caught her hand, rough warmth closing over her fingers. "But the part that loved you then never left."

Her throat tightened. "Have you ever—" She faltered. "Other women?"

His head snapped toward her. "No." The word fierce, raw. "Never."

Her chest shook. "I used to think that if I saw you again, I would fall apart."

The thought broke something open. She kissed him again, hard, almost desperate. Her hands in his wet curls.

He gathered her in, arms locked firm around her waist, his mouth tracing her temple, cheek, the hollow below her ear where her pulse stumbled fast.

"You're trembling," he whispered, rubbing her arms.

Her breath came unsteady. "Not from cold."

The heat rose—sharp, reverent. Earned. She lifted her gaze. "If we do this…"

His eyes didn't waver. "Then no lies. No shadows. Only us."

Her heart hammered. "I want you."

"You have me. Always."

Their mouths met again, slower, searching. His hands curved at her waist. She leaned closer, relearning the shape of him in touch, in breath.

When the carriage lurched to a stop, neither moved.

His arms stayed wrapped around her. Her head rested against the warm bend of his shoulder, their legs intertwined. She allowed herself to believe in safety.

Outside, the rain had gentled, no more than a hush against the glass. Inside, their breath lingered in the space between them.

She tilted her head. His eyes were closed, though he wasn't sleeping. His thumb moved in slow circles against her back, absent, steady.

"I thought I'd forgotten what it felt like," she whispered.

His eyes opened. "What?"

"To be wanted. Not as a benefactress. Not as someone's aunt. Just… myself."

He bent, kissed her forehead, let his lips rest there a moment. "You are the only woman I've ever wanted. Then. Now. Always."

Her throat tightened, tears threatening, but she forced them down. "I was afraid you'd see how much I've changed."

"I do see," he said quietly. "Every wound. Every strength. And I love you more for them—if you'll let me."

Her chest cracked open. It was enough. More than enough.

They stayed like that, not in silence so much as a stillness that held them both. She traced idle lines across his chest, feeling the heat beneath his damp coat.

At last, the outside world pressed in. The carriage had come to a stop before a tall townhouse, gaslamps throwing their glow across the wet stones. The horses stamped, shook their manes, impatient.

Felix stirred, blinking toward the window. "Where are we?"

Maisie reached for her gloves. "The Marquess' townhouse." She unlatched the door just as the driver came down. "Come inside," she said.

But Felix hesitated, cleared his throat. "I… haven't told you about Lilly."

Maisie froze. Her breath caught. "Lilly?" she repeated, voice a little too bright.

He nodded, solemn. "I need to make sure she's well at home."

Home. With Lilly.

A low sound escaped her, half growl, before she could stop it.

She folded her arms, her tone clipped. "I want to meet Lilly. Now."

Felix blinked, startled, then leaned out into the rain. "To 87 Harley Street, driver!"

$$\diamond$$

Chapter Twenty-Eight

FELIX HELPED MAISIE down from the landau, their hands still joined. Neither seemed ready to let go, as if the air between their palms might fracture if broken too soon.

"You'll like it," he said, nodding toward the narrow townhouse. "Treatment rooms in the back, waiting room in front. Just me here now—except Lilly."

Maisie's mouth curved, though her eyes thinned. "Lilly."

He gave a quiet laugh. "She's just learned how to howl. Come on."

Before she could press further, he turned the key. The door swung open, filling the air with the scent of antiseptic and beeswax, sharp and clean. From somewhere inside came a faint whimper.

And then—

Crash!

A door slammed upstairs. Heavy boots pounded down.

Felix spun. "Alfie?"

Maisie froze where she stood.

A man appeared, papers clutched in one hand, a golden puppy trembling in the other. Not Alfie. Not anyone she knew.

Felix went taut, the change in him instant. "Who let you in?"

The intruder smiled, thin and deliberate. His accent curled around the words. "That's who let *you* in, milord?"

The notorious Baron Wolfgang von List? Dangerous.

Felix's body angled, a barrier without touching her. Maisie felt the shield of him, though her arm remained free at her side.

List's gaze skimmed the room, noting details, storing them, before catching on her. A flicker. The barest pause. Then his mouth curved with a mockery that cut. "Well. You've been busy."

Felix stepped forward. "What are you doing here?"

List didn't answer. He crouched and set the puppy down. Lilly yipped once and tore across the floor straight into Felix's arms. List stayed where he was, eyes on the papers he carried—one page in particular.

Maisie Morgenschein.

Felix snatched it before he could blink. "Put that down."

List's gaze slid back to Maisie. Longer this time. Searching. "Who is she?"

Maisie's spine straightened. She walked to a chair, sat, calm as if she'd done this before. "Doctor?" Her voice carried clearly, steady. "Are you ready for me? I don't have much time."

Felix's heart lurched. A mix of fear. And awe. Her mask slipped on without a seam.

List's smirk twitched, faltered. "Doctor," he repeated, his distaste curling sharp. He let the rest of the papers spill from his hand. Turned toward the door. "You protect this woman from Vienna. I'll find out why."

Felix's voice struck hard, edged like steel. "Get out."

The door shut with a slam. The bolt shot home, its echo ricocheting through the hall—less a sound than a warning fired.

Maisie hadn't moved. Not until Lilly nosed her way into her lap, warm fur pressing against her skirts. Maisie bent her head, whispering, "So you're Lilly." Her fingers clung to the pup as though touch itself could steady her.

Felix dropped to one knee beside her, eyes fixed on the door. "That man—Baron Wolfgang von List. Prussian. A hound for the Kaiser. Suspicion alone is enough for him to ruin a man."

Maisie tightened her hold around Lilly's trembling body. "If he knows who I am—if he questions John's guardianship—John could lose everything."

Felix's tone turned grimmer still. "And your protection. He stole my papers, my search for your name. He'll use it against you."

Maisie drew herself upright, voice steady though her hands shook. "Then let him believe the story. I'm your patient. Nothing else."

Felix shook his head sharply. "Maisie—no. I've only just found you."

"You're not shielding me," she said quietly. "You're shielding the boy. And I will too."

His jaw clenched, muscle taut beneath the skin, rage banked but burning. "Then every record of you here, every trace—gone."

She reached for his hand, fingers light on his. "That won't be enough. If they uncover the truth, they'll strip John's name away simply to blot me out."

The silence closed in, heavy as stone.

At last, Felix broke it. His vow cut through like a blade. "Whatever mask we wear, I'll protect you. But I will never pretend I don't love you."

Lilly sneezed—tiny, indignant, the sound startling in the thick hush.

Maisie looked up, met Felix's eyes across the small weight in her arms. "Then we fight," she said. "Quietly. Together."

⟫⟪

"THAT'S NOT RIGHT," Felix said, his voice low, roughened. "I can't even take you home. Not without painting a target on you."

Maisie didn't answer.

He stepped toward her, then stilled, as though closing the last inch between them might undo everything. "If anyone sees us—

really sees us—they'll know you're not his aunt. They'll ask questions. About you. About us."

Still, silence.

Felix looked at her. *The woman who once counted his pulse after kissing him breathless. The girl who lived within earshot of Vienna's white horses yet never dared to climb astride one.*

"I just found you," he said, quieter now, ragged around the edges. "And already I'm told to pretend I haven't. What kind of freedom is that?"

Maisie crossed the room—three quick steps—and caught his hand. Her grip was firm, familiar, too much and not enough.

"We can't be seen," she whispered. "Not yet. If List even suspects the truth about John, he'll tear it all down. The marquisate, the boy's future—it'll vanish overnight."

The name *List* burned through Felix's chest. Always prowling and circling. He felt the old instinct rise: fight, shield, strike first. Not this time. Not with her in reach. He would take the blow himself before letting it fall on Maisie or John.

"But I want to be with you," he said, raw.

"And I want you." Her voice dropped, trembling but sure. "Every second. In daylight, not in shadows. But not if it costs the boy."

His throat tightened. "I thought you were mine."

Maisie's eyes shone. She leaned close enough that he felt her breath. "Then prove it. Protect me *like* I'm yours. Hide me because I matter."

His jaw locked. "So that's what we are now? First lost… now hidden?"

Her smile was small, aching. "No. We're a promise."

He drew her closer—slow, deliberate—his lips brushing the crown of her head as if sealing a vow.

"Then I promise this," he murmured against her hair. "When the boy is safe—when no one can twist our love into a weapon—I won't just take you home. I'll walk beside you in daylight. Every day. For the rest of my life."

Her face pressed against his chest, hidden in the damp wool. Her arms cinched tighter, as though she could anchor herself in the rhythm of his breath. "Until then," she whispered, steady but aching, "we endure the shadows."

After Felix kissed her one last time, he opened the door and she left Maisie behind but became Lady Spencer as soon as she crossed the threshold. The coach had been waiting, and Maisie got in. Felix raised his hand in a signal, and the door creaked open to the lamplight.

She gathered herself, shoulders straightening, her expression calm as porcelain. One careful step, then another—down into the gaslit street with the grace of a woman who belonged everywhere.

But Felix knew. Knew how her fingers had clutched, how her voice had trembled when only he could hear. They were already acting a part. Pretending strength neither of them felt.

And somewhere out there—in the dark beyond the circle of lamplight—List was listening. Lurking and waiting for their missteps.

Chapter Twenty-Nine

I T WAS SPLASHED across the morning papers before the sheets had cooled from the press.

Baron Wolfgang von List of Königsberg, Prussia, has lodged a petition before the Lords Commissioners in Chancery, disputing the legitimacy of John Spencer, Marquess of Stonefield.

The article dripped with venom:

Serious doubts surround the boy's guardianship. His household, it claims, is directed by a woman of questionable repute, possibly masquerading under the name Lady Spencer. If such charges prove true, neither his fortune nor his future can remain safely in her hands.

Thus, the issue was set. The Peerage Committee would hold a public hearing at Chancery to decide whether John's guardianship would stand or whether scandal, sharper than law, would strip it away.

For Maisie, the words cut deeper than any blade. It was not her name she feared losing, but the boy's very future. She had promised his father he would never be left alone. And she knew, with the same certainty she knew her own breath, what it would mean if John fell into List's hands.

Rachel Pearler laid the paper flat, her rings catching the lamp-light. "It's confirmed. The committee meets tomorrow. Chancery rules. Lord Kettering presides."

Maisie's hand stilled on the arm of her chair. "Then it has begun."

"You mustn't go," Rachel said at once. "They won't hear a woman. They won't even see you. To speak would only draw fire onto yourself—and onto John."

Maisie's throat closed. "So I am to stand aside while List twists John's inheritance into scandal?"

Rachel's gaze softened. "Someone with standing must answer. A gentile man with a title—or a witness they cannot dismiss."

"Felix cannot speak," Maisie whispered. "He's a Jew. They'll use it to ruin him—and pull every other doctor on Harley Street down with him."

Rachel did not deny it.

From the hearth, Deena's voice carried, steady despite her youth. She stood, her hands clenched at her sides. "John isn't hiding. He's preparing to stand before lords as if he weren't thirteen—because he has a name and a title. And you—" her eyes brightened, "—you gave him that courage."

Maisie pressed her palm to her ribs, where the ache lived. "I thought I was protecting you. Protecting him. That if we stayed quiet long enough, the world would let us belong."

"And has it?" Deena asked—not cruel, only unflinching, the way a girl spoke when she had seen too much already.

Maisie's gaze dropped. Her fingers curled into the folds of her gown. "No. Silence only takes. It took Father. It nearly took Felix. And if I stay silent tomorrow, it may take John too."

Rachel crossed to her, resting a hand over hers. "Then let John speak. Even if you cannot enter that chamber, you will be present in every word he speaks."

Maisie turned to the window, rain streaking the glass. Out-side, the city went on with its gray indifference. Somewhere across town, Felix bent over his work, still mending what life had broken. And here she stood, with nothing but silence to offer.

She closed her eyes.

Ghosts might hide, but they did not raise boys.

"I didn't realize," Maisie murmured, "how long I've been vanishing into silence." She lifted her chin, the spark reigniting. "And I won't vanish again."

At 87 Harley Street…

ANOTHER DAY BLURRED past, and still he and Maisie had only stolen moments—quiet, half-lit meetings at the Pearlers' where the walls listened too closely.

The carriage hadn't moved in an hour.

From the surgery window at 87 Harley Street, Felix watched the blurred oval of its rear glass, the shadow of a man seated too still to be waiting on anyone. The harness sagged. The horse half-dozed. Only the watcher's attention lived—coiled, patient, trained.

Enough.

Felix set his quill aside and dragged both hands through his hair. He had lived too long shrinking himself for safety—head lowered, voice measured, always stepping aside for men who carried titles like blades. But this—being stared at like a specimen while the woman he loved hid two streets away—this he could not bear.

A knock. "Felix?"

Alfie slipped in, rain still glittering on his lashes, a folded sheet in his fist, darkened where it had soaked through.

"The summons?" Felix asked.

Alfie nodded, passing it over. "Committee of Privileges. Chancery. Nine tomorrow. List petitioned to 'examine the propriety of guardianship and trust administration.'" His mouth flattened. "Not the title—he can't reach that. But he means to shame the household and wrench authority from it."

"From her." The word landed in Felix's chest like a weight. "He stole my papers. He's put men outside the Pearlers' and outside here. He lurks in shadows and calls it justice."

"That's his tactic," Alfie said quietly. "He can't win clean, so he tries to win loud. If he paints Maisie a deceiver, he pushes the lords into overreach. If he paints you as dangerous, he chills your allies. He's after control."

Felix let the summons fall to the desk. "We are not criminals," he said, low, almost to himself. "And not children to be watched."

He turned back to the curtain. The watcher's head shifted, as if he could tell that he was watching him back.

Felix's pulse steadied. "I'm no longer a specimen."

"Felix—" Alfie began.

But Felix was already moving. Coat shrugged on, door flung open, he strode down the stairs. The hall smelled of carbolic. Rain-silvered air rushed his face as he pushed outside.

Across the street, the watcher stiffened.

Felix stepped off the curb, not fast, not slow—the gait of a man who belonged to his own street. Alfie kept pace at his shoulder, the summons tucked into his breast pocket like a shield.

At the carriage, Felix fixed the watcher's gaze through glass. "You've sat long enough," he said even as a diagnosis. "If you have business, speak it. If not, go."

The man flinched.

He had not expected to be met head-on. Not by a Jew who did not lower his eyes.

The latch clicked. The watcher looked down, then up again—measured him and Alfie—and chose retreat. He flicked the reins once. The carriage rolled into the mist.

Felix watched until the wheels vanished around the corner. Cowards always preferred corners. And shadows. They never came alone. They always came in packs just like the *Burschenschaft*.

Alfie exhaled sharply. "That's why they haunt the edges. They push where the law is thinnest, pick at the least defended, and call it order."

Felix's jaw locked. "Not today."

A figure moved at the far end of the street. Then another.

Raphi Klonimus, hat brim jeweled with rain, lifted a hand and came to Felix's right. From the other side, Nick Folsham appeared with Wendy on his arm, her nurse's cloak neat, her eyes flint. Andre crossed from the mews, black case swinging at his side.

"We saw you through the window," Wendy said. "What happened here?"

"I was just about to talk to you, but you're all outside?" Raphi added.

No one pretended it was a coincidence, but Felix just swallowed, and they understood him. As did he: They came because this was the moment. They took their places beside Felix and Alfie—a line across Harley Street, shoulder to shoulder, as if fear itself had been called to account.

Silence stretched. The city breathed around them—wheels hissing on wet stone, drizzle pattering down, a costermonger's cry carrying thin through the fog. In the glass panes along the terrace, their reflections stood: five men and one woman in her dark nurse's cloak, a line across Harley Street.

Alfie broke the quiet, voice edged but steady. "He'll never forgive me for poisoning him that night. Every shadow he sends is another reminder."

Wendy's chin lifted. "Then he hates me just as much. I'm betrothed to the prince whose gold he bleeds from Transylvania. He knows exactly what I stand for."

"From our own trade routes," Raphi said, voice low and grim. "He isn't only a parasite—he's a thief. Every coin he moves weakens the crown I serve. And he cannot stand that we Jews earned our place at court."

Nick gave a sharp laugh. "Despicable doesn't cover it. He's

tried to ruin me—and yet the patients who matter most to his schemes still walk through our practice door."

"They need us. They barely tolerate him." Felix looked across the street at the practice they'd built.

Andre folded his arms, broad shoulders dimming half the lamplight. "And the people he manipulates are the same ones who trust us. He hasn't broken through yet. He won't."

Felix looked from one face to the next, the ache in his chest shifting—less the solitude, more the gravity of belonging. He had walked this city for years with silence at his back.

Raphi's voice steadied the damp air. "Then tomorrow, we stand together."

The rain tapped harder against the cobbles, like an oath being sealed.

Felix drew breath as though for the first time all day. His voice came firm, unshaken.

"We do. For everything we've built despite people like him."

THE STREET HELD still for a heartbeat—just drizzle, lamplight, and the faint hiss of wheels turning far off. Then the sound grew clearer, a steady approach over wet stone.

Raphi pointed at his carriage right in front of 87 Harley Street. The Klonimus carriage. He tipped his chin toward it, rain dripping from the brim of his hat. "Come. We'll talk where walls keep our words, not glass."

Felix hesitated. "I won't drag your house into this fight."

Raphi's reply was quiet but immovable. "Felix, you've never had a fight that wasn't already ours."

Alfie clapped his shoulder, solid and brotherly. "And tomorrow," he added, "we'll stand the same way at Westminster. A line. Let List count us."

Felix thought of Maisie—how she had trembled in a carriage yet lifted her chin; how she had taught a boy to be brave by living it. He nodded. "Then we make a plan."

Together, they climbed into the Klonimus carriage.

And just a few minutes later, on Regent Street, the Klonimus workshop glowed with lamplight, every surface alive with the quiet ache of work. Metal rasped under the file, drawers slid with soft clicks, and the space smelled of oil and warm brass. On a velvet pad, diamonds gleamed—old mine cuts, each one holding light as if it were breath.

Chawa Klonimus stood behind the central bench, her scarf pinned neatly, her calm presence settling over the room like a hand on a restless child's shoulder. When Felix entered with Raphi and Alfie, her eyes found his. She looked at him the way a mother does when she already knows the end of the story, and only waits for her children to catch up.

"You have the summons," she said.

Alfie placed it in her hand without ceremony. She read once, then again—eyes narrowing not from fear but in cold assessment. "He dresses the same old malice in respectable words." She set the paper flat. "When a man like this aims at one of us, he aims at all of us."

The truth of it loosened something in Felix's chest. "I wanted to warn you," he said. "He's watching the Pearlers. He watched my door today. He stole my notes. If he cannot put the pieces together or find proof, he will invent it."

Chawa's mouth softened. "You think we did not see the watchers outside our shop?" She nodded toward Raphi. "He moved the boys through the alleys all morning. We've been in this city longer than the baron has dreamed of trespassing here."

Raphi slid open a drawer and lifted a narrow tray. Diamonds lay in rows—small as frost, one larger stone cut to catch and return light.

Felix blinked. "Raphi—what—"

"For your vow," Raphi said.

Felix shook his head, heat tightening his throat. "I didn't—We don't need—It feels too… modern."

Chawa smiled, a private warmth. "Finding the woman you have loved since you were a boy is not modern. It is ancient." She pushed the tray closer. "But giving her a circle of light—that is a promise the world can see."

Felix reached without meaning to, brushing the largest stone with his fingertip. It flared—steady, quiet, unshowy. It made him think of Maisie's laugh when she forgot to guard herself, of her hands cupping a child's face and making the whole world gentler by nothing more than looking.

"I can't ask her to bear more danger," he said.

Chawa tipped her head. "You are not asking her to bear it. You are telling her that you will carry it with her."

The door opened. Rain clung to the shoulders of a footman, and then Rachel Pearler stepped inside—with Maisie at her side, Deena close behind. Cloaks damp, cheeks bright from the chill. Wendy moved at once, drawing Deena to the hearth with a brisk kindness. Rachel joined Chawa at the bench as if she had always belonged there.

Felix couldn't speak.

Chawa leaned close to Maisie, pressing both of Maisie's cold hands between her own. "My dear, at last I meet you, darling." She hugged her gently. "Listen to me. When men like the baron try to frighten a house, they start with the woman who keeps its lamps lit." Her voice gentled. "But there are more hands for those lamps than he can imagine."

Maisie's eyes went to Felix. He saw the tremor she hid for Deena's sake, and beneath it, the steadiness that had carried her this far. She didn't glance first at the diamonds. She looked at him.

Raphi cleared his throat. "Tomorrow is not a court to strip a title. It is an inquiry to embarrass a household, perhaps to unseat a guardian. Maisie cannot be heard in the chamber. So we send what cannot be ignored: men with standing—and a boy who knows his own mind."

"John will speak," Rachel said. "He will say he trusts the woman who raised him, and fears the man who would tear him away. That truth cannot be dismissed."

Maisie crossed her arms. "And when the bravery shakes after, we'll be near enough to steady him."

Alfie looked across the table. "And you, Felix?"

Felix's gaze dropped to the tray Raphi had set between them. Diamonds gleamed in orderly rows, each one a shard of light caught and kept. His hand hovered, then he reached—hesitant, reverent—and touched the largest stone. It flared once, a quiet brilliance, steady as a heartbeat.

He looked up, not at the jewel, but at Maisie. The fear inside him was not of List. It was of asking her to believe that together could be safety, not another burden. His voice roughened. "I'm done hiding. But I won't decide for you."

Maisie stepped closer, the lamplight striking the damp ends of her curls, gilding them as though the light itself had chosen her. She looked down at his hand on the stone, then back at him. Her voice was steady, her eyes unflinching.

"Then decide with me. If they try to divide us tomorrow, let it be after we've chosen one another today."

The room stilled. Felix closed his hand around the stone as if sealing an oath, then kissed Maisie's hand. With Raphi's quiet nod, he took the simple setting from the tray. His fingers trembled—more from joy than nerves.

He lifted Maisie's hand, again cold and without gloves, fingers red from the chill. He slid the ring home, careful to make sure the diamond wouldn't fall out before it was set. It fit as if it had been waiting for her all along.

A sound broke from Deena, half laugh, half sob. Wendy clasped her shoulder. Alfie cleared his throat like a man blinking back grit. Raphi tilted his face toward the ceiling, muttering something about dust, though his sleeve brushed quickly across his eyes. Rachel only smiled, quiet and immovable as stone.

Maisie laughed softly, astonished, a tear slipping free. "Yes," she whispered, answering the question he hadn't managed to form.

And Felix, at last, let himself breathe.

$$\sim\!\!\diamond\!\!\sim$$

Chapter Thirty

AN HOUR LATER at the Pearlers', Maisie couldn't stop fiddling with the new ring on her finger. The diamond was already on her hand. Raphi had set it quickly in the band, his craftsman's touch sure and steady, and Rachel's carriage carried them back to the Pearlers in silence. Felix's palm had rested against hers the whole way. By the time they stepped down at the gate, men were already watching, their stillness too practiced to mistake. Maisie had felt the brunt of it—but this time, she did not hide her hand. There was no longer any point in denying the bond between Felix, the Klonimuses, and the Pearlers. List would strike. Let him. They were ready.

Maisie didn't leave the window after. From the upstairs front room she could see the narrow gate that opened onto the Pearlers' garden, ivy-framed and usually quiet. But today, a man leaned too long against the lamppost across the street. Earlier that day, it had been another—shorter, with his hat tugged low and a cigar that never quite burned down.

She had stopped believing in coincidence as soon as she'd noticed them. And for hers and Deena's safety, Rachel had asked them to stay. The household of the little marquess wasn't ready for an ambush by List's men. The Pearlers lived ready.

Behind her, Deena shifted on the settee. The girl's breathing stayed slow, and Maisie forced herself to turn. The shawl had slipped from her shoulders; Maisie tucked it back and smoothed a hand over her curls. Her sister hadn't asked for this upheaval. Neither had John. *Yet here we are*, she thought—*hiding behind lavender curtains while men with sharp shoes and sharper eyes wait for one of us to slip.*

She pressed a kiss to Deena's brow.

On the desk lay a letter, half-finished. Addressed to John at Eton. *Are you well? Have they asked questions? Are you safe?* She had not yet chosen how to close it. "Your aunt" felt like a lie. "Your Maisie" felt too much like a vow. And Eleanor… Eleanor was gone. *Perhaps I am no one now*, she thought—*just a shadow with a pen.*

A knock startled her.

She crossed quickly, heart tight. Rachel Pearler's voice came softly through the door. "It's Dr. Fernando and his fiancée. The princess."

Maisie opened. Rachel stood with a tray and a faint smile. "He claims it's a patient call. I say he's carrying a message from Faivish… ahem, Felix."

Maisie followed her into the parlor. Dr. Fernando rose at once—noble bearing, warm eyes—and bowed low. But it was the woman beside him who made Maisie falter.

Princess Theodora. Here, in Rachel Pearler's parlor. Accepting tea in her gloved hand, speaking gently with Fave Pearler, as though such visits were routine.

Maisie's mind reeled.

And yet—this was not the first. They had come in sequence, one after another, as if taking watch. Alfie with Lady Beatrice, leaving behind vials of oil for "the nerves, not the lungs." Nick Folsham and Lady Penelope with their shortbread and stories of Faivish searching for her, their laughter carefully ordinary. And now this—royalty at Rachel's table, her name spoken aloud by a princess.

Maisie's breath caught. "You're all… connected to him."

Dr. Fernando smiled, kissing her hand. "Felix has more

friends than enemies. To us, he is family." He glanced toward Deena. "Which, I understand, now includes you both."

The princess lifted her cup. "Felix never forgets a promise. Neither do we."

Rachel lingered a moment at the threshold, her look saying what words did not: *You are not alone here.*

Later, when the parade of guests had gone and the rain thickened against the glass, Maisie sat by the fire while Deena read nearby. She unfolded the letter again; the ink had blurred slightly at the edges. She added a single line: *I will never stop protecting you. No matter what happens next.*

She didn't sign it. Only folded it, pressed it once to her lips, and carried it to Rachel's study to ask a footman to deliver it discreetly. The air itself felt tighter now, as if the city held its breath.

And beneath it all, a question pulsed with each tick of the clock: *Where is Felix? Why has he sent everyone else—but not come himself?*

The next time Rachel passed through, Maisie stopped her. "There's a man outside. By the gate. He's been there since morning."

Rachel didn't flinch. "We'll send someone to check. Quietly."

Maisie held her gaze. "If he's out there, they've seen Felix. Or soon will."

Rachel only nodded. "Whatever comes, we'll be ready."

Maisie's throat tightened. "Thank you."

Outside, the rain fell harder. Inside, she stood before the fire, arms folded tight, her breath shallow but steady.

Come soon, she thought. *Please.*

◆

Chapter Thirty-One

THE HOUSE HAD gone quiet at last, but Faivish had sent her a message to meet her at midnight. Upstairs, doors clicked shut, and Deena's even breathing rose through the stillness. Maisie had no rest in her. When it was finally almost twelve, she slipped through the corridor and out into the courtyard—a place walled in by brick and ivy, shut from the street, locked from both sides. Safe, at least for this hour. A sanctuary at the Pearler's fortress.

The air was soft and damp. Ivy curled along the brick, peonies hung heavy and fragrant, their velvet heads bowed as though listening. The fountain whispered over stone, its silver ripples catching the moonlight.

Faivish was already there, waiting by the fountain like the night itself had carried him in. The lamplight from the hall had not followed—only moon and shadow—but she would have known him even in darkness. Broad shoulders, coat dark with rain, eyes lit with the same ache she felt in her heart.

She walked to him in silence, her skirts brushing the cobbles, her breath steady only because she forced it so. When she reached him, her hand rose—hesitant, trembling—before she pressed it flat to his chest.

His heart thudded against her palm.

Faivish let out a breath that sounded like surrender. He lowered his forehead to hers. "You came."

"I will always come when you call," she whispered as he already leaned in.

His first kiss was soft—testing, almost unbelieving. The second lingered, her lips parting, his breath tangling with hers. Then hunger found them both, long-starved, long-denied. She kissed him like thirst meeting water, and he kissed her like a man who had walked through deserts to reach this well.

Her shawl slid from her shoulders, pooling at their feet. She didn't care.

His hands framed her face, reverent, aching. Her fingers gripped his lapels, tugging him closer, clinging as if he might vanish if she loosened her hold.

She broke for air just long enough to murmur, "There's nothing here but a bench and a wall."

"And you," he said hoarsely. "That's everything."

He kissed her again—deeper, unguarded, claiming. Her hands slid into his hair, damp curls catching between her fingers. His palms found the curve of her waist, then higher, skimming the silk of her gown as though to memorize the shape of her.

"I can't lose you again," he said against her mouth. "Not to List. Not to fear. Not to anything."

"You won't," she breathed. *At least not tonight.*

She backed against the fountain, cool stone firm at her spine. One foot lifted to the rim, skirts shifting, baring the pale line of her calf. Faivish stilled at the sight, his breath catching, then stepped between her knees.

"Tell me to stop," he whispered, though his hands already trembled against her hips.

Maisie did not answer. She caught his hand, guided it to the hem of her skirt. Her fingers brushed his, sure and unflinching. "I've hidden long enough."

His throat worked. *"Mayn sheyns..."* My beauty.

Her smile was fragile, radiant. "Say it again."

"You are beautiful," he said, his voice breaking. "Brave.

Mine."

His mouth traced her jaw, her throat, the hollow where her pulse leapt. Each kiss was slower, heavier, heat coiling like banked embers. She gasped when his hand slid beneath her bodice, his thumb grazing the rise of her breast through the thin chemise.

He froze—just a heartbeat—then bent, kissing her skin there with aching reverence. She arched into him, fingers fumbling at the buttons of his waistcoat.

"I want to feel you," she whispered, breath ragged. "I've lived for safety. But you—" her lips trembled against his ear, "—you make me feel alive."

"You will," he promised.

Her bodice loosened under his hands, silk slipping down her arms. Moonlight found her skin—warm, flushed, freckled, glistening faintly with the garden's cool damp. His rough breeches pressed against her thighs as he leaned closer, heat sparking everywhere their bodies touched.

"Still cold?" he murmured, his voice ragged with restraint.

Her answer was only a soft, urgent sound—half gasp, half plea—as she pulled him to her again. "No," she whispered. "Not with you."

He smiled—soft, boyish, startled. For that instant, she saw only him. Not the doctor, not the exile. Faivish. Hers.

He gathered her chemise at her hips, palms steady, reverent against her thighs. When his fingers touched her fully, she moaned—a sound unguarded, unshaped, as natural as breathing. It broke something in him. He bent to her, arms tight, her face pressed into his neck as she clung back.

"I've missed you," she breathed against his skin. "I dreamed of every part of you."

He trembled, his lips brushing her hairline. "I never stopped wanting you."

Their mouths found each other again, slower now, deeper, the kind of kiss that says nothing has ever been lost. He shrugged free of his coat, his waistcoat—clothes falling carelessly at their feet—until only the thin linen clung to him, damp and open at the throat.

Maisie's gaze followed him, dark and steady even as her hands shook. When he dropped his breeches, she made a soft sound—half astonishment, half hunger—and reached for him with instinct that had waited years.

"Wait," he rasped, his restraint almost breaking. He gathered and then folded the fabric and slid it behind her back, where the stone pressed cold. "You shouldn't have to feel stone."

Her throat caught.

"Better?" He cupped her cheek, his thumb stroking the damp heat of her skin, lingering as if he could weld both their heartbeats with that one touch.

She gave a nod.

"I thought I hadn't forgotten anything, but I have. Forgot how your skin smells when it's warm. I forgot how your eyes go dark when you ache for something. I forgot how strong you are, even when you think you don't have the strength."

Her chest rose sharply, breath trembling. "Too many memories buried by time."

"And tonight," he whispered, his voice rough with need, "I'm unearthing them all."

His hand slid higher along her thigh, anchoring her against the fountain's cool stone, guiding her as he pressed closer. She gasped when she felt him—hot, solid, hovering at her entrance. The anticipation alone unraveled her.

Every muscle in her body tightened, waiting. Wanting.

"Faivish…" Her voice cracked on his name, her lips brushing his jaw as she pulled him nearer.

But he waited. His eyes held hers, asking without words.

"Faivish," she whispered, desperate now. "Please."

"Are you ready for me?" His voice cracked, prayer more than question.

Her nod was sharp, certain. "I've been ready since the rain and the carriage."

HE KISSED HER once more, then moved—slow and steady as each inch mattered. Her body took him in, heat folding around heat, and she cried out—relief, hopefully not pain, the sensation of being found and claimed again.

Her arms locked around his shoulders, nails biting into his skin. He groaned—pleasure and longing tangled—one hand bracing her thigh, the other cradling her spine as though she were precious enough to break.

She closed around him—tight, slick, alive. Every thrust he gave her was slow, deliberate, like vows pressed one atop the other.

When she whispered his name—"Faivish. My Faivish"—it gutted him. He bent over her hand, caught her ring finger in his mouth, and kissed the band glinting faintly in the moonlight. His lips trailed up until she shivered.

"That night in Vienna," he rasped, voice shaking with more than desire, "we made a promise no one else could see. I have honored it every day since. And I will honor it all my life."

Her body arched into his, lips trembling as his words sank deeper than his touch. "Yes," she whispered, joy breaking through her voice. "Yes."

He moved again—still slow but deeper.

Their rhythm built without words. Only sound: her breath breaking in waves, his groans rough against her throat, the fountain's steady murmur, the soft thud of petals slipping from peonies above.

She wrapped her legs tighter around him, tilting her hips to draw him deeper still.

He kissed her everywhere—her temple, her shoulder, the corner of her mouth. Each kiss spoke what his heart had shouted all these years: *I found you. I missed you. I will never let you go.*

Her fingers clawed onto his shoulders, her body clutching

him so tightly he thought he might break—she felt so much better than even his wildest dreams. Faivish let out a low roar, the sound torn from his chest, one hand bracing her thigh, the other steady at her spine. She was heat and silk and trembling strength, and he drove into her slowly, deliberately—each thrust another vow, another piece of the life he meant to give her.

When she whispered his name—"Deeper."—it undid him. He bent to her hand, caught her finger in his mouth, kissing the ring and then the skin around it until she shook. The rhythm between them built in silence—her breath in his ear, the fountain's murmur beside them, his own groans ragged in her hair. The wind stirred, petals brushed against his calves like benedictions, and still he moved, his control fraying with every stroke.

Her body trembled around him, holding him so fiercely he thought he could never leave her again, not in this life or any other. And then he felt it—her tightening, the quake of her climax breaking through them both like lightning splitting the sky. She cried his name, and he held her through it, whispering in Yiddish, in English, in fragments of breath he couldn't even shape into words, only devotion.

When the shudder passed, she slumped against him, glowing with heat, trembling in his arms. He stayed inside her, still, unwilling to surrender the bond. He wanted to fuse himself into her bones, never again to know the absence that had left him hollow for too dreadfully long.

She lifted her hand to his cheek, her thumb brushing the damp edge of his mouth. Her words struck like a blessing and wound all at once: "I built my life around your absence. Let me build something new with you in it."

Her voice broke, and he bent closer to catch it. "Don't move."

"I won't," he promised, his vow hoarse, absolute.

He brushed a strand of hair from her temple and kissed her there, his chest rising hard against hers.

"You were never the danger," she whispered against him, and

the words burned through his chest. "You were the place I didn't believe I deserved."

His own voice cracked. "You're mine. You always were. I was only waiting for the day you'd let yourself believe it."

Her tears glittered in the moonlight as she breathed, "I do now."

He kissed her again—slow, reverent, tasting her, tasting them. No masks. No disguises. No more stolen corners of time.

When she told him she loved him, not hidden, not false, but in the open, Faivish trembled. "And I will never let them erase that."

Petals drifted down around them, scraps of silk on stone. The courtyard fell utterly still, as though even the world bent to witness them.

He cradled her tighter, her head tucked into his shoulder. Her chemise clung in folds at her waist, her thighs bare against his hips, and yet she seemed not exposed but *home*—safe where she belonged.

He bent to her hair, his murmur breaking softly into the night. "*Mayn sheyns.*" My beauty.

He felt the warm slip of her tear against his chest, joy this time, not grief.

They didn't need words after that. They simply stayed, their bodies entwined, his hand tracing circles at her back in rhythm with the beat of her heart.

Two souls, no longer starved. No longer hidden.

By morning, the world might fall apart. But under the drifting petals, with the fountain singing its quiet hymn, they were whole.

Chapter Thirty-Two

THE MORNING OF the hearing came on pale and thin over St. James, and Maisie fastened the last glove button with hands that would not quite obey. *Love last night. War today.* She caught the faint trace of rose pomade on her skin and lifted her chin.

Downstairs, the Pearlers' front parlor had turned into a campaign map. Westminster sketched wide across the pianoforte, routes penciled in dark strokes, names matched to times. The house breathed that particular hush before a storm.

Rachel stood at the window. "Five minutes. Keep the carriage moving. Do not let them pen you at the main gate to Eton."

"Fave said the driver is trusted?" Maisie asked, voice steady enough.

"He is," Rachel said, eyes still on the street. "He'll take the court entrance, not the crowded street side."

The bell chimed. A beat of stillness, then Fave appeared. "Mr. Alfie Collins. He's ready."

Ready? Alfie?

He stepped in, rain jeweled on his sleeve, briefcase tucked close—tired eyes, clear purpose. "I'll stand with you," he said quietly. "At the hearing."

"Alfie—"

"For the boy," he cut in, gentle but immovable. "List has petitioned to call him illegitimate and wrench his guardianship. If he manages it, he gets custody—and with custody, a schoolroom of orphaned heirs trained to his prejudice. That's his game."

Heat climbed Maisie's throat. She knew it; hearing it still hurt.

Alfie's mouth tightened. "I entered my name with the clerk. They will call me. A gentile voice saying love makes a family. Saying safety is owed to a child—not to a title."

She stared at him. "You'll paint a target on your back."

"I've been a target for List for a long time. And I'd rather be marked for standing up than live ducking List." A breath. "Felix would speak himself; they will not hear him or any other Jews. Let them hear me."

Her ribs ached with a sense of gratitude. *For them he is Felix. For me—Faivish.* She looked around the room—Fave at Rachel's shoulder; Raphi in the doorway with two of his brothers behind him; Nick and Andre arriving with their cases; even Prince Stan in a plain coat, gloves tucked in his belt. Faivish's circle. Loyal to the man and to the future his work promised. Jews and gentiles together, craftsmen and physicians—men who had built a corner of London on skill instead of pedigree. She wished they didn't have to fight for it. But better to have something worth defending than to run again.

"This is dangerous. These men, Fave, Raphi, their wives, and children—" Maise started, but then she saw Rachel squeeze Fave's arm.

"We're proud to stand together and show our children that we have nothing to be ashamed of. Or else, List would win." Rachel turned from the window. "They'll try to intercept Alfie before he reaches Westminster. Or John is on his way in with you. So we make it difficult."

Raphi nodded once. "We ride out dressed alike—black coats, black hats, matching mounts. We leave in a block and scatter on signal. Let List's men chase shadows."

"And if they choose a rider to stop," Nick added, "they'll stop the wrong one."

Again, dangerous. Maisie hated that.

"As long as it's long enough for me to reach the chamber," Alfie said. "Long enough for John to walk to the table and be heard, it's enough time."

Maisie's fingers tightened at her side. "He must speak," she said. "They will try to drown him in the room. But if he stands there, they'll have to look at him. A titled boy telling them whom he trusts."

Rachel's hand found hers for a brief squeeze. "We'll put him in front of Lord Kettering before any of List's men can blink."

Outside, the driver cleared his throat by the open door. The sound carried like a summons.

Maisie drew a breath that settled her bones. She met each man's gaze in turn—the Klonimus brothers with the Pearlers, Nick, Andre, Prince Stan—and saw the same promise looking back: *we stand together; we don't run.*

"Very well," she said, voice level. "You ride. Alfie speaks. John walks in on my arm."

She glanced once, quick and tender, toward the hall where Faivish appeared next—black hat in hand, wet brim, eyes like storm light—then faced the day waiting for her.

⤜⟩⟩⟩⟨⟨⟨⤛

FAIVISH HAD BEEN waiting in the Pearlers' stables for what felt like an hour, though the clock in his pocket showed it had been only a minute. The place smelled of the sour tang of horse and hay. Harness buckles rattled as men adjusted straps for the tenth time, anything to keep their hands busy.

Raphi and his brothers bent over a tack bench, murmuring in Yiddish too low for outsiders to follow, their fingers quick, sure. Nick and Andre kept to the wall, silent as sentries. Even Prince Stan was there, jaw set, gloves tucked into his belt like a man about to march rather than a man of rank.

The horses stamped again, one after another. The sound

caught in Faivish's chest. He felt as though he were back in Vienna, a Jewish student watching the white Lipizzaners dance for emperors. Jews weren't allowed inside the ring. He had stood marked, excluded. And now—here he was, about to ride himself, not into a performance, but into a fight. The audience, however, was the same.

The servant's door gave a low groan and Maisie slipped out with Alfie. She kept her head down, her bonnet pulled tight, and moved quickly. She bent over the Pearlers' carriage, tugging at a latch that refused to catch. Her gloved fingers looked too pale against the brass.

"Maisie."

She froze. Shoulders rose, fell, before she turned to him. He nearly broke then, almost dragged her away—through the mews, out of London, far from List and his lackeys. But Westminster was already waiting. Nobles with sharp eyes and sharper knives. He couldn't run. Not this time.

She vanished toward her carriage. Felix stayed, listening to the silence grind. Horses snorted, shifting weight. Leather squeaked. He could taste the danger in the air.

By the time he pushed into the front hall, rain clung to the brim of his hat.

"Is she gone to fetch John now?" Rachel didn't look up from her map. "Twenty minutes. Three carriages together. They split at Aldwych."

Felix's shoulders sagged, just a fraction. "So List won't know which to follow."

"He'll try. His men, too," Rachel said. "But they won't win."

Alfie would take the shortest way there, coat buttoned, papers clutched. His mouth was tight, grim.

"I don't like this," Felix muttered.

"Nor I," Alfie said. "But I'm going."

"I won't lose a brother."

"Then help me make it count."

They stepped into the yard—

And Felix stopped cold.

Nine riders, all in black coats and white cravats, horses snorting steam into the damp air. Not soldiers, not quite. Shadows made flesh.

Chawa Klonimus stood among them, her sons flanking her like sentinels—Raphi, Aaron, Gideon, Ben, Caleb, Nati. Their faces were proud, unyielding.

"This is our answer," she said. "To List. To the committee. To every man who says we don't belong here."

Faivish's eyes swept wider: Nick astride a dark gelding, Andre mounted beside him, even Wendy steady at Prince Stan's stirrup, the prince already on a tall bay.

Nick spoke first. "We ride together. Same clothes. Same hats. When it's time, we scatter."

Andre added, his voice iron-steady, "Let them follow. They won't find Alfie."

Chawa pressed a black hat into Faivish's hands. "One hour. That's all we need. Enough for the young marquess to stand and speak for himself and for your love to stand by the boy."

She looked to Alfie. "You go inside, but hear me, Faivish, make them think you never did."

Felix looked around him—doctors, craftsmen, even a prince. Jews and gentiles, bound not by law or blood but by something harder to break. None of them is here for coin. All of them for a boy. For Maisie. For the right to stand upright in England without being cut down.

"We're doing this for our future. Our children and grandchildren's futures," Chawa said. "You're doing this for her, for love."

He shook his head. "No. Because she would have done it for me."

Raphi's mouth curved, tight. "She already has."

The silence that followed was heavy, sacred.

Felix swung into the saddle. The leather groaned beneath him, his pulse hammering like a drum. "And if they fire?" he asked.

"They won't," Chawa said. "Word's already out—we made it look like the young Marquess of Stonefield rode at dawn, with Prince Stan beside him. Which one of you is he?"

Raphi's grim smile answered. "Let them guess. Fire at one, fire at us all. And the committee is watching List. He can't afford a misstep of attacking English nobility or foreign royals."

Felix closed his eyes for one breath. Then opened them and mounted a horse that had been readied for him.

"Let's ride."

And they did.

Chapter Thirty-Three

To Maisie's relief, John slipped out through Eton's back doors exactly as Rachel had arranged. Cap pulled low, satchel bumping at his hip, boots barely crunching on the stones—he moved like a boy trying to be invisible and almost managing it.

Maisie held the carriage door open. He climbed in without a word and dropped into the seat across from her.

"So this is about my father?" he asked, his tone brisk as he swung the satchel onto his knees. "I'm missing geometry and history for this."

Maisie's throat tightened. She tried for a smile, but it barely formed. "John, your father asked me to protect you."

His gaze fixed on hers, steady, too old for thirteen. "You told me once we protect each other."

Her heart twisted. Nails hold like trust and love. And she had held—through fear, through hiding, through exile. But this boy was her last nail, her last piece of promise. If he slipped into List's hands, she knew in her bones he'd be bent and hammered into something unrecognizable. And it would be her fault.

"Yes," she whispered. "We do."

He shifted, frowning. "When this is over... will we be a family? Properly, I mean. Will you marry the dentist now that you found him? Deena wrote it so cryptic but I understood."

The question landed like a stone dropped in still water.

Maisie blinked hard. "John—"

"I've never had a father I knew," he said, softer now. "Not really. And I trust the dentist. He's kind. He doesn't scold me when I fidget. He explains things. He…" His face reddened slightly. "He smiles with warmth that reaches his eyes. I've seen it. He's not like others."

Tears pricked hot at her eyes. How had he seen so much? She had tried to guard him from all of it—and still he knew.

Her hands trembled in her lap. "I don't know what the committee will do," she said at last. "But I know this: I will never let anyone take you from me."

John shrugged, though the motion was stiff. "If this baron gets me, he won't just take the estate. He'll take my freedom. And I don't want to go. He was at school and the headmaster made me greet him. He looked at me like a piece of bread he meant to tear in half."

The words broke her. She reached across the carriage and drew him close, wrapping her arms around his narrow shoulders, pressing his head under her chin. He smelled of ink and chalk dust, of boyhood, of a future she couldn't bear to see undone.

"I will never let that happen," she whispered fiercely into his hair. "Not only because I promised it to your father but because you are my family just like Deena. And yes, I'll marry and you'll have us all to protect you." He leaned into her, solid and real, and she thought she might shatter from loving him. Then, muffled against her collar, came his small attempt at humor:

"I didn't think I'd have to defend my marquisate before lunch on my first Wednesday at Eton."

Maisie laughed—an uneven sound, part joy, part ache. She pressed a kiss into his hair. "You won't do it alone. Not now, not ever."

John sat back, straightening with a dignity that startled her. His jaw firmed. His fingers curled around the satchel as though it were part of him. "I won't let them take it," he said. Then, sharper: "I won't let them take you away from me. Not Deena. Not the family I've always wanted."

Maisie's eyes blurred. She managed a smile, tender and fierce all at once.

Nails hold, she thought. And this boy—this brave, unyielding boy—was one of the four corners of what would make them hold: She, Faivish, Deena and John.

✦

Chapter Thirty-Four

THE CHAMBER AT Westminster echoed with whispers, a restless tide of voices rising beneath the Peerage Committee's vaulted dome.

Maisie sat motionless in the gallery, veil drawn, her gloved hands knotted white in her lap, gloves forgotten again. She wasn't supposed to be here. No woman could speak before the Lords. Yet they had permitted her to sit—under the false name Lady Eleanor Spencer.

Below, Baron von List waited like a wolf at the kill, chin high, pale eyes glinting.

And across the floor, John. Alone. The leather satchel pressed to his chest like a shield. His back was straight, but Maisie saw the boy he still was—forced to carry what no child should bear.

"Who raised you, Lord Spencer?" asked the chancellor.

"There was always staff," John said.

"And your father?"

"I didn't know him. He lived in exile. Sent money. From Austria."

"And why was that?"

"I don't know for sure," John said carefully. "He was charged with lies."

Laughter rippled across the benches—sharp, unkind.

"Treason, adultery, theft—those are crimes," a peer scoffed.

"Lying isn't."

John's jaw lifted. "Adultery, I think. But I'm not certain what it means."

More chuckles. List smiled, thin and poisonous. Maisie's stomach lurched. He was circling, waiting for his moment.

"And your mother?" someone asked more gently from the podium next to the chancellor.

"She was always there." John cringed when he said it but Maisie knew it was true, she'd been there. Bedridden but alive for most of his life.

"Where?" List's voice cut the air. "In spirit? After her death?"

"Order!" barked the chancellor.

But List pressed forward, voice ringing like a whip. "The boy speaks to ghosts. Let me assume the estate's management on his behalf—"

"Hey," John cut in, clear and sharp. "Not so fast."

Maisie's heart clenched.

"My mother," John said steadily, "was sick. But she always loved me and made sure I was looked after. She stayed upstairs. I read to her—'The Tortoise and the Hare.' She said I was old enough to defend my name. Slowly but surely."

"Was your mother Miriam Morgenschein?" asked the chancellor.

"No, milords. My mother was Henrietta Elsbeth Vancourt. She married my father in 1795."

"Do you have proof?" another Lord demanded. "That you are not the son of Miriam Morgenschein?"

John hesitated. His fingers worked the satchel strap, then steadied. "No. But I'm related to her niece, Maisie Morgenschein."

Gasps stirred the chamber.

Maisie gripped the bench so hard her nails bit through the fabric of her gloves.

"Explain," the chancellor ordered.

John opened his satchel. His hands did not tremble. "There's a letter—from my father to my mother. He wrote that Miriam and Ephraim Morgenschein were his best friends in Vienna. Miriam died early but Ephraim married and had a daughter, Maisie. My father wrote that if anything happened, Miss Maisie Morgenschein should raise me. He called her kind. Said the Jews could be trusted with my name and estate."

He passed the papers forward.

Maisie closed her eyes, her mumble of home cracking like a thin egg.

The chancellor scanned the page. Another paper followed. "This bears the seal of the Marchioness of Stonefield, your mother. Signed by the Archbishop of Canterbury."

John's voice piped up again, soft but unflinching. "It's in Latin. I don't take Latin till next term."

A ripple of laughter, gentler this time. The chancellor nodded. "It is a marriage license. Your parents wed in England. Before your birth."

John pulled out one last paper. "This is from my headmaster at Eton. My birth certificate. He said I ought to return it."

The clerk took it, examined the seal. "Legitimate. English-born. Registered peer of the realm." In other words, John had no Jewish blood and his title was safe.

A hush fell. For a heartbeat the whole chamber stilled.

John lifted his chin, his small hands tightening over the satchel in his lap. The chamber had gone so still that Maisie could hear her own heartbeat.

"I don't want to give up my inheritance," he spoke as steady as he could though his lip trembled. "I don't want to lose my life in England. My loyalty is to the Crown. But one day—"

List barked a laugh. "Listen to him—he parrots what she feeds him! He's a boy. A frightened boy!"

John flushed but didn't look away. "One day," he pressed on, louder now, "I'd like to visit Vienna. The place Maisie Morgenschein came from." He glanced up toward Maisie in the gallery, eyes bright with both fear and defiance. "She protected me. She taught me about the nails that hold a family together—trust, and love. She held when nothing else did."

"Enough," List snapped, stepping forward. "This is sentiment, not testimony. He has been deceived by a woman who isn't even his kin—"

John's voice cut sharp over him. "She is my kin! She is my family. And she loves a man like Dr. Leafley—and I want to find a love like that one day."

The words hung in the chamber like a bell struck true. Gasps rippled through the gallery. The boy's shoulders heaved, but he didn't sit down. He stood there, shaking, a child in front of men who had mocked him—and he did not yield.

Maisie's throat closed. Tears burned, but she held them back. He was defending himself, defending her. And she knew in that moment: John was not only her charge. He was her son.

The doors banged open.

Alfie Collins strode in, coat dripping, hair plastered to his forehead as he removed his hat. "Pardon the delay," he enunciated each syllable, his voice carrying through the large hall. "I am here to vouch for Lady Spencer—and for the boy."

"You?" a Lord exclaimed.

"A peer by marriage," Alfie said. He turned toward Maisie deliberately. "And a witness. I know her. I know her character. I stand for her."

List leapt to his feet. "You were deceived! She is a fraud!"

The gavel cracked. "Order!"

Alfie's voice rang stronger. "I met Maisie Morgenschein in Vienna when I studied. She worked beside her father, Professor Ephraim Morgenschein. And with Dr. Faivish Blattner—now Dr. Felix Leafley. They saved me when I was refused care. Without rights, without recognition—only kindness."

Gasps, whispers. Names that could not be ignored.

Alfie opened his case. "Here. Proof of our degrees. Diplomas. Records. Leafley had better marks than I did."

He looked straight at the Lords. "Her only crime was compassion. She took another woman's name to protect this boy. And in so doing, she gave England back its marquess."

List's shout cracked the air. "She's a liar! Didn't flinch to take the name of a woman who'd been cast out of Society by scandal and—"

The chancellor raised a hand. "Then let us hear from her."

Maisie rose. Slowly, trembling, she lifted her veil. And it wasn't just a veil but Lady Eleanor Spencer who came off like the skin she'd be ready to shed now, just as the late marquess' letter had predicted the night Father died.

Gasps rippled through the chamber.

"I am Maisie Morgenschein," she said. "I confirm it all. I have protected him. I have taught him. I have loved him. But he did the same for me."

"You are not noble," the chancellor replied. "And you are a woman, thus unfit to manage his estate even if we grant you control over his person."

"Yes," Maisie said, her voice breaking but firm. "A woman. A Jew. And yet I gave him a home, when no one else would. Not his title. Not his wealth. Only love. And I wish to give him a family to protect him for all time."

John rose from his bench, climbed the steps to her side, and wrapped his arms around her waist. Maisie's knees nearly gave out. He had chosen her—openly, before them all.

The chancellor cleared his throat, gaze sweeping the room. "Mr. Collins. You claim close knowledge of Miss Morgenschein— of Lady Spencer, as she has lived. Tell me—who is your wife?"

Alfie lifted his chin. "Lady Beatrice Wetherby."

A murmur rippled. Recognition sparked across several faces.

The chancellor nodded slowly. "I know her father. A man of principle."

"Indeed," Alfie said softly. "A man I try daily to be worthy of."

"And your connection to Miss Morgenschein is known to your wife?" the chancellor pressed.

"Indeed. My wife is very fond of Miss Morgenschein." Alfie didn't hesitate. "Her betrothed, Dr. Leafley, is as a brother to me. That makes me—" he allowed himself the faintest smile, "—an uncle, of sorts, to the young Marquess."

Gasps stirred again, softer this time, like the chamber itself was recalibrating.

The chancellor leaned back, studying John with keen eyes. "So you would claim, sir, that you will stand as guardian in all but name? That you would manage his estate and grounds until he comes of age?"

"It would be my honor," Alfie said firmly. His gaze slid to John and warmed, steady as an oath. "I would. Not to possess—but to preserve. Until he is fit to do so himself."

John's shoulders squared.

The chancellor let the silence stretch, then nodded once. "Then it seems to me the boy is surrounded—not by pretenders, but by men and women who have risked name and safety to see him grow to his inheritance."

Maisie's throat ached. She could hardly breathe.

The chancellor's voice rang out, sure and solemn. "Any soul—man or woman, gentile or Jew—who protects a peer of the realm so faithfully should be honored, not punished."

He raised the gavel. The crack echoed like thunder. "In light of the extensive evidence offered in support of the authenticity of the young marquess' parentage and his devotion to the family he's found, chosen and approved by his late parents, there is no need for extensive deliberation." A hush washed over the bench and finally the other men nodded. "This committee finds no cause to remove the Marquess from his title."

The chamber erupted—shouts, protests, the shuffle of robes and the clatter of canes.

List staggered, pale with fury, his mouth twisting like a blade. Maisie met his eyes through the storm. He wasn't finished. She knew that.

But for this moment, they had won.

John's arms clung tight around her. And Maisie let herself believe, just for a breath, that she had not failed him. That the nails still held.

Chapter Thirty-Five

THE GREAT OAK doors of Westminster Hall swung wide.
Maisie descended the steps with John's hand clutched tightly in hers, the sunlight striking the courtyard into brilliance. Beyond the wrought-iron gates, the crowd surged forward— voices hissing, calling, judging. At the foot of the stairs, a line of riders waited in black coats and hats, horses pawing at the stones, reins taut.

Among them—Faivish.

His eyes found hers through the throng. Hat in hand, rain still on the brim, his gaze burning and unshaken. For a moment, Maisie could not breathe. He was not hiding in the shadows this time. He was here, standing in the open, surrounded by brothers who had chosen to stand with him.

Baron von List's voice slashed through the noise. "Look at them! All dressed alike—rats in the same coat, indistinguishable, scurrying from their holes. You cannot tell one from another!"

The crowd rippled with cruel laughter.

Then, with deliberate calm, Dr. Nick Folsham stepped forward out of the line. He drew off his gloves and held them loosely at his side. "Tell me, Baron, is this what you feel each time you consult my work? When you accept my treatments for your health and your pride? Do I look like a rat to you then?"

A stir went through the gallery. List faltered, but only for a breath.

And then another voice rang out, rich and measured.

"Nor to me." Prince Stan stepped forward from his place among the riders, his cravat immaculate, his bearing regal as he placed a hand to his breast. "As royal delegate and ambassador to Transylvania, I will inform my fellow diplomats that Baron von List cannot distinguish loyalty from treachery, nor justice from spite."

The courtyard hushed, thunderstruck.

Maisie's heart pounded. She turned—and Faivish was there, closing the distance. His hands reached for hers and it seemed that he had never belonged anywhere else. The world and its stares fell away.

She pressed close, her veil slipping as she whispered fiercely, "Lady Eleanor is no more. I step into the light now—as your wife."

His breath caught, his forehead lowering to hers. "We stand in the light. All of us. Together."

And she kissed him—before the eyes of London, before the Lords, before the crowd that would judge her. A kiss not of secrecy, but of claim.

Then—

A crack split the air.

Gunfire.

Faivish shoved Maisie hard to the side, dragging John against him as he turned to shield the boy.

Stone shattered in a burst of dust.

Maisie screamed.

Faivish crumpled against her. Blood bloomed dark across his breeches.

THE DOORS SLAMMED, the reins snapped, and the carriage jerked forward so hard Felix's vision went white. Pain knifed up his thigh. He would've slid if Maisie hadn't hauled him upright, arms around his chest.

Her hands were wet. Not rain, but his blood.

John pitched into the opposite seat, satchel crushed to him like a shield. His cap crooked, one ear sticking out, but his eyes—too wide, sharp, fixed on the red soaking Felix's leg.

The wheels clattered hard. The window shivered open and let in horse sweat, fog, a ghost of gunpowder.

Felix tried to sit straighter. Fool. His teeth snapped shut on a hiss. Head slammed back against the cushion.

"Stay still," Maisie breathed. Her palm pressed hard against his thigh. He felt the tremor in it.

The silence lasted too long. Then John's voice, high, stretched too tight: "I saw it. List. Someone grabbed him—the pistol too. What happens now?"

Maisie didn't look up. Her eyes stayed on the spreading red. "Not much," she said, rough. "Men like him slip through. Always."

Felix barked a laugh that broke halfway, ended on a groan. "Bad ones always do," he muttered.

Vienna flickered in his head—the parade ground, white Lipizzaners stepping perfect circles. Nobles applauding. Jews in the shadows. Always shadows.

"Not if I ever sit in Parliament," John said suddenly. His chin jutted, too old for his face. "I won't allow it."

Felix turned his head, caught Maisie trying to smile at him, failing. Her hand shook. Her face didn't.

Another jolt. Pain shot higher, stealing his breath. "Missed the bone," he rasped. "No bullet inside. Better not be or else Andre will have to cut it out."

Maisie snapped at him. "You're in good hands."

"That doesn't mean comfort. Infections kill. This will hurt worse before it eases."

"They are riding ahead to the practice." Her voice steadied

him more than her hand.

Marvelous. A surgery specially prepared for him.

Maisie heaved.

No, no! Rope in a storm. He could take pain. He could even take dying. What he couldn't take was her fear and tears.

John lurched forward, grabbed his sleeve with both hands. "You can't die. You hear? You can't. I finally—" His mouth worked, then words spilled, too fast, tripping. "I finally want parents. Not tutors. Not governesses. Not lies. Just you two and Deena. Please."

Felix's chest burned hotter than his thigh. He raised a shaking hand, laid it on the boy's shoulder. Weak grip, still enough.

"I'll hold on," he whispered. His eyes found Maisie. "For you. For her. For us." Not all infections killed, he had at least a twenty percent chance to avoid infection altogether with Alfie's burning salves. *Argh!*

The carriage ride dragged and he felt a shiver down his back. Pulse dropping. Her lips touched his temple. Her cheek pressed to John's hair. In that moment, it was only them.

The carriage hit a stone. Pain split him in half. He groaned, but forced his mouth to twitch—half smile, half snarl. Anything, so the boy wouldn't see only fear.

"You'll live," Maisie said fiercely. A command, not a plea. "You have to heal."

"Bossy," he rasped. A surgery and stitches at least before he could think of healing.

"Too stubborn to disappear," she shot back, voice breaking. "That's why you'll heal."

John shifted on the seat, clutching the satchel like it could shield him. His voice came out low, uneven. "At school... I just tell them my parents would come visit. Easier that way. Not sure when but that they will. Makes them stop asking."

He ducked his head, scuffing the toe of his boot against the carriage floor. "But now—" His throat worked. "Now I don't have to pretend and yet I fear—" He heaved.

Felix's chest tightened, worse than the wound. He couldn't find words. Couldn't shape them past the ache. All he managed was to lift his hand—shaking, clumsy—and rest it on the boy's shoulder.

The boy leaned into it without hesitation, shoulders stiff at first, then softening.

Felix forced his voice through the pain, barely a whisper. "You've got us. Both of us. That won't change."

John sniffed, straightened. "Good. Because Maisie would kill you if you had died taking a bullet for me. That's even worse than cavities!"

Felix gave a breathless laugh. Weak, but real. "True."

Maisie let out a broken laugh that twisted into a sob. She folded them both in her arms, shaking.

The carriage rattled on. Streets blurred past—fog, shopfronts, the warm tang of bread somewhere close. But inside there was only blood and pain and the two faces pressed to him. Nails hammered deep. Trust and love. Holding.

❦

Chapter Thirty-Six

THE LAMPS BURNED low at 87 Harley Street, shadows thrown long across the walls. Every room seemed to move at once—doors banging, boots thudding, voices snapping and fading—but in Andre's surgery the noise thinned to nothing.

Felix sat in the high-backed chair, his leg stretched across a stool stacked with folded linen. The bandage was already blotched through. His shirt clung damp to his chest; his curls stuck to his temple. He looked steady, but only because he forced himself to.

Maisie hovered close. She hadn't changed from Westminster—the same torn gown, the same streak of dust at her jaw, her hair fallen loose in curls she hadn't noticed. Her eyes kept darting: his leg, his face, Andre's hands, back to his leg. As if she could hold him together by watching hard enough.

Andre leaned against the wall, arms crossed, expression flat. "He stays awake," he said again, to no one in particular. "Awake means alive and fighting an infection."

On a blanket near the hearth, the little mongrel pup had her head on her paws. She didn't whimper. Just watched him.

Felix's gaze slid to Maisie. Her lips parted, soundless. Then: "I thought—" She broke off, shook her head. Started again. "I thought I'd lost you today." A confession now that they were not terrifying John.

He rasped something like a laugh. "You nearly did." He swallowed. "But this house... these people..." His eyes steadied on hers. "And you. You always drag me back."

The door pushed open. Rachel entered first, her shawl clutched, Deena behind her. Then Raphi and Gideon with coats slung over their arms, and finally John, his satchel left behind, his hands empty for once. He lingered by the door, shoulders square, eyes too old.

No one said anything. The silence itself was heavy enough.

Felix looked at them all—Raphi, Gideon, Rachel, Alfie with lips pressed into a line, Andre grim and waiting as Wendy changed the basin of water for new compresses. They had risked everything. Not for him. For her. Because she had chosen him, and so they had, too.

His throat felt tight. "Miracles," he muttered, half to himself.

Alfie's brow furrowed. "What?"

"Is he hallucinating? Feverish?" Nick asked, stepping forward to feel Felix's forehead.

"No," Felix's mouth tugged faintly. "Still here. All of you. Me. That's a miracle."

Wendy made a wet sound and pressed her sleeve to her eyes once she'd set the basin of cold water down.

Maisie caught his hand before he could slip further down the chair. Her fingers twined with his, firm. "Don't make me laugh," she whispered, though her chin shook.

His lips twitched. "Not laugh. Feel. I've been stitched together by everyone here even beyond Andre's apt hands... but you, Maisie—" his grip tightened, surprising even himself—"you're the one who makes me whole."

Her breath shuddered out.

With effort, Felix fumbled at his side, fingers closing on the folded cloth Raphi had given him earlier. He drew it out, slow, every motion costing him.

He reached for her hand, clean and cold again. Then he kissed the finger with the diamond ring.

"For every name you carried," he said, his voice rough, "every danger you shouldered—" He stopped, swallowed, forced the words out. "I want you to have one name that's yours. I want you to have mine. Maisie Leafley."

She made a sound between a sob and a laugh and dropped to her knees so she could see him level. "Yes," she said at once, breathless. "Yes. Always yes. Faivish—always my Faivish."

He slipped the ring onto her finger with shaking hands.

No one cheered but everyone shifted. Rachel let out a long breath she seemed to have held for years. Alfie touched Felix's shoulder gently. Andre, still severe, inclined his head.

And John—John stepped forward. He looked at Maisie, then Felix. "So… you're really my family now?" His voice cracked on the word.

Maisie's hand went to his cheek. Felix lifted his own trembling hand and laid it on the boy's shoulder.

"Family," he said simply.

John leaned awkwardly into both of them, fierce like he meant to hold them there by force.

Felix let his head tip back against the chair, breath catching. For the first time since leaving Vienna, he didn't feel exiled. He felt home.

Chapter Thirty-Seven

Two weeks later, at 87 Harley Street…

FELIX LEANED ON his crutch, bracing against the edge of the chair as he closed the leather satchel at his feet. For once, the bag wasn't for leaving—it would only carry papers back and forth. Harley Street wasn't ending. He would instill work here. But he would no longer live inside its walls but with Maisie, Deena, and John at the townhouse.

Alfie held up a jar of lavender lozenges. "Do these go with you or stay with the practice?"

Felix squinted. "I can't remember if they're medicinal or just sweets."

"They're from Paris. Definitely sweets."

Felix waved it off. "Then they stay. Harley Street deserves a stash."

Andre chuckled. "You're the only man I know who thinks leaving candy behind is a sign of maturity."

Felix shook his head. "Not maturity. Balance. For years, I only had the work. Now… I have a life beyond these walls."

Wendy appeared in the doorway, cheeks pink from the cold. "I hear this is the last official packing day?"

"Not quite," Alfie said. "Patients still need us. But from now on, we'll work here, not live here."

Nick tied off a bundle of texts. "The practice remains. The miracles remain and some we get to carry with us."

Laughter rippled, gentle but real, as if they all needed to let it out after too much waiting, too much fear. The walls of Harley Street had heard weeping, shouting, and even blood hitting the floorboards. But today it heard laughter, and Felix thought Professor Morgenschein would have approved.

Just then, Maisie stepped into the room, John at her side and Deena trailing shyly behind, her hands clasped tight. Lilly, the little pup, bounded ahead of them, ears too big for her body, tail wagging furiously until she made her usual beeline for Felix's good leg.

Felix bent stiffly to rub her ears, and the sight made Maisie's chest ache. All this time, she had imagined him swallowed by these rooms, by pain and ghosts of patients lost. Now, he stood here alive, with a future. With her.

Alfie nodded to Maisie. "Your father would be proud of you all," he said simply.

The room quieted. Felix leaned heavily on his crutch, steadying himself as Alfie's words hung in the air. He saw Maisie's breath catch, the way her lashes fluttered, and he knew what those words meant to her. Professor Ephraim Morgenschein's dream—science and compassion, carried forward and it was alive before them. And Maisie stood at its center, no longer hidden. Not Lady Spencer, not a shadow, but his life partner.

Then Deena, who had been hovering by the door, suddenly blurted: "I want to learn. To be a nurse. Like you all do."

Every head turned.

Her cheeks flushed crimson, but she pressed on. "I used only to want to survive. But now... I want to help. To be part of this. If you'll let me."

Felix felt a pull in his chest. The girl who once shrank from every footstep in the hall now stood taller, her voice clear.

Maisie crossed to her sister, taking her hands. "Deena, this isn't just work. It's long hours, sorrow, and sometimes failure. It's dangerous."

Deena lifted her chin, eyes shining. "So we were hiding and

lying about who we were. At least this way, I'll be of some use. And Father would be proud of me."

Alfie stepped forward, his voice soft but sure. "I'll train you with the others like we did with Wendy. From bandages to tinctures to keeping a cool head when a room fills with panic. You'll never be alone."

Felix's voice cut through the hush, low but steady. "Then it's settled. Deena will join us at Harley Street. A Morgenschein here always. This place will never be just walls and charts—it will always be family."

He caught Maisie's eyes then. She was pale with exhaustion, but her gaze burned bright. Even now—especially now—she carried herself with a strength that humbled him.

She came toward him and took his hand in both of hers. "Balance," she whispered. "I once read war is only postponed. But love… love is what endures."

His throat tightened. He pulled her closer, lips brushing her temple, not caring who saw. John straightened beside them, his voice quiet but sure. "Then we're a family. At last."

Felix felt the boy's words sink into his bones. Family. A word he had not dared claim in years. Maisie's arm went around John and Deena, and Felix shifted closer, folding all into his side.

Lilly nosed her way between their feet, let out a single triumphant bark, and sat on Felix's boot as if to anchor them there.

It was messy. Loud. Improper. And it was everything Felix had ever wanted.

For the first time in years, Felix didn't feel like the boy shut out of Vienna's halls, nor the exile ducking into shadows. He was Faivish. He was Felix. He was Maisie's. And John's. And finally—finally—free.

Chapter Thirty-Eight

T HE PEARLERS' MORNING room opened onto Green Park like a theater box. The pale light of the sun struck the damp lawn; the trees along the path steamed a little where last night's mist lifted. Inside, Rachel had set a breakfast worthy of a coronation—silver urns breathing tea and coffee, a chocolate pot near the hearth; platters of cold cuts and sliced fruit; a dish of devilled eggs kept cool by a tray with ice; fried trout under clarified butter; apple tartes in a wide crystal plate; baskets of buns and a large celebration challah with at least eight braided strands, their sugared tops shining; jars of marmalade and quince jelly; a compote of stewed gooseberries bright as jewels.

Felix took the chair nearest the windows—back to the light, leg propped on a low stool in deference to Andre's orders—and tried not to smile at how every plate that passed near him acquired a Bath bun by some act of providence. Lilly had already wriggled under the table; Raphi's little boy, Joseph, dropped to all fours after her with a whisper of "Sh—I'm a tiger," and disappeared between chair legs and tablecloth like a small, determined comet.

"You are not a tiger," Raphi said mildly, without looking down. "You are a Klonimus. We do not hunt puppies at breakfast."

Joseph reappeared under Felix's stool, cheeks flushed, one

sock half-down. Lilly licked his wrist and darted away, a gold blur. Joseph giggled, then sat cross-legged beside the stool, satisfied with proximity if not conquest.

Felix let the sound of it soak in. The room held nearly every-one who had stood with him on Harley Street and on the steps of Westminster—Fave and Rachel Pearler hosting as if they did not, between them, run half the city; the Klonimus brothers in a neat dark line; Andre and Nick already arguing in low voices about a new ligature; Alfie topping off cups with the confidence of a man who believed tea could solve nearly anything; Wendy passing a plate with a quiet "Eat, or I shall make you carry this home later."

Maisie slipped into the chair beside him, fresh muslin, hair pinned in a softer way that made him think of late evenings rather than committee hearings. She set her napkin, looked toward the window, and he caught it again—that quick, astonished look she'd worn the first moment after the hearing, as if the world were slightly larger now and somehow hers.

She met his eyes. No mask. No borrowed name. He felt the ground come steady under him.

"Try the tarts," she said, as if offering a truce to the day.

"I'll obey my bride," he murmured.

"And I'll follow you around the world should you ever need to travel again," she said, and the corner of her mouth tilted.

On the far side of the table, Rachel lifted the chocolate pot. "Before we say the blessings over the wine—Raphi?"

Raphi rose. He did not clear his throat or make a production of it; he simply held his glass, waited for the room to still, and spoke in the same voice he used at his bench when a stone finally caught the light.

"We've eaten together often," he said, "through years none of us expected, in places none of us meant to go. Today we are here together for a different reason." He glanced at Felix, then at Maisie. "We are together and united because the world tried to make shadows of you, and you stood in the sun instead."

A murmur went round the room—agreement, not applause.

Raphi went on, eyes on John now. "We sit together because a boy spoke plain in a room that prefers lies polished into law." John's ears reddened; he straightened anyway. "Because his guardians were brave enough to be seen as they are. Because friendship held." His glass lifted a fraction. "To the Morgenschein courage, to the Leafley stubbornness, to the Spencer line we shall all protect, and to the Pearler table that kept us fed through all of it."

"To all of it," Alfie echoed, and glasses met softly.

"And to Lilly," Joseph added, under the table.

"Especially to Lilly," Nick said gravely, as the puppy resurfaced near his boots and put one paw on his instep like a stamp of ownership.

Plates began their circuits. Felix let the warmth of fish and spice and buttered rolls put small, sensible weights on the morning—the kind of ballast ordinary happiness requires. Conversation braided itself in the easy way of people who had faced something and survived.

Andre, without looking from his plate, said, "If you limp on that leg out of pride, you'll limp longer."

"I do everything out of pride," Felix said. "Ask anyone."

"Not true," Wendy said, pouring tea. "Sometimes you do it out of temper."

Alfie leaned into the exchange with a grin. "Mostly out of love, which is more inconvenient than either."

Felix tipped his head toward the window. "Green Park disagrees. It looks perfectly convenient this morning."

"Green Park," Rachel said, "has no idea how many notes I sent to keep this room quiet while the city treated our friends like a curiosity." She said it with lightness, but her hand, resting on Fave's sleeve, tightened.

"Not curiosity," Fave said. "Example."

"Both," Chawa Klonimus answered from near the urns, helping herself to a second heaping spoon of sugar for her tea. Her scarf was pinned more elaborately than usual; the silver at her temples made her look, Felix thought, like the matriarch in a painting—except the eyes were sharper. "Eat," she added, and entire platters obediently advanced, receiving a nod from Eve Pearler.

Deena had been quiet at the end of the table, eyes moving as if trying to memorize everyone at once. When the laughter tipped into a lull, she stood. Not a dramatic stand—just that small, decisive rise he had learned to recognize as a Morgenschein choosing.

"I want to say something," she said.

Forks paused. Joseph stilled under the table without being told.

Deena lifted her chin. "I'm going to begin an apprenticeship," she said, each word placed down like a card. "I'll alternate weeks at 87 Harley Street and at Cloverdale House. I want to learn to nurse properly." She glanced at Maisie, then Felix, then Wendy. "It's… it's what our father would have wanted. And it's what I want."

A beat—then Wendy smiled. "We'll train you."

Nick, dry as salt: "Twice, if necessary."

Andre: "Three times, if you're stubborn."

Alfie, hand to heart: "And four, if you insist on learning anything from me."

Deena's laugh broke loose; the room followed. Her face, when it sobered again, was brighter. "Thank you," she said, and sat, and Felix watched Maisie's hand find her under the table and squeeze.

John cleared his throat. "I'm missing Latin for this," he said, perfectly solemn.

"You're excused," Rachel told him. "Prince Stan will put in a good word with the headmaster."

"I rather like Latin," John confessed, and then, almost as if he surprised himself, "But I like this better."

"This?" Felix asked.

"This," John said, gesturing at the table, the room, the morning. "Being… seen." He glanced toward the window, where Green Park opened wide and ordinary. "I thought titles made people look. It turns out truth does it better."

"Keep saying things like that," Alfie said, "and you'll send your headmaster into apoplexy."

"Not before I sit in the House of Lords," John replied, straight-faced.

"You'll sit there," Felix said. "But you'll come home to us."

Something in Maisie eased at that. He felt it in the way her shoulder settled against his for a breath, then lifted again to pour Rachel more chocolate.

Conversation turned; plates changed hands again; Joseph and Lilly negotiated a truce over a fallen Bath bun that involved Joseph breaking it in half and Lilly pretending she had not wanted the larger piece anyway.

When the clatter had softened and the tea had gone to refilling rather than pouring, Chawa rose. No glass; no script. She set one palm flat on the linen, as if feeling for the bones of the table itself.

"*Genug geredt,*" she said—enough talking. "Time for a *brokhe*, a blessing."

Silence gathered itself.

She looked to Maisie and Felix. "*Zol eyer hoyz zayn ful mit likht un gelekhter,*" she said, the old words worn smooth by use. "May your house be full of light and laughter. *Zol Ihr zan gezunt un mit mazl*—health and luck—*and mit kind un mit sholem*—children and peace." Her gaze ticked to Deena, then to John. "*Un zol ir keynmol nit hobn moyre tsu zayn vi ir zent*—may you never fear being exactly who you are."

She reached across and, with a practicality that always undid him, straightened Maisie's napkin. "*Nu,*" now, she said, softer. "*Ests.*" Eat.

It let everyone breathe again; a few throats were cleared; Nick made a show of examining a potted trout to dislodge the lump in his. Felix looked toward the window so no one had to see him do the same.

Later—after second cups and small slices of cake, after Prince Stan promised letters to Vienna and Warsaw and somewhere else entirely "where a certain man's name will not open doors for quite a while," after Raphi's boy fell asleep under the table with Lilly's chin on his knee—people began to stand in ones and twos. The brothers kissed their mother's cheek; Andre promised to check Felix's wound "only if you let it be a wound and not a trophy"; Wendy warned Alfie about the dangers of experimental tooth powder with the seriousness of a sermon.

Felix stayed where he was. He liked rooms most in the hour when a party exhaled—chairs askew, cups forgotten, the air warm with everything that had been said. Maisie laid a hand over his where it rested on the arm of the chair and looked at the chaos with a satisfaction that had nothing to do with tidiness.

"Stay for a minute," she said.

"I'm not moving," he answered. "Doctor's orders."

"Which doctor?"

"The one I married."

A quiet beat held between them. The park beyond the glass was a calmer green now; a boy in a cap chased a hoop along the path and fell laughing when it outran him. Someone along Piccadilly shouted for a cab. The city did what cities always do: it went on.

Rachel drifted by and touched Felix's shoulder. "You'll bring her tomorrow?"

"To Harley Street? Try to stop her," he said.

"Not to Harley Street," Rachel returned, eyes kind. "To choose fabric. Married women must attend to terrifying matters." She flicked a glance at Maisie's sleeve. "You, my dear, are now obligated to own at least one gown that is entirely impractical."

"I just owned five years of impracticality," Maisie said. "I'm thinking stout serge."

"Silk," Rachel decreed, and vanished with a laugh.

Felix reached for his cup and found it empty. Maisie topped it off without asking—tea, not coffee—and set it back in his hand. He watched the steam rise, thinking briefly of a small courtyard and peonies and the plop of water against stone; of a boy's thin, furious voice on the steps of Westminster; of the weight of a promise all those years ago.

"Faivish," she said.

He looked up.

She didn't speak immediately. She simply placed her palm over his wrist, feeling for his pulse with the same steady touch she had used the first time he kissed her breathless in a Vienna hallway. Her face softened, as if the gesture reassured her.

"Still here," he said.

"Still here," she answered.

Joseph snored softly under the table. Lilly, offended by the indignity of someone sleeping during what might yet be a meal, slid out, stretched, and put both front paws on Felix's boot.

"You've a friend," Maisie said.

"I have a house full of them," he answered. "That's grand."

"I dare say." She smiled. "Finally visible."

He let that sit. He had been visible often enough in the wrong ways—his name, his nose, his skill when it made the wrong man feel small. But this—this was different. He could feel it in the way Fave spoke to him as to a peer in more than profession, in the way Prince Stan did not puff up to compensate for foreignness, in the way John did not look right or left before he reached for Maisie's hand at a public table.

Raphi came by last, coat over his arm, Joseph's abandoned sock tucked absurdly in the pocket. He bent a little closer than necessary. "We'll walk you home," he said.

"We're at home," Felix said.

Raphi's mouth tipped. "Then we'll walk you to your other home, the one on your letterhead now."

Felix nodded. The Pearlers' shutters threw slats of sun across the parquet. Outside, Green Park widened and then narrowed again where the trees met. He rose carefully—crutch under his hand, Maisie at his side, the room shifting into that soft chatter of leave-taking that always made him think a second act might still be ahead.

At the door, Chawa waited. She took Maisie's face between both hands and kissed her brow, then did the same to Felix, as if he were also her child and always had been. "*Azoy*," she murmured. "So."

"So," he said back, because sometimes the small words were the only ones that fit.

They stepped out onto the landing. Green Park breathed. The city went on. Behind them, the Pearlers' morning room hummed with the last of the clearing away—cups stacked, chairs nudged back under tables, laughter still caught in the curtains if anyone wished to go listen for it later.

Felix leaned into the crutch and into Maisie both. At the foot of the steps, John waited, hat in hand as if he meant to escort them himself. Deena stood with Wendy, already discussing gloves and sterilization as if it were gossip. Joseph tumbled out of the doorway with one sock on and one sock off, and Lilly shot past him to reach the sun first.

"Ready?" Maisie asked.

"Yes," he said, and meant the whole of it. "Let's go home."

Epilogue

Eight years later

O N A BRIGHT morning, the carriage traveled the last mile to Oxford as John watched the towers grow closer and pretended his stomach wasn't acting up. "No chocolate at bedtime," Felix said from the facing seat, as calm as ever—father for all that mattered. "I won't, I promise." Maisie stroked the curve of her belly through her pelisse. "You'll come home when the baby arrives, right?"

"I'll come home as often as I can," John said, and reached for her hand because it felt wrong not to. He called her Mother now. Not because he had forgotten the woman he'd started with, but because a life can hold more than one truth. More love. Soon, more family. The house had been whole this summer—Nurse Wendy ruling Cloverdale House like a benevolent tyrant, Uncle Alfie forever repairing a window latch, Andre declaring a chair unfit for human posture, and Deena so busy at the practice she came home smelling of clean towels and pride.

The carriage jolted over a rut. He thought he'd kept the flinch inside. Apparently not, judging from his parents' pinched lips and sad smiles.

"I'm afraid I won't fit in again," he said, and only knew he'd spoken when the words sat in the air between them.

"You don't need to fit in anywhere if you know your place," Felix answered, mild and sure.

John let it land. Know your place. Not as the world meant it. As Felix did: the place you make by being useful and steady, by keeping your word when no one looks.

He looked out at the quad's edge. He wanted what was ahead—lectures, the reading rooms, the quiet thrum of academic work. He wanted the law and understood how to use it like Felix's sharp tools. Uncle Alfie had taught him that law was like a muscle, the way it could bend toward fairness if someone insisted or punch justice if it was abused. And there was the estate; Uncle Alfie had carried more than his share for years. On their last tour of cottages and fields, John had said he'd take on the ledgers himself this term. He meant to keep that promise.

The carriage turned by the gate and followed a path with a few puddles. A porter stood with a squeaking pen and a ledger that looked older than half the undergraduates. Bells marked the quarter hour. A boy in a coat too big for him wrestled a trunk up the steps and pretended he wasn't losing.

And when the carriage door opened, John could almost smell the changed air. He was going to study here, among others who'd be his peers. But he was Marquess already and wasn't preparing for a future riddled with responsibilities—he was trying to catch up.

Felix got out of the carriage first and offered Maisie his hand; she laughed at herself when she took it and held her belly as if to keep the unborn baby safe under her heart. John followed, boots on stone.

This is Oxford.

"Write when you settle," Felix said, straightening a sleeve as if it were urgent work. "And when you need books. And when you don't."

"I will."

Maisie tugged him in. "Eat properly. Sleep." Her voice dropped. "And be kind. That's the only rule that never fails."

"Yes, Mother." He wished his voice didn't falter when he said goodbye to her.

He hugged them both hard. It wasn't graceful and didn't need to be. Felix's arm came down to his back with the pressure that said I've got you. Maisie kissed his forehead. She now smelled faintly of soap and ginger tea, the new favorite because it eased her. They didn't ask him to be anything he wasn't. They never had. And their love had always been unconditional.

And before he could blink again, his parents returned to the carriage with a nod. Oxford was for him, for peers of the realm, for gentile aristocrats—not for Jews. It stung to think of his parents not belonging anywhere he did because they were inseparable—if not in person, then in their hearts. And that's why he swallowed that lump in his throat when he saw Maisie pat her eyes with a handkerchief, not the dainty lace one but the sensible ones Felix carried in his coat pocket.

John inhaled deeply, hoping to make room for courage, and set down his valise and crossed in front of another boy offering to help with trunks. "Take the strap; I'll have the heavy end."

"No need, sir—students don't carry. Leave the portage to the lads," the porter called, pencil squeaking over his ledger.

Somehow, he felt as though he'd been watched.

"It's my heavy luggage; he can help to carry it—and I'll take the other end," John said without looking up.

The boy blinked, surprised into a grin. "Cheers."

"This way?" John said, and they heaved together. Two steps, then four, then the landing in front of the dormitory for new students.

"Name?"

"John Spencer, Marquess of Stonefield," he offered, and didn't care what the porter thought. The man ran a finger down the ledger and nodded him through. It felt like something opening.

They left the trunk at the door, and John turned back to his parents. Maisie had pushed her face through the open carriage window and waved with the already saturated handkerchief; Felix was saying something to her that made her mouth twitch in an unwilling smile. John savored the sight and then made himself move, because standing still never helped.

The quad spread neat as a bookplate: clipped grass, pale stone, the long shadow of the library tower laid like a ladder across the flags. He stopped before he entered the building—not to gawk, but to mark it. People like my parents couldn't have stood here as students, not when they were young. Oxford's doors had been shut to Jews. They'd built lives anyway. I can walk in. I can ask questions out loud. He could use this for good. He would.

"Go on, milord," the boy said behind him, as if he'd heard the thought.

"I'm going," John said, and meant it, but he couldn't shake the sensation that someone was following him. Or why else were the tiny hairs on his neck pricking up?

He turned back once more because he couldn't help it. Maisie pressed her hand to her heart. Felix tipped the brim of his hat with two fingers, and the carriage moved through the gate and out of sight.

He waved until he was certain they couldn't see him anymore, but the tight place under his ribs squeezed.

"Is the library open?" he asked the boy, who'd set down the strap.

"Yes, milord. Shall I wait for you here?"

"Please set this aside, I'll return soon." John crossed the quad with his hand on his chest and a list of instructions clattering pleasantly in his head: come home often; write first, worry later; eat; sleep; be kind.

The porter's pen squeaked faintly as he mumbled to another new arrival behind John. Geese argued somewhere beyond the wall. John looked up at the great windows of the library, bright as Maisie's polished silver candlesticks in the sun—

—and caught a flicker from the inside.

Blond hair, quick as a match-flare. A profile turned half away. A book held close to a blue-clad chest. The slightest tilt of a mouth, as if a private joke had just landed.

It was a breath, no more. Enough to set the air inside him

humming in a most unfamiliar way.

A swift beat rose where the ache had lived. Good, off to the library. Begin the work, he thought, and the tempo evened as he allowed himself to explore a little.

He entered the library and found a staircase open to a dark tower. Perhaps that's where she is.

He climbed. The old treads answered each boot with a hollow thud that sounded like a secret he needed to uncover. At the landing between two floors, where the windows faced the court, he paused one last time and looked back across the court. Carriages delivered more new students to the new dormitory, but he was already at the library.

John smiled and went up to where he'd seen the blonde girl.

The room he found at the end of the staircase was small and bright. A desk with a nick in one corner. A window overlooking the court. Books in an uneven stack, a blue shawl slung over the chair back, a mug ring on the sill as if someone had been here often and in a hurry. Someone lived in this forgotten corner.

"What are you doing here?" The voice came from the shadow near the shelves—clear, bright, with a faint lilt that felt instantly like home. Like how Maisie and Deena sounded after a long spell of German.

Hm. Curious.

"I didn't know there were girls in the library," John said, turning toward the sound. Another ridiculous rule. Why should girls and Jews be barred from rooms built for thought? In his house, both owned half the shelves.

"I saw you arrive, you're new," she said.

"You watched me with my parents?" he asked.

A shape moved. She stepped into the shaft of light: fair hair pinned as if it refused to behave, a blue dress that matched the quick glance he'd caught from the quad, ink on the side of one finger.

HIS HEART LEAPED once—clean and startling.

"I'm not supposed to be here," she said, chin up, eyes steady.

"You're right about that. What are you going to do about it?"

Three thoughts arrived at once. One, kiss her and keep the secret. Two, tell on her—nonsense. Three, say something clever—nothing came.

"I'm John," he managed. "I'll keep your secret if you..." He searched for terms and found honesty. "If you let me sit in this room sometimes. And if you don't vanish before you tell me your name."

A quick smile—gone almost at once. "Names travel. In here, we use subjects."

"Then give me one." He had grown up bickering with Deena, so this was a well-practiced game.

"Latin prose. And another: people who think titles outrank sense." She tipped her chin toward the stairs. "And you?"

"Law," he said. "And whether kindness is optional."

"That will do."

He moved a step closer to the desk, careful not to crowd. "You were watching."

"Yes." She glanced toward the window. "Your parents are the first I've seen to escort you with tears, hug you, and return to the carriage."

He'd already shown that his family was different and hoped it wouldn't matter at Oxford, but of course, it would. John's mouth went tight, not from offense. From recognition. "That's accurate."

"You helped the boy with your trunk." She nodded toward his cuff. "And got dust on your sleeve. The porter will hate that."

John looked at the blot on his breeches and didn't brush it off. "It was my heavy luggage. He could barely carry it. Why not help?"

"That question will not make you popular here."

"That's not what I'm here for. I'd rather be useful than popular."

She considered him, then the empty chair. "Very well, Useful. Sit. Five minutes. The porter walks past the tower on the quarter."

"You know his route?"

"I know every dull habit around here." Her eyes warmed, then cooled again, practical. "If anyone asks, you didn't see me."

"Understood," he said, meaning that he had seen her and it had done something to him he couldn't quite name. "But I'd like to see you again."

A small breath. Not quite a laugh.

"I watched you," she said, as if it were the simplest answer. "From the window. You caught my attention." She spoke as though she was so much more than a girl hiding in the library tower, and he was aching to find out who she was.

Heat moved through his chest; not the old ache. A quick, sure beat.

"Good," she said, as if that settled something. "Then you'll do."

"Who are you?" The question slipped out. *Why are you hiding here?*

"Not today." A small smile. "If you want to see me again, come when the bells strike the quarter."

"I'll keep your secret."

"Come alone," she said. "I'll teach you one lesson—how to keep a secret when it hurts. Are you ready for everything Oxford has to offer?"

"I am." John was ready to give his studies everything—time, energy, the long nights—and to give his cause the weight of his title and his steady support. Yet as the moment between them settled like a dream turned reality, he thought this girl—whatever her name—might be the one he was ready to give his first kiss, and perhaps his heart.

On the quarter, I'll be here. I'll do the work. And if she returns, I'll ask her name—and, if she'll let me… more.

Mind open. Heart awake. Ready for all of it.

If you loved John, he will get his chance at romance in *The Name of Love,* a short story in the Anthology titled *Dukes in Spring.* Even Deena gets her love story in the *Hearts of Hope* series by Sara Adrien.

Stay up to date with all of Sara Adrien's new books and the next series by signing up for her newsletter at www.SaraAdrien.com

The series continues with *Bring Me A Winter Miracle* (book 6), where Prince Stan and Princess Thea aim to reunite their families for a dazzling winter double-wedding. All of the characters from the *Miracles of Harley Street* series are snowed in at an elegant country castle. But when love and adventure intertwine, they will need one more miracle that could change everything.

Author's Note

Thank you for picking up this book and stepping into the Regency era with me. I've always been captivated by this period, not just for its elegance and romance, but because it appears so tangible to me. The warmth of candlelight, the comfort of beautifully crafted furniture, the steady rhythm of horse-drawn carriages—in many ways, life was developed enough to imagine ourselves right there. I've been honored to hear from readers and fellow writers that I bring this world to life, and that connection to the past is something I treasure deeply.

Yet, even as I've immersed myself in this glittering age, I couldn't ignore a gap in its stories. Where were my people? As a Jew, I knew we were there, but history so often left us in the shadows. The fact is, Jewish life during this time was fraught with barriers. In Eastern Europe, Jews were confined to the Pale of Settlement, unable to leave. On the Continent, they lacked basic citizenship rights. Even in England, while there was more freedom, Jews couldn't own property or study at universities. This world was as beautiful as it was flawed for many people, and I've long been exploring that nuance.

I touched on this theme in my *Diamond Dynasty* series, which followed six Jewish brothers from London who studied at university in Edinburgh, where Jews were allowed to attend. Writing that series showed me how much these stories mattered—not just to me, but to readers like you, curious about the voices history has often overlooked. With this book, I've taken on a new challenge, bringing to life characters who come from Vienna, a city with its own unique and complex Jewish history.

Researching the story you just read was both enlightening and heartbreaking. I turned often to Robert S. Wistrich's *The Jews of Vienna*, a resource I can't recommend enough to those wanting to learn more. He recounts that even in the mid-18th century, Empress Maria Theresa believed Jews should be kept as far from "civilized life" as possible. Just decades later, however, Emperor Franz Joseph II recognized their contributions to society, albeit still viewing them through a pragmatic lens rather than an equitable one. These contradictions between progress and prejudice were at the heart of Jewish life in the Regency era, and they resonate deeply with me.

For me, this isn't just history; it feels powerfully current. While writing this novel, I've watched news of the ongoing existential war against Israel and witnessed devastating antisemitic incidents, including the murder of a Jewish couple in Washington, D.C., right outside the Holocaust Museum. These events weigh heavily on my heart. They remind me why it's so important to tell these stories—not just to honor the past, but to reflect on our present and imagine a better future.

To my readers, thank you for coming on this journey with me. I hope this book not only opens a door to the Regency era but also introduces you to a world you may not have explored before. If you're new to my writing, I invite you to check out my *Diamond Dynasty* series with the Klonimus brothers for more stories of resilience, love, and faith woven through history. And although in real history, the first official Crown Jeweler was appointed in 1843, and during the Regency, commissions for the Prince Regent were not considered work for "the Crown." In this fictional world, I imagined an earlier appointment and what might have happened if a Jewish family had risen to hold that title in the early nineteenth century. This small alteration allowed me to explore how such a position might have shaped lives, love stories, and intrigue during the Regency.

May my books bring you joy, intrigue, and perhaps a new perspective. Thank you for reading, and for making space in your heart for a story like this.

Deena's song:

You might wonder which song Maisie, Deena, and Felix hummed that bound them together. It was a Yiddish one and there's a lot of history hidden here that I'd like to tell you about: Yiddish folk songs are an intricate element of Jewish culture, filled with the emotion, humor, and wisdom of everyday life. While I find many of them sad and they move me to tears, they are not meant as such. Rooted in the experiences of Ashkenazi Jews, they not only entertained but also served as a way to preserve traditions, transmit values, and tell stories across generations. Often sung at gatherings, celebrations, or in private moments of reflection, these songs encapsulate the joys, sorrows, and quieter moments of a people navigating history in both their homeland and the diaspora.

What makes Yiddish folk songs so special is their storytelling nature. They are rich with imagery, often filled with metaphors or riddles, and feature characters grappling with universal emotions like love, loss, hope, or yearning. With melodies that evoke both laughter and tears, these songs hold a timeless quality that continues to resonate even today.

One exceptional example of this tradition is the classic Yiddish song, "Tumbalalaika." This beloved folk song is essentially a dialogue between a young man and a young woman, where the man tests the woman with riddles to see if she is the one for him. The riddles are poetic and philosophical, with answers that reflect wisdom and depth of thought that would fit the vibes between Maisie and Felix as they tried to find one another. The interplay of questions and answers reflects not only the playful courtship rituals of the past but also a deeper longing for connection and understanding, making the song uplifting yet profoundly meaningful.

Lyrics of "Tumbalalaika"

Yiddish:

Tumbala, tumbala, tumbalalaika,

Tumbala, tumbala, tumbalalaika,

Tumbalalaika, shpil balalaika,

Tumbalalaika, freylekh zol zayn.

English Translation:

Tumbala, tumbala, tumbalalaika,

Tumbala, tumbala, tumbalalaika,

Tumbalalaika, play balalaika,

Tumbalalaika, let us be happy.

The melody, with its repetitive phrases and inviting rhythm, creates a sense of intimacy between the singers and the listeners. Though modern audiences may enjoy the song as a lighthearted ditty, its riddles carry a contemplative undertone, reminding us of the depth inherent even in seemingly simple Yiddish folk songs.

By preserving songs like "Tumbalalaika," we honor the voices of those who came before us, carrying their stories into the present. These songs are not just music; they are fragments of history, echoes of love, laughter, and wisdom that continue to inspire. If you find yourself humming along to "Tumbalalaika," take a moment to reflect on the generations who sang it before you, weaving their lives and their dreams into the fabric of this enduring tradition.

Attribution for lyrics and translations comes from public domain archives and academic compilations of Yiddish folk songs, ensuring the preservation of these cultural treasures.

Dentistry in Vienna—A Note on History:

In reality, formal dental education in Vienna began in 1821, when Dr. Georg Carabelli was granted permission to give the world's first university lectures on *"Zahnarzneykunde"* (modern dental medicine). These early courses were theoretical only; practical training remained in his private surgery. It wasn't until much later in the 19th century that dental societies, clinics, and eventually a university institute were established in Vienna, with full professionalization coming toward the end of the century.

In my story, I chose to shift this timeline slightly earlier because there's no record that would deny Felix the education he pursued. This allowed my characters to encounter the beginnings of dental medicine within the Regency period. This is a deliberate artistic choice: while it bends historical fact by a few years, it stays true to the general moment in history when dentistry was first emerging from barber-surgeon craft into a more scientific, university-based discipline. There have always been outliers who combined medical training with other areas of science and traveled to perfect their crafts just like Noah Gordon described in *The Physician*.

Felix, my fictional dentist, is thus imagined as a rare exception of his time—a man who studied under physicians, learned anatomy and surgery, and reached far beyond the limits of a barber's training to specialize on teeth. Thus, he represents what a Carabelli-trained dentist might have looked like if the seeds of professional dentistry had taken root just a little earlier.

It's also worth remembering that many of the great leaps in medicine and healing came not only from the names preserved in official records, but also from those whose contributions were overlooked. Jewish physicians and healers across Europe often stood in the shadows of history, carrying knowledge across borders at a time when universities were closed to them. They apprenticed, traveled, and adapted techniques from one region to another, uniting classical learning with lived practice. Noah Gordon's *The Physician* dramatizes this beautifully: the Jewish scholar moving from place to place, gathering fragments of knowledge, and creating a holistic art of healing.

Felix, in this sense, also honors that legacy. He is imagined as one of those rare, self-taught and well-traveled men who, though excluded from official institutions, pieced together a formidable education from the margins—studying with physicians, learning from observation, and carrying skills across communities. His story is fiction, but it reflects the reality that innovation often came from those whose names never made it into the history books.

Historical Context of Felix's Trouble at the University:

While writing this story, I wanted to reflect the historical climate in which a Jewish dentist like Felix might have lived and studied. The University of Vienna, one of the most prestigious medical schools in Europe, has a long and complicated history—one that included deeply ingrained anti-Jewish sentiment.

The Billroth Affair (1870s): In 1875, the celebrated surgeon Theodor Billroth proposed reforms calling for a "German medical elite," explicitly excluding "Eastern Jewish" students, whom he referred to as "unfortunately not completely exterminable weeds." This moment—known as the "Billroth affair"—is remembered by historians as a turning point in the formal, institutionalized discrimination against Jews in Vienna's medical faculty.

Secret Anti-Semitic Networks ("Bears' Cave"): By the 1920s and 1930s, a covert circle of nationalist, Christian-Socialist professors—nicknamed the "Bears' Cave"—actively worked to limit Jewish academic participation. They imposed quotas and blocked Jewish scholars from advancing to habilitation (earning their doctor titles), the qualification necessary for a university career.

The Anschluss and Mass Expulsions (1938): After Austria's annexation by Nazi Germany, the university imposed a "numerus clausus" that capped Jewish enrollment at just 2%. Within that same year, thousands of Jewish students and faculty were expelled or barred from completing their degrees. Many would be deported and murdered in the Holocaust.

Against this backdrop, Felix's skill, persistence, and success carry even greater weight. Thus, despite the fact that medical and dental techniques were not the exclusive domain of the nobility, and there is no historical evidence that procedures such as gold-foil dental fillings were "reserved" for the aristocracy, there were private letters and accounts that explained that the newest and best resources at university were often reserved and inaccessible to Jewish students. Felix's use of this rare, highly specialized method—making a gold and porcelain fused crown—still known to only a handful of dentists today—is a reflection of his dedication, mastery, and artistry, not a mark of noble privilege.

Although I borrowed from documented history and many primary sources, I have also taken artistic license to imagine what could have happened earlier than our surviving records show. The truth is, not many Jews dared to speak openly against the injustices they faced; fear, exclusion, and systemic prejudice often silenced them. Society was different then—its restrictions, unspoken rules, and casual cruelties shaped people's behavior in ways that can feel frustrating to us today. As much as we embrace the ballrooms, the gowns, and the glittering London setting of the Regency era, it is important to acknowledge the shadows that existed alongside the sparkle. That reality, uncomfortable as it may be, informed these characters and the world they inhabit. Historical fiction like this book lives between these lines of the history that was written down, so that imagination can illuminate the silences, explore the untold, and give voice to those whose truths were never fully recorded.

Dentists vs. Doctors—A Historical Clarification

Why don't we call a dentist "Doctor" in the UK?

Historically, dentistry evolved from the trade of barber-surgeons rather than physicians—so in Britain, dentists were not granted the same academic status as physicians. It wasn't until the mid-19th century that the professionalization of dentistry gained traction: the Dentists Act of 1878 began regulating practice, and in 1860, the Royal College of Surgeons introduced the License in Dental Surgery (LDS) as the first British dental qualification. The University of London followed only much later: it awarded its first Bachelor of Dental Surgery (BDS) degrees in 1921.

By contrast, in countries like the United States, Canada, and parts of Europe, dental education integrated more readily into higher academia. Degrees such as Doctor of Dental Medicine (DMD), Doctor of Dental Surgery (DDS), and Bachelor of Dental Surgery (BDS) are common, and dentists are fully licensed medical professionals with prescribing authority.

Isn't that unfair?

Absolutely.

Dentists are (or after all their training, should be) highly skilled clinicians—performing complex diagnostics, surgeries, and prescribing medications. And yet, in the UK, the title "Doctor" was long reserved for those with a medical degree or a doctorate. Interestingly (or sadly) British surgeons still use "Mr." or "Ms." as a badge of historical trade distinction.

That's why, in *Miracles on Harley Street*, I've portrayed my hero Felix as a rare exception—not merely a barber with a forceps, but a man who pursued advanced medical study on his own initiative, earned the respect of his mentors, and mastered techniques well beyond what most dentists of the era knew. He truly embodies the depth and responsibility deserving of the title Doctor.

But even outside this story, the dental profession's reputation has long straddled science and suspicion—some historical practices rightly deserved that stigma, but others emerged from men and women deeply motivated to heal. I've been privileged to be related to a handful of modern dentists—true artisans of care— who, like Felix, self-financed further studies, pushed beyond standard training (and traveled around the world for that training), and advanced compassionate, minimally invasive treatments.

This book is dedicated to those exceptional healers. Through Felix, I hope to shine a light on what dentistry could have been—elevated by character, innovation, and humanity.

Thank you for joining me in giving these "unsung doctors" the respect they deserve in this story.

On Names, Gold, and Felix Leafley:

In the Jewish tradition, surnames as we know them today are a relatively recent development. For centuries, many Jews had no fixed last name at all, using instead patronymics (son of, daughter of) or identifiers linked to their place of origin. When surnames became legally required—often by edict in parts of Europe during the late 18th and 19th centuries—families sometimes adopted names tied to geography, natural elements, or trades.

Felix Blattner's name carries a playful nod to this history. Felix—which happens to sound a little like "fix it"—suits a man who repairs not only teeth, but also smiles, and ultimately, the broken hearts in this story. Blattner comes from *Blatt*, the German word for "leaf," as it would have been used in Vienna when he was in university. But in the world of dentistry, that leaf imagery holds an even richer meaning: the highest art of direct gold foil fillings uses thin, delicate sheets of pure gold leaf to restore small cavities.

This technique, known since ancient Egypt, involves crumpling the gold leaf into a ball and pressing it into the hollow of a tooth, where it compresses and locks into place. Gold is uniquely suited for this—it doesn't corrode, has unique properties, and when carefully worked, it can last a lifetime as a filling. In fact, museum specimens of ancient Egyptian skulls still display these glittering restorations, a testament to both the skill of their makers and the enduring beauty of the material.

Today, only a handful of dentists still practice this demanding craft. It's precise, patient work, requiring both a gentle touch and a mastery of technique—much like Felix himself. *A taste of gold* from his *golden touch* seemed the perfect wordplay for his role in this book: a man who doesn't just fill cavities, but restores what's missing, leaving something precious behind.

I hope my story—and the *Miracles on Harley Street* series—did the same for you, filling a spot in your heart and leaving something precious behind. For more books like this, please visit my website at www.SaraAdrien.com.

Acknowledgments

My deepest gratitude goes to Marion L. of Vienna, who became my eyes and ears in grounding the backstory of these characters in authentic detail.

To Susan B., Andrea, Emily, Ariele, and everyone at Dragonblade for their steady guidance and partnership in bringing this book into the world.

And especially to my readers—Jo, Terri, Dominique, Nicole, Lyn, and so many others—your encouragement and enthusiasm give my Jewish characters a voice to champion in the world of Regency romance.

And special thanks to Morgan and her little Lilly! I hope you both liked being in this book! To many more!

About the Author

Bestselling author Sara Adrien writes hot and heart-melting regency romance with a Jewish twist. As a law professor-turned-author, she writes about clandestine identities, whims of fate, and sizzling seduction. If you like unique and intelligent characters, deliciously sexy scenes, and the nostalgia of afternoon tea, then you'll adore Sara Adrien's tender tear-jerkers.

For more information and exclusive sneak peeks, new releases, and more, sign up for Sara Adrien's newsletter at www.Sara Adrien.com.

Catch up with Sara Adrien here:
linktr.ee/jewishregencyromance
saraadrien.com
instagram.com/jewishregencyromance
facebook.com/AuthorSaraAdrien
bookbub.com/authors/sara-adrien
goodreads.com/author/show/22249825.Sara_Adrien
youtube.com/channel/UCK9OLp1wN6IaGkXe7OugfHg

www.ingramcontent.com/pod-product-compliance
Lightning Source LLC
Chambersburg PA
CBHW071241300726

48975CB00002B/517